Tanya Jones was born in Lancashire in 1965 and grew up in Stafford. She read English at King's College, Cambridge, where she was received into the Catholic Church and met her husband Martin. After a brief period working in London, she in charity fundraising and PR, they moved to Ampleforth and she took an MA in Medieval Studies at York University. She then went on to study law and served her articles in Cleveland, qualifying as a solicitor in 1993. She now divides her time between writing and working with her husband in their companies Cathedral Software and Wireless Networks. They have three sons, Gawain, born in 1987, the 1996 British under-ten chess champion, Rory, born in 1993, over whose head most of the *Mortgage Bandits* was typed, and Aidan, born in 1997, just in time to help with the proofs of *Trotter's Bottom*. One and a half labradors (the other half is believed to be a whippet) complete the family, now living in Gilling, just across the valley from Ampleforth Abbey. *Trotter's Bottom* is her third Ophelia O. novel and the first two, *Ophelia O. and the Mortgage Bandits* and *Ophelia O. and the Antenatal Mysteries*, are also available from Headline.

Also by Tanya Jones

Ophelia O. and the Mortgage Bandits
Ophelia O. and the Antenatal Mysteries

Trotter's Bottom

Tanya Jones

HEADLINE

First published in 1997
by HEADLINE BOOK PUBLISHING

First published in paperback in 1998
by HEADLINE BOOK PUBLISHING

10 9 8 7 6 5 4 3 2 1

ISBN 0 7472 5672 1

Printed and bound in Great Britain by
Clays Ltd, St Ives plc

HEADLINE BOOK PUBLISHING
A division of Hodder Headline PLC
338 Euston Road
London NW1 3BH

For Gawain

Chapter One

An English Opening

Ophelia's first thought was that Chequers had come back to haunt them. There she sat, plump and black, on the top of the flight of steps which led to Parrish Snodsworth Ranger, defying, with her eight remaining lives, the ebullience that had fatally propelled her under the wheels of the butcher van. Ophelia peered through the fog and caught the heel of her unfamiliar court shoe between the cobbles of the Market Square. She decided to concentrate on where she was going.

So it was that, having successfully negotiated four or five fish-and-chip wrappers and the odd broken brown ale bottle, Ophelia reached the stone steps, thick, as ever, with pigeon-droppings, and looked up again. There was no sign now of the cat, who was, presumably, slumbering in the celestial arms of her deceased owner, the eponymous Mr Parrish. Instead, there bobbed, in cheerful fashion, a large and luxuriant fur hat, black, with the occasional fleck of cream, well-groomed and healthy.

But beneath the hat stretched a wide, Slavic face that was anything but cheerful.

'Aahhh,' said the face, but it was not an 'Aahhh' of anticipation, still less of satisfaction, rather the 'Aahhh' of a deep and justifiable gloom. 'You are working here?'

'Um . . . yes,' said Ophelia and then, thinking this to be scarcely the war-cry of a dynamic legal desperado, returning to the fray, 'Yes. Certainly. How may I help you?'

The trouble was, that however much she had looked forward to this moment, to the exhilaration of striding, untrammelled by sling or pushchair, into her own office again, she could not help but worry about what she had left behind her. Could her husband Malachi really manage to measure out the right amount of formula milk for his sixth-born, little Adeodata, whilst simultaneously keeping two-year-old Innocent out of the septic tank? How she wished that she had persevered with the electric breast pump instead of allowing her eldest, Pius, to turn it into an automatic slow-bowling device. It wasn't even as though it was still the cricket season.

The fur-hatted man seemed as dubious as she, for he had still not answered her question but stood, hands in the deep pockets of his overcoat, and rocked from side to side. 'How to begin? How to begin?'

'Why not start with coming inside?' suggested Ophelia, feeling the first cold scrapes of a Rambleton autumn against the back of her fifteen-denier shins. She took the large, flat key from her pocket and, with the insouciance of twelve months' experience, executed the complex sequence of twists and thumps that would persuade the door to open. Antiquity, in this instance, had provided Parrish Snodsworth Ranger with a more efficient burglar alarm than any technology could offer, for only Ophelia herself and her secretary, Polly, had perfected the routine. Not, Ophelia thought ruefully, that the disparate collection of cereal boxes and biscuit tins that constituted the office filing system contained much of interest to the potential burglar, while the petty cash box had, at the last reckoning, contained three halfpennies, still accepted as legal tender in most of Rambleton's shops, a couple of Polly's hairgrips and an I.O.U. for twenty-seven pence from the landlord of the Ram's Leg.

Inside, the building was as dank and musty as it had been five months before, when Ophelia had departed on her maternity leave. The blue paint with which she and Polly had done their best to lighten the atmosphere was already peeling away, revealing the immutable solicitors' brown beneath. She waved the man through, past the remains of Polly's sandwiches and into her own office in the corner. Here her visitor seemed to relax a little, for this room, which had formerly been that of Mr Parrish himself, was at least traditionally shabby, with a wide treacly desk, frayed leather blotter and rows of olive-backed volumes upon which dust clung in bluish bobbles, undisturbed by the years. Ophelia flicked the switch of a small plastic fan-heater and motioned the man to sit down. This he did, gingerly, settling his broad base into the semi-circular embrace of an ancient chair and letting his short legs, in a hairy grey tweed, swing slightly above the lino. Under the glare of the fluorescent light his face seemed to sag. She had, upon first seeing him, plump and sturdy, guessed his age at about sixty-five, but now realized that he was probably ten or fifteen years older.

'How to begin?' he repeated, and then snapped to his feet in an unexpectedly military manner. He thrust out a pale plump hand.

'Name, of course. Alexander Illyich Zhukovsky. But to you – Zuke!'

He smiled, for the first time, and into his khaki-coloured cheeks came a shadow of crimson. His eyes, as grey as his suit, lightened.

'I am Russian – you can tell?' The question was evidently rhetorical for he continued without pausing, 'I am grandmaster of chess. I win many, many tournaments, many, many prizes. Not the very top – you understand? I am not Kasparov, I am not Karpov – as you see!' He gestured towards his ample stomach. 'But in my time – I win plenty.'

'And now?'

'Now – aahh. Now is coming of democracy to my country.' He spoke the word 'democracy' as if it were 'plague', and seemed to realize this, for he stood up again, and gave Ophelia a neat little bow. 'Not that I do not believe in democracy, you understand, cradled in your own England. Is very great thing, great as Buckenam Palace and, how is it? – murphins?'

'Muffins?'

'Murphins, yes. Very good. But democracy for me, means ending of my salary. The Communists, they pay me to play chess. Sometimes, they pay me not to play chess. But Mr Yeltsin, he have more on his brain than merely chess players. The Russian Federation, it cannot spare the roubles for old Zuke.'

'So you came to England?' Ophelia was confused. She knew nothing about professional chess, but had the idea that Britain, and Rambleton in particular, was unlikely to be an effective springboard to a lucrative career. 'Are you sure that . . .'

'Oh, not for playing chess. There is no money here, I know that. For chess I would have gone to France, Germany, America, even. No, I come with my wife.' As he said these words, his face fell back into its greenish folds and his eyes turned dull again. 'My wife, she is English. Is – you say *Rambletonian*?'

'You could do, certainly.'

'Good. I do not wish to make mistakes here. My wife, Hilda, I tell her when the salary is gone. She is very worried. Then, she jump up, like this.' Zuke sprang from his chair for a third time, but with his eyebrows raised in pantomime of feminine enthusiasm. 'She say, "Silly me, for I have land at home, from my father. We go home, we find. Will be house, maybe, rent, pension. All will be right." Then she bring a map, of her land, I think. I do not understand it, but I say, very well, we come. And so, yesterday, we arrive. The Grand Hotel, you know?'

Ophelia did, although she had always thought 'Grand' a particularly inappropriate sobriquet.

'We stay, have dinner, bed. Is quite like Russia, in fact.'

Ophelia could well believe it.

5

'This morning, we order breakfast-in-bed. Bacon, sausage – you know all this?'

'Only too well.'

'You mean is not tasty? I think also the same. The egg, it sit on my stomach like a jellyfish. Is right, jellyfish?' Ophelia nodded. 'But is much, much worse for my poor wife.'

'She's ill?' asked Ophelia, wondering whether he was under the impression that Parrish Snodsworth Ranger was the local Tourist Information Office or, perhaps, Trading Standards Department.

'Is worse.' Zuke gripped the arms of the chair and rolled his barrel chest towards her. 'Is dead.'

'Dead? What, from the breakfast?'

Ophelia had for some time been developing doubts about the proliferation of the law of negligence, but even she could concede that Zuke sounded to have a good case. Rambleton's breakfasts were not generally distinguished, either for savour or nutritional value, but their deleterious effects were not normally quite so swift. She wondered whether Zuke could be said to be resident in Britain for legal aid purposes.

'No, I think not.' He sounded almost regretful. 'I think she had not eaten at all. We sit up in bed, the manager bring trays. I begin, say, "Hilda, how is it that this is called coffee? Even in the worst days in Moscow we do not drink such mud." She makes no reply and I fear that I have offended her. Is her home town, you know, maybe she likes not for me to insult. "Forgive me, my love," I say, while I am thinking very fast of something to praise. "These shirthangers" – is right, shirthangers?'

'Coat?' suggested Ophelia, not sure now whether he was addressing her or the unfortunate Hilda.

'Ah. Coat, indeed. "These coathangers are very fine. Most high quality woods." And still is no answer. So I give her nudge, you know, friendly little show-yourself-woman." He demonstrated, digging a plump elbow into the unyielding arm of his chair. 'And then it is that I know.'

With this simple statement he seemed to have finished, and sat back in the chair, watching Ophelia with round and trustful eyes.

'That must have been terrible for you. What did you do then?'

'I telephone to the manager, ask him "Please come quickly" and he does, up stairs two at a time, bearing many things, salt, napkins, milk. He is thinking that I wish to complain of the breakfast. I think there are maybe many such complaints. But when he sees Hilda he is very much sympathetic, very sad. Again he calls the doctor.'

'Again?'

Zuke flapped his stubby fingers. 'Is not important. We will come to that. So, the doctor, he arrives, says yes, she is dead, it is heart attack.'

Ophelia nodded vaguely. 'Yes, I see.'

'No!' exploded the little man, propelling himself completely out of the chair so that he had to catch hold of the desk edge for support. 'No, you do not see! You do not know! My Hilda – she had no heart attack. She was strong, healthy, like oxen, you say.'

'But the doctor had been called before?'

'Last night, yes. But this was by no means necessary. Hilda, she went out in the evening, she did not tell me where. She was, I think, seeing a person about her land. I, perhaps, would have been too excitable to be of help. Also, I was very tired. I, you see, was tired, not my wife. I am five years older than she. It is I who should be dead. But yes, you ask about the doctor. Hilda, she comes back last night, comes through the reception where the manager sits. "Mrs Zhukovsky," he says, "you look ill. You must sit and take something, some brandy, perhaps." "No," says my wife, "I do not care for spirits," and this is quite true, for all our years in Russia she would never approach the vodka. "I am maybe a little tired," she says, "for it has been a long journey." But then, I think, she trips on the stair, and he is worried, so calls the doctor for the first time.'

'And what did the doctor say then?'

'I think, nothing much. Is hard for me sometimes to understand English when all are talking at once. He tells her to take aspirin, and she has them already in her handbag. Then they leave, and we sleep. So, she was not really ill, you see, not so ill that she should die in the morning-time. No, my friend, I fear that Hilda is murdered.'

Ophelia, unusually, could think of nothing to say. Wild accusations had, she was sure, often passed across the scuffed surface of the desk during the past century, but she had heard none so stark and blatant. 'But why me?' was all that she could eventually manage. 'I mean, I'm a solicitor, not a private detective. If you have any suspicions, then you ought to talk to the police.'

'The po-lice? Bah!'

Ophelia missed his next few words, fascinated by the fact that he had actually managed to say the word 'Bah'. She had been trying to slide it into her conversation for years, but somehow, from a native speaker of English, it never quite seemed to work.

'I'm sorry, you were saying?'

'Are almost certainly, you know, in the pay of the culprits. Most likely it is themselves who are the assassins. We have seen much of this in Russia. You hear of KGB?'

'Oh, absolutely. But the police force here . . .' Her voice tailed off as she tried to imagine the ineffectual Constable Booking, preoccupied as ever with his conjugal affairs, forming a hit squad.

'. . . Are same as everywhere. Believe me, my friend, it is certainly not safe. You will investigate, kind Mrs O. Will be much better.'

'No. I'm sorry, but it won't. We just don't do things that way in England. Not even in Rambleton. I really must insist that you contact the police first. If they're . . .' She was going to say 'incompetent' but thought she had better not prejudice him even further . . . 'unsatisfactory, then you'd better come and see me again.'

'Very well, if this is necessary. But also, I have special reason to come here.' He dug in one of the pockets of his overcoat and brought out a crumpled piece of paper. It was an old compliments slip from the firm, dating back to the time, before the merger of a year before, when it was known as Parrish, Stanmore & Parrish. 'This is yourselves, yes?'

'Yes. At least, it's what we used to be called.'

'Good. This I find in Hilda's handbag. Is certainly then you who will find Hilda's land, I think. Also her murderer. Is meant to be.'

Ophelia was looking more closely at the slip of paper. Although the actual letter-head had apparently not changed for fifty years, until she and Malachi had introduced the first PC and integral graphics package to the office, there were other clues which suggested that the slip dated back to the 1950s or before. Only one telephone number was given, with no fax or DX number, and this was described simply as *Rambleton 456*. Also, the list of partners was headed by William Parrish, the last Mr Parrish's father, and followed by James Stanmore, whose name was now immortalized only on the door to the office lavatory. 'How long had Hilda had this, do you know?'

Zuke looked a little offended. 'How is it I should know? You think that I would be rummaging in my poor wife's handbag if she were here to be asked? It was, I think, with the map. Oh, silly old Zhukovsky! I am now forgetting to give you the map itself.'

He delved again into the commodious pocket and handed Ophelia a folded piece of heavy cream paper. She opened it to find a hand-drawn map, carefully outlined in red, which showed an oddly shaped piece of land. The landmarks within the boundaries, mainly fences and trees, were meticulously recorded, but there was no hint as to which property it bordered, or as to the location of the land itself. At the bottom right-hand corner two words were neatly blocked, **TROTTER'S**

BOTTOM, and below them was a small ink drawing of a very pink pig.

She looked up to find Zuke smiling at her with an expression uncannily like that of the pig. 'One last thing,' he cautioned, raising a broad forefinger. 'Despite our setbacks at home, I am not, as yet, a poor man. I am willing to pay well, yes, to the last rouble, to find the killer of my dear Hilda. Many monies, you understand?'

Ophelia tried to look detached, as though the question of payment was a matter of perfect indifference to her.

'But of one thing I must be sure. Is very likely, you see, that my poor wife was done to death – you can say "done to death"?'

'A bit melodramatic, but in the circumstances, I think so.'

'Done to death,' repeated Zuke with satisfaction. 'Done to death by one of my enemies in the world of chess.'

'Oh, do you have many?' said Ophelia in surprise, thinking of the girls in her school chess club who seemed notable, apart from their attachment to upswept spectacles, by their comparative immunity to the usual round of intense friendships and quarrels.

'That, I cannot tell.' Zuke's expression darkened. 'It is the nature of the game. One thinks, analyses, calculates. One makes one's plan, secretly, silently. Only when one is sure, when the hands of the clock are moving forward and there is no more time to waste, only then is the move made. And then – *mate*!' He clapped his hands together at the last word and the sound echoed across the room to the empty stationery cupboard. 'And that is why,' he

continued as the sound died away, 'that is why my
lawyer must, as a great necessity, herself be a chess
player.'

'Oh,' said Ophelia.

'So we lost the job, then?' Polly, the secretary, was
perched beside her typewriter, swinging electric-blue
legs impatiently while the kettle wheezed to its climax.
'He's gone to Nick Bottomley's firm, I s'pose?' She
hugged her fuchsia-pink anorak closely to her, for the fan
heater had burned itself out shortly after Zuke's depar-
ture, and they could not find the matches for the gas fire.

'Certainly not. I didn't intend to celebrate my first day
back by turning work away. Not *paying* work.' The
distinction was important, Parrish's having several times
had to go without new supplies of Jammy Dodgers while
waiting for the petty cash to be replenished by the Legal
Aid Board. 'No, I just – crossed my fingers a bit.'

'So you told him that you did play chess?'

'Well, I'm sure I must have learned sometime. I
mean, it's one of those civilized things that you just
know, isn't it? Like where Middle C is and the War of
Jenkins' Ear.'

'Ooh, did you hear about that, then? Right outside the
Ram's Leg, it was, a month or so back. My Gary was
there an' all. Mind you, he said as Ned were right
exaggerating.'

'Who's Ned?' Ophelia was out of practice in translat-
ing Polly's particular brand of Yorkshire. She covered
her knocking knees with a couple of affidavits.

'Ned Jenkins, as said he had his ear bitten. Gary said it

were only a graze. Couldn't hardly even see the tooth-marks, so it seems a bit much to call it a war. Just a bit of a scrap, really. Gary'd gone by the time the police came, mind. Got to watch his reputation these days, what with being an entree.'

'*Being* an entree?' Ophelia knew that Gary, whose van had despatched poor Chequers, was trying to cater for Rambleton's more esoteric tastes, but had not imagined that he was serving himself up alongside the venison and ostrich steaks.

'Yeah, you know, like your Malachi. Got his own business.'

Ophelia considered embarking upon either a translation of *entrepreneur* or a history of Anglo-Spanish maritime conflict, but decided that both were unspeakably trivial in comparison with the exertions of the kettle, which showed definite boiling tendencies. She leapt upon it before it could change its mind and poured out two large mugs of strong instant coffee.

For a while there was silence as the caffeine oozed through their cold and aching muscles, sending little tingles of wakefulness to the ends of their numbed fingers.

'Couldn't we buy some matches?' begged Ophelia. 'I'll pay for them, if there's nothing in petty cash.'

'Half-nine.'

'What?'

'Ophelia, where've you been? You know nothing in Rambleton ever opens before half-nine. More like ten if it's been a good night in the Leg. It's only quarter-past, now. So come on, about this Russian. You lied, then, did you?'

'Not exactly. I told him I was a bit rusty, couldn't remember whether a gambit moved forwards or diagonally.'

Polly nodded.

'But then I said . . .'

'Go on.'

'I said that one of the children was very keen, played all the time and dreamed of being a professional chess player like him.'

'Oh yes. Which one's that, then?'

'Which one's what?'

'The one of your children that wants to play chess. Funny, I can't quite imagine any of them sitting down for long enough. I s'pose Urban's the quietest, isn't he, but I thought it was all dinosaurs with him.'

'That's just it. It isn't any of them. That was the little, er, fib that I had to tell. But I did have my fingers crossed behind my back.'

'That's okay, then.' Both women realized that the demands of social etiquette, not to mention those of the Solicitors' Professional Practice Rules, could invariably be overridden by the rituals of the playground. It was really the only way to survive, with sharks like Nick Bottomley of the bright, successful and, no doubt, adequately heated, firm of Canards ready at any moment to snatch their hard-won clients. 'So, you'll have to get one of them to start, will you?'

'Looks like it.' Ophelia shivered again as she put down her empty coffee mug, and considered the prospect without relish. Since their move to the dilapidated Moorwind Farm some eighteen months before, the O.

children, never notable for their cleanliness or industry, had run almost completely wild, filling their spare time with complex plans, of which she only heard tantalizing encryptions, and the husbandry of various unsavoury animals. The only one who could be relied upon to stay in one place was little Dodie, but even Ophelia's limited knowledge of chess prodigies suggested that they rarely began at three months. At the thought of the baby she pulled her coat protectively around her, but it was too late. Already she had felt the familiar tingling sensation in her breasts, and two neat circles of damp cloth had appeared on her blouse, shiveringly cold where they met the chilly air of the office.

'Damn,' she said, with a vague mental apology towards the heavens, and reached into her new handbag, matronly capacious to deal with just such crises, for a fresh pair of disposable breast pads. Polly watched, aghast, as Ophelia dived into her blouse and removed two dripping discs.

'I never knew you could do that. I'll not bother with the Coffeemate next time, then.'

'Bit sweet, I'm afraid,' said Ophelia, 'but very nutritious. That is, if you want a selection of my antibodies.'

Polly paled beneath her oyster-coloured foundation. 'P'raps not. Anyway, you're going to do this Russian case, are you?'

'The land side of it, yes. Just the kind of thing I like, sorting through piles of dusty old deeds. But not the so-called murder.'

Polly's face fell. 'Spoilsport. I thought we'd be dead good as detectives. You know, Miss Marple and that. Eee

– I forgot! Talking of old folks, Mr Snodsworth wants to see you over T'other Side.'

When, nearly a year before, the ancient Rambleton firms of Parrish, Stanmore & Parrish, and Snodsworth & Ranger had merged to form Parrish Snodsworth Ranger, a name of such eminent dullness that no one, least of all Polly, who had to answer the telephone, could remember it unprompted, it had proved impossible to dispose of either of the shabby offices which faced each other across the Market Square. The three remaining solicitors, Mr Snodsworth, Mr Ranger and Ophelia (Mr Parrish having mysteriously passed away while the ink on the merger documents was still tacky) had accordingly spent the next few months flitting between the offices like substantial butterflies, referring in each case to the opposite premises as 'T'other Side'.

'Wants to see *me*? He's never wanted to see me. I'm still not convinced that he even knows who I am. Are you sure?'

'Oh yes. I was surprised, too, with him being such a dreadful male chiropodist, but he was quite cheerful about it all. "Trot along," he said, "and have a look at the jolly old ropes." '

'I suppose I might as well go now, then,' said Ophelia with feigned reluctance, sure that Mr Snodsworth's *amour propre* would not allow him to go matchless, and suspecting that even the autumn wind outside would be warmer than her office. 'Sort out the post while I'm gone, would you, Poll?'

Polly jumped down from the desk and stood to mock attention, her natural four feet ten enlarged by the five-inch strawberry-blonde spikes of her newest hairstyle.

'Aye aye, Cap'n. And you'll pick up the matches on your way back.'

'Uh-huh.'

The journey across the Square was easier than it had been an hour before, for the frost had been melted by the intermittent sun and Ophelia had exchanged her court shoes for a sensible flat pair, found in her filing cabinet, whose only drawback was that Malachi had polished them in the dark with a tube of lime-green touch-up paint. Something sharp was digging into her left little toe and she had a nasty feeling that Innocent had at some stage used them as storage receptacles for his smaller Sticklebricks.

No concession to the firm's merger had been made in T'other Side's window, which was still bathed in faded blue silk, from which a small card made its discreet announcement.

W. R. G. SNODSWORTH, M.A.
L. N. RANGER
SOLICITORS & COMMISSIONERS FOR OATHS

The dark waiting room was empty but for a small middle-aged man in a quilted jacket, staring between his knees at the red tiled floor.

'Is someone seeing to you?' asked Ophelia.

'I've come to see Mr Ranger,' said the man in a hopeless monotone, 'but I don't suppose as he's in. He's not generally in when I come.'

'I'll find out for you if you like. Your name is . . .?'

'Phlutt. With a Ph, not an F. But I wouldn't bother if I were you. I'll just wait. I'm generally waiting for something or other, so it won't make no odds.'

Mr Phlutt gave a sigh, insufficiently marked to indicate any particular disappointment, and returned to his observation of the floor.

The heavy door of Mr Snodsworth's room opened slowly, hampered by the luxuriant pile of his Persian carpet. From behind an enormous mahogany desk his iridescent baldness arose above a copy of *Barchester Towers*.

'Damn fine writer, this young Trollope, despite his tomfool name,' murmured the old solicitor. 'Wonder which club he belongs to. Ah. The infant Oliver. Wondered when you were going to make an appearance. Punctual and punctilious, that's the way to succeed in the law, my boy. Polite and parsimonious. Never mind all this newfangled typewriter nonsense. Well, stand up straight, lad, make a man of yourself.'

'I . . . beg your pardon?'

'Squeaking little voice you've got, haven't you? Won't make much of an impact on old Judge Hebblethrower with that warble. Sounds like a damn woman.'

'I am a woman, sir.'

'What's that? Speak up, won't you? And another thing – get that hair cut. We don't want any of those Rolling Beetles here, you know. Not to mention – Good God! Scotch, are you?'

'No, sir, I'm . . .'

'Then why in the name of heaven are you wearing a skirt?'

'Because I'm a woman.'

Mr Snodsworth lifted a pair of gold pince-nez from a chain about his neck and peered at Ophelia through them.

'So you are,' he said in deflated disgust. 'Well, I don't need polishing this morning. I told that snippet on T'other Side that I wanted to see the new man. Give him the benefit of my experience. How many years is it that I've been in practice?'

'Sixty-two, I believe.'

'Sixty-three. There you are then. Young man, first day in the office, bright, bobbing and ready to go, all he needs is a few wise words from an attorney of sixty-four years' standing. Well run along, run along, my dear and fetch him.'

'Fetch who, I mean whom?'

'Why, this Oliver O., of course. That popsie told me that he was starting this morning.'

'I'm afraid you must have misheard, sir. I'm *Ophelia* O. Don't you remember? I'm the solicitor on T'other Side. I've just come back from my maternity leave.'

'What the devil's maternity leave?'

Ophelia explained, as delicately as possible.

'But . . . but,' Mr Snodsworth's round face fell into a drooping parody of bewilderment. Ophelia was reminded of Innocent, her two-year-old, so often baffled by the irrational explanations of his elders. 'I'd heard a rumour there were lady solicitors, but, *married women* . . .' He picked up his fountain pen, and shook it, apparently drawing strength from the shower of ink spots which fell across the desk. 'No, we can't have that sort of thing here, madam. I fear that you must consider yourself bowler-hatted.'

Ophelia raised a tentative hand to her wiry curls. 'I don't think I've . . . Perhaps a headscarf?'

'Cashiered, young lady. Chasséd. In short, I am dismissing you. Kindly return to your offspring and send young Oliver in.'

'I've been trying to tell you, Mr Snodsworth. There is no Oliver.'

'Poppycock. Of course there's an Oliver. Smart young lad, starting work today. Look here; I've even noted it in my journal.' He pushed a leather-bound diary towards her, his finger indicating an illegible entry in pale brown copperplate. 'Just what we need around here. I once had high hopes of that shaver young Ranger, but it doesn't look as though he'll ever make anything of himself.'

Ophelia forbore to point out that Deputy District Judge Ranger had been Mr Snodsworth's partner for the past twenty years. It was occurring to her that it might, after all, be useful to keep the mythic Oliver alive. Her sacking was, of course, in blatant contradiction of all sex discrimination legislation, and she was confident of her success, other things being equal, in achieving reinstatement and compensation from an industrial tribunal. What such a tribunal would make of Mr Snodsworth's evidence, however, she dreaded to imagine. Its members might well end up so bewildered that they would dismiss the case in pure self-defence, or might decide that Ophelia, in even wanting her job back, was demonstrating certifiable lunacy. More significantly, it would take so long for the tribunal machinery to grind into action that by the time the case was heard she would have lost all hope of retaining the lucrative business of Mr Zhukovsky. She would just have to keep out of Mr Snodsworth's way as much as possible, and be prepared to impersonate the fictive Oliver in an emergency. Ophelia glanced down at her still globular stomach and sighed. She had hoped to avoid trousers for the next ten years or so.

'Well off you go then, missie, off you go. You won't get me to change my mind, you know. Feminine wiles never got anywhere with William Reginald G. I well remember the last popsie to try anything of that sort. Flapper like you she was, as well, but she soon found out she'd picked on the wrong chap. Yes indeed.' The corners of his eyes crinkled with malicious reminiscence as he picked up a folder from his desk.

'Of course, Mr Snodsworth. Oh and sir?'

'Hmmm?'

'I've just remembered. Oliver's in court all day today. Said he wanted to start as he meant to go on, working hard for the firm from morning to night. Keen as mustard, that young fellow.' She bit her lip, wondering whether she might have overdone it, but Mr Snodsworth was equally impervious to contradiction or parody.

'Excellent. *Excellent.* Now then, I think counsel's opinion is called for on this one.'

Ophelia closed the door gently, leaving Mr Snodsworth with his beloved directory of barristers, *circa* 1922. It was not until she was out in the Square again, having completely failed to notice the patient and phlegmatic Mr Phlutt, that she realized that Mr Snodsworth had been referring, not to the case of *Re Geranium Trusts* which had been his constant companion for the past half-century, but to the new folder on his desk, with the more prosaic title of *Podd*. She trudged back across the cobbles deep in thought, and forgot all about the box of matches.

Chapter Two

The Chicago Gambit

By a quarter-past five that afternoon, Ophelia was racing up the pot-holed road which led home, equally oblivious of the outraged squawks of the starlings bathing in the puddles and of the defunct suspension of her ancient Volvo. Through the deepest crater, over the rusty cattle-grid and she was there, manoeuvring through the gate-posts and into the grim yard of Moorwind Farm. Above her, a battered sign was creaking on its rusty hinges. *Wet Nose Solutions*, it read, *for all your PC needs*. Ophelia gave the sign a little push, so that it flipped over to reveal its banana box origins, and set off towards the front door, flanked by dead geraniums, of the concrete bungalow.

As she grew closer to the door her trudge became a trot, and then a sprint, as the faint sounds which could at first have been the screeching of far-off seagulls were clarified into the screams of a small baby.

'Dodie!' she cried, wrenching the rotten wood of the door from its frame. 'Mal?'

Malachi, small and damp in a sweatshirt and jogging trousers that were more hole than trouser, emerged from the bathroom. With one hand he pulled ineffectually at his waistband while the other clutched a furious bundle in a grubby Babygro.

'Thank God,' he panted, and his balding head faded to a crimson several shades paler than the baby's. 'Here, hold her a moment, would you, while I . . .' He thrust the child at Ophelia and plunged both hands down the back of his trousers. 'Ridiculous boxer shorts, been twisted like that since half-past three, couldn't put Dodie down, been screaming . . .'

'You or the baby?' asked Ophelia, unbuttoning her blouse with a practised hand while jogging the still frenetic infant on her shoulder. She pulled aside the cup of her bra and three delicate jets of repressed milk shot out at different angles.

'Both,' said Malachi, mopping at the front of his sweatshirt with his sleeve.

Ophelia, still standing, attached the baby's mouth, which had been popping like a frustrated goldfish, to her nipple. There was suddenly silence, except for Dodie's breathless gulping and a small, cheerful voice from the other side of the sitting-room door, chanting, 'One piggy, two piggies, five piggies!'

'Oh good,' said Ophelia. 'You've managed to fix the video, then?'

'Not exactly. You must admit, it showed a generous spirit in Innocent, feeding it all those peanut butter sandwiches. He made them himself, as well. Perhaps it wouldn't have been as bad if it wasn't the crunchy sort.

There's something about those little bits that defeats the Japanese completely. Now if the Americans had known that before Pearl Harbor . . . What? No, no, it's a leaflet-thingy that Lady Tartleton gave him. She's got a new scheme, I'm afraid.'

Ophelia opened the door, Dodie clinging to her lapels with a desperate and sticky grasp, and went into the sitting-room. In the middle of the scarred linoleum squatted a little boy of two-and-a-half, surrounded by the components of a dismantled disk drive, and leafing happily through a brightly coloured booklet.

'Six piggies, seben piggies, ten piggies!'

'Hello, Innie. Had a nice day with Daddy?'

The toddler looked up, beamed at her, and returned to his booklet, which, Ophelia could see now, was entitled *Pig Breeding the Hygienic Way*.

'Big purple one.'

Ophelia sat down on the large sagging sofa, its geri-atric springs complaining gently, detached Dodie and plugged her on to the other breast. Before replacing the vacated nipple in the decency of her blouse she gave it a sharp stab with her forefinger.

'What's that for?' asked Malachi, who had followed her in. 'Bit masochistic, isn't it? You should have told me you liked that sort of thing.'

'Don't be silly, it's to stop the milk flow. African women do it on buses.'

'Sounds like one of those slogans people have in their rear windows. *African women do it on buses. English-women prefer* . . . Hang on, wasn't there a National Express coach in Cornwall . . . ?'

'There was, yes,' said Ophelia, feeling rather warm even in the chill of the irresolute electric fire, 'but we were very young then and it *was* at the terminus.'

'So was I by the time we'd finished,' grinned Malachi, showing at least three unnecessary dimples.

'Four!' cried Innocent.

'Not quite,' admitted Malachi, 'but I was getting there.'

'Rubbish,' said Ophelia briskly. 'One-and-a-half, then a man came down the aisle with a broom. And my stiff neck didn't clear up until Falmouth. So,' she continued, with a little jerk of efficiency, 'Dodie wouldn't take her bottle, then? Did you try the carrot purée?'

Malachi silently indicated a long orange smear which extended from his shoulder downwards.

'How about the baby rice? Strawberry yoghurt? Chocolate pudding?'

At each suggestion Malachi pointed to the appropriate stain on his sweatshirt.

'Ah. Well, I expect she'll be all right after this feed. What were you saying about Lady Tartleton?'

'This my bagoota,' announced Innocent, having abandoned *Pig Breeding* and returned to the disk drive. 'Boken.'

'I think it's something to do with her American nephew. Do you want a sandwich, by the way? Apparently he's a . . . Hold on, this sounds like them back now. I'll leave her to explain.'

And Malachi fled, with an agility reminiscent of his rugby Blue days, into the kitchen. Moments later the front door was rammed open by someone or thing whose ferocity made Ophelia's own tussles with it look like gentle coaxing, and seven large and variegated Labradors bounded through it. In a few seconds the sitting-room, distinctly grubby to begin with, was transformed into a pandemonium of mud and flying paws. Innocent was knocked over in the first onslaught, his affronted squawks mingled with the dogs' excited woofing, while Dodie was swiped with three or four wagging tails, totally independent of their owners' control. The baby, accustomed to this after three months at Moorwind, merely flapped a tiny hand in their direction and continued to guzzle.

Ophelia did her ineffectual best to impose discipline.

'Meg! Gigabyte! Virgil – no, you're Horace, aren't you? Rea, down!'

The chasing redoubled and the air was filled with floating dog hairs, dancing in a sudden burst of sunlight.

'Sit!' came a voice from the doorway and, as if quite different dogs, the seven Labradors arranged themselves into a neat row, each tidy on its haunches, muzzle raised in military precision, eyes bright with enthusiastic loyalty.

Innocent continued to sniff.

'And stop that snivelling, child!' snapped Lady Tartleton with such a realistic bark that one of the younger dogs began to thump its tail on the floor.

'Lavatorium!'

One glance from those eyes, glittering fierce on either side of the sharp violet nose, was sufficient. Lady Tartleton, tweed and corduroy whistling, strode over to the sofa and stood over Ophelia. 'Suckling again?'

'I've been at work all day. It's her first since breakfast.'

'Hmmm. Well, you won't have to go to that appalling place for much longer. As I've been trying to explain to that husband of yours, I've had a letter from my nephew in America.'

'I didn't know you had a . . .'

'One hardly likes to advertise, Ophelia, that one's relations have been forced to the colonies, particularly the rebellious ones. India's bad enough, and one knew some quite decent people who'd been out there. But that's by the way. Even Australia would be an improvement. Apparently the boy, Stephen is it, or Mark, something dreadfully dull, has done all right for himself over in the States. Professor of Hydro-Porcine Agriculture at the Hank B. Thrupenberry University, Illinois. What d'ye think of that, then, eh?'

'Hydro-porcine . . .' mused Ophelia, trying to dredge together the remnants of her classical education. Dodie seemed to have fallen asleep and so, gingerly, she licked her little finger and carefully inserted it into the baby's mouth, to break the seal upon her breast.

'Wet pigs,' explained Malachi from the doorway. His mother, in the pre-Vatican II days of his infancy, had intended him to be a priest, and had rocked his cradle to gently murmured declensions.

'Exactly,' said Lady Tartleton and then, fearing to demonstrate approval for Malachi, whom she considered a peasant, and suspected of laughing at her, looked around for something to criticize. Her gimlet eye fell on Ophelia.

'I'd just yank it off, if I were you!' she roared, and Dodie's face crumpled in readiness for a fresh scream. Ophelia quickly replaced the nipple and grimaced.

'Thank you so much. So that's what Innocent was looking at, was it? Hydro-Porcine Agriculture.' She looked towards the booklet, abandoned now, along with the disk drive, in favour of an investigation of Horace's genitals. 'Lovely.'

'Oh, d'ye think so?' Lady Tartleton gave a short sniff. 'Thought it sounded a bit bogus myself. But it turns out there's a practical point to it all. Young Matthew's made a fortune with the system in America, apparently, so it ought to work here, even the way this country's going to the dogs.'

The Labradors raised their muzzles slightly higher in exaggerated obedience while Malachi edged past them to join Innocent on the floor, a haphazard bundle of bread and cheese in his hand.

'Not you, my darlings. Metaphorical dogs. Not a decent pedigree among them. So.' She swung her attention back to Ophelia, who was trying to see her watch through Dodie's ear. 'Are you in, then?'

'In what?'

'Brain turned to mush, all this whelping. In the System. In the business.'

'Using this hydro-pork?'

'Exactly. Pig Breeding the Hygienic Way. It's quite brilliant, really, when you come to think about it. Young whoseit, David, obviously outshines all those dreadful gangsters. First of all, instead of keeping the pigs in mud, or straw, or whatever the yokels use, they live in a kind of giant paddling pool. So much more pleasant for all concerned. And, of course, they are fed a strictly vegetarian diet, spoonfed, all natural yoghurt and green vegetables. So wholesome.'

Ophelia was slightly perplexed. All this talk about cleanliness and vegetarianism would normally be anathema to Lady Tartleton, who relished feeding her dogs on raw offal and riding through a dozen newly ploughed fields before breakfast.

'And of course doing it this way won't put the dogs' noses out of joint,' continued the lady. 'Poor blighters, imagine what it would do to them to see a horde of pigs being allowed to wallow in mud all day and gorge themselves on left-overs. Like opening one's house to the *hoi polloi*. Not to mention,' here her face became, if possible, even sharper than usual, 'the economic advantages of this method. Think about it, Ophelia, spoonfeeding, so no waste, none of that expensive pig-food, just greens that are past their sell-by date . . . Do you know, I discovered something last week that no one, not even Father, had ever told me? If you go down to the Market Square on Friday evening, after the stalls have gone, you can sometimes find cabbage leaves on the cobbles, *absolutely free*!'

'Incredible,' said Ophelia, who had twisted her ankle more than once on these instances of heavenly manna. She was only half-listening, for she could hear, through the window behind her, the sounds of her four elder children on their belated return from school.

'Looks like the Witch is here!' came six-year-old Hygenus' ringing and tactless tones.

'Sshhh,' advised Urban, a year younger, but infinitely more adept in the avoidance of trouble.

'I can't face her really, not after a long day at school, can you, Pius?' said Joan with the world-weariness of having just passed her eighth birthday. Pius, the eldest at nearly ten, had evidently nodded his assent, for Ophelia heard the sounds of rustling backpacks and sweet papers as the children settled down on the grimy concrete.

'. . . knows about these things, even if he does look like a corner grocer,' Lady Tartleton was saying.

'Oh, I'm sorry?'

'Mental capacity of an earwig, that's what all this childbirth does for you. Not to mention incontinence. D'ye know, I can go twenty-four hours on horseback without once needing a piss?'

A row of delighted splutters could be heard from under the window.

'And that baby should be weaned by now. You can't tell me noises like that are natural. Anyway, I was saying, if you can concentrate for long enough to listen, that Edgar thinks it's a good idea.'

Malachi looked up with renewed interest. Edgar Pottlebonce, erstwhile farmer, now Agricultural Consultant, was renowned for his ability to predict the most lucrative departures for the farming business.

'Oh yes, what with all this mad cow twaddle, as if cows, even mad, didn't have a damn' sight more sense than the idiots out there. And he thinks there'll be a small fortune just in the EU grants. Just think, Ophelia, *money*!'

'I suppose so,' said Ophelia vaguely. Dodie had

finally finished feeding, but was still clinging to the nipple with her hard little gums. A draught was coming through the ill-fitting window pane across Ophelia's exposed breast, and she was very hungry. The tantalizing vision in Malachi's hand was now blocked by the row of dogs and she wondered whether it might after all have only been a discarded nappy. 'We manage, though. And isn't there something about not laying up treasures on earth.'

Lady Tartleton looked around the room with its scuffed lino, splintered paint and ominous brown patches appearing through the wallpaper.

'If you had laid up a few more treasures on earth,' she suggested wryly, 'your poor dogs might at least have a bit of carpet to lie on, in front of a respectable fire. If you're sure that you won't come to live with me at Yardley Farm,' Malachi and Ophelia gave simultaneous shudders, 'then you could at least take this opportunity to get yourselves something more appropriate. As for treasure, everyone knows these days, so whatsisface, Daniel, tells me, that it's quite all right to go straight for the – what do those vulgar young men on the television call it? – *dosh*. Sign of God's approval, apparently, and one can quite understand. Don't suppose the Almighty went to all the trouble of creating good honest sterling for it to be splashed about by the oiks. So, you two,' she looked dubiously at Malachi, fearing that, again, her hauteur might be mellowing, 'I'll expect you in with me. Got to dash now. Come on, chaps!'

The four male Labradors, three fully grown and one

large puppy, broke ranks and bounded after her. Ophelia and Malachi heard the door slam, one of its plywood panels fall to the floor and Dodie give a little sigh. Then there was silence, broken by the opening of the kitchen door.

'Well, what d'ye think?' asked Malachi, through a mouthful of cheese.

'Is that my sandwich?'

'Sorry. Sounds a good plan, I would have thought. She's got her head screwed on, really, hasn't she, that Lady Tartleton, even if she is a bit of a battle-axe?'

'I don't think so, Mal. It's quite true that we could do with a bit of extra money, especially the way your business has been going lately . . .'

Malachi opened his blue eyes very wide and gave a pout that was fractionally genuine.

'I made three sales last week.'

'Two floppy disks and an ergonomic arm-rest. Hardly enough to keep us in luxurious splendour. But even if this pigs idea would work, and I can't see it, wouldn't they all catch cold, knee-deep in water through a Rambleton winter, she's going to want capital to start it up, isn't she, to buy the piglets in the first place and set up the paddling pool? We can just about get by on what I earn, but we certainly haven't got anything spare that we can afford to risk. I'm sorry, Mal, but someone has to be practical.'

' "Someone has to be practical." You heard. People only say things like that when it's *really* bad. We must be on the sink of starvation.' Pius, his stomach comfortably filled with a purloined half-packet of Jaffa cakes, spoke with a certain relish.

Urban gave a long sniff.

'Now look what you've done,' said Joan. 'Come here, Urbs and have a digestive. Pius doesn't mean it.'

But Urban stayed shivering on his bottom bunk, arms wrapped around his bony knees in silent martyrdom.

'He does mean it, you know,' said Hygenus. 'We'll all be skelingtons and ghosts. Woo-oooh!'

'Sshhh,' cautioned Joan with a nod towards the party wall with their parents' bedroom. The conference was taking place during the brief hiatus between Dodie's midnight and two o'clock feeds and the sounds of grateful snores would have been audible, had not all the children been trying to talk at once.

'All I was saying . . .' began Pius.

'Urbs'll probbly die first,' said Hygenus.

'I don't like skelingtons,' snuffled Urban.

'Sshhh!' said Joan again.

'Want a bit-git,' declared Innocent, waking up for the first time and the Jaffa cakes and digestives were duly passed around.

'Well, what about this idea of the W— Lady Tartleton's?' said Pius, as soon as his tongue was free to move.

'*Breeding Pigs the Hygenus Way*!' cried that young man, only to be told, rather scathingly, by his sister, that there was a world of difference between Hygen*us* and Hygien*ic*.

'You only have to look at your hands to see that.'

Hygenus squinted at his palms by the dim bedside lamp. 'They're okay. Aren't any atchull *lumps* of dirt, only sort of smears. You can't go around worrying about just smears. And I think pigs is a good idea, anyway.'

There was a general consensus of this opinion, inspired mainly by Lady Tartleton's references to feeding the pigs on left-over vegetables. All the O. children were under the firm impression, probably derived from bedtime stories, that they were forced to eat large quantities of cabbage, broccoli and swede. In fact they had only slight and fleeting inklings as to what these horrors even looked like, for Malachi's idea of a balanced meal consisted of dolloping extra tomato ketchup on the Pot Noodles.

'But we need that, what Mum said, capital,' objected Joan.

'I can do capitals,' said Urban, shuffling forward on his bed. 'Mrs Clarke says I'm really good.'

Hygenus was sceptical. 'In Reception? I don't think so, Urbs. I don't think you do capitals in Reception. Not *really good* capitals.'

'We do,' Urban's lower lip was pulsing ominously. 'I do U for Urban and I do O. And M for Mummy and . . .'

'It's not that kind of capitals, anyway,' said Pius. 'It means money. Everyone go and see how much they've got.'

There was a general scampering and creaking of overloaded drawers as the little boys searched for their money boxes.

'I know mine anyway,' said Joan. 'Three pounds eighty-two.'

'*Three pounds eighty-two!*' Hygenus could scarcely

have summoned up more righteous indignation had he
been Dennis Skinner himself, surveying the Crown
estates. 'How'd you get three pounds eighty-two? I've
only got eight and a quarter pence, and five of that's
French.'

'What's the quarter?'

Hygenus looked more closely. 'A dead ladybird.'

Urban painstakingly counted out twenty-six pence, all
in two pence pieces, while Pius contributed two rather
sticky pound coins. Innocent had been forbidden to have
any money until he was three, as he always ate it.

'Dodie's got loads of money,' said Hygenus
morosely, 'but it's in that china pig and we can't get it
without breaking the silly thing. You'd think that a
china pig would want to help us get some real ones,
but I don't s'pose Mum and Dad would be very
pleased.'

'I don't think they would,' agreed Pius. 'But we can't
do much with six pounds whatever it is. Pigs cost ever so
much, I bet, probably fifty pounds each or something
like that.'

The children sat in unaccustomed gloom and Dodie,
perhaps disturbed by the lull, began to cry.

'I'd better get back to bed,' said Joan, 'before Mum
starts wandering about. Everyone think how to raise
some money and we'll have another meeting next week.
'Night. God bless, boys.'

'Bless,' repeated her brothers automatically, their
minds buzzing with commerce.

But it was not the children's melancholy which woke

their little sister but the preparatory whirr of the old-fashioned telephone before it began to ring. Malachi stumbled through, his pyjama legs, as ever, precariously long, while Ophelia scooped up the soggy and squalling Dodie.

''Eyyo?' yawned Malachi. ''Oo's it?'

'Please, I would like to be speaking to Mrs O.?'

'Would you? I suppose you'd better then. Oaf? Kraut for you.'

Ophelia stumbled through with difficulty, trailing cot sheets and damp extremities.

'Don't be such a xenophobe. Kraut? Are you sure? Hello?'

'Is Mrs O.?'

'Yes. Oh, Zuke.'

Malachi, over Dodie's head, gave a pantomime of incredulity. '*Zuke?*'

'Shhh. No, not you. What did you say?'

'I fear I wake you up. I forget, you English like to be, what is it, *early to bed, early to rise*?'

'*Makes a man healthy, wealthy and wise.* It hasn't worked so far, so I wouldn't worry about it. Has something happened?'

'I go to police, as you advise.'

'What, just now?'

'Oh no. In afternoon. Respectable English time. Since then I am thinking.'

Ophelia supposed that, as a chess player, he was used to this, but she could not help wishing that his thoughts had either ceased earlier or gone on to the morning. Feeding Dodie now might encourage her to sleep until five or six but was far more likely merely to stimulate her appetite so that she would wake again at hourly intervals throughout the night.

'And what did the police say?'

A note of triumph came into Zuke's voice. 'As I thought, is same as everywhere. "Go away old foreign man," they are telling me. "Your wife, she die of heart attack, is all. Now go away, go away, we have many important forms to fill." '

That, thought Ophelia, sounded authentic enough.

'So, after all, you must be finding murderer for me, yes? Is very good pay, do not worry. Is agreed? Is agreed, Mrs O.?'

'Hang on a moment. And by the way, you'd better call me Ophelia if I'm to call you Zuke. As I said before, I'm a solicitor, not a private detective. I wouldn't know where to start in finding a murderer.'

'*Murderer?*'

'Quiet, Mal. I tell you what I'll do, Zuke. I'll go and see the police myself for you and try to persuade them to investigate a bit further. And meanwhile, of course, I'll be looking for Trotter's Bottom and I'll let you know if anything suspicious comes up. Okay?'

'Okay, Ophelia. I am like a small piece of clay in your hands. You are my only hope.' Zuke replaced the receiver with a dramatic click, leaving Ophelia standing in the cold hall, listening to the dialling tone. The line had, she now realized, been unusually bad, even for Rambleton.

Malachi was standing behind her, practising his masterful expression, which was not easy, with his pyjama jacket buttoned up all wrong.

'Murderer? Zuke? Trotter's Bottom? What is all this, Oaf? I hope you're not getting involved in anything *dangerous*.'

Ophelia smiled. He was irresistible really, with his little fringe of blond hair sticking up and nice bits of solid torso peeping out from the disordered pyjamas. Dodie had fallen asleep again as Ophelia had talked on the phone, for which she was suddenly glad. She had just remembered that there were other things her body could do. She slipped her spare hand around to the base of Malachi's spine, just where the frayed cord was edging downwards.

'Come along then,' she whispered, 'show me exactly how dangerous I'm allowed to be.'

Chapter Three

The Moscow Variation

''Ello, love,' said the policeman cheerily.

'Hello, yourself,' replied Ophelia, pleasantly surprised. The last time that she had visited Rambleton police station the desk had been manned by an ancient and embittered sergeant whose policy towards all intruders was to assume their guilt until he was inevitably proved right. By contrast, this genial young man, broad and blond, had rather the demeanour of a wedding reception D.J., enticing guests on to the dance floor.

'Did you want anything special,' he asked now, 'or just a sit down? We've got new chairs.'

Ophelia followed his proprietorial gaze towards a pair of chrome tubular chairs, blindingly upholstered in turquoise nylon.

'They're lovely,' she began, but was saved from the social obligation to lie further by a bellow from the screened-off area beyond the desk.

'Pigeon!'

'Yes, sir?' The boy's expression froze. 'What've I done now, sir?'

'How many times must I iterate this, Pigeon: *Those chairs are not for use by the General Public*. Those chairs are a symbol, Pigeon, a symbol of a new era, of the modernization, digitization, technologicize . . . technize . . . technicalize . . . computerization of this station. They are not for the flea-ridden bums of Rambleton riff-raff.'

'But it's not riff-raff, sir and I don't think her bum's got fleas. Sorry, madam, bottom.'

'That's not the point, Constable, and you should know it. How long had Sergeant Warner been requesting new reception seating? Eleven years and eight months. How many requisitions in triplicate on Form Four-hundred-and-three-A had he submitted? Fourteen.'

It was rather like the old Catechism, thought Ophelia. Quite soothing, really.

'And when did the chairs appear in the reception area? On the day after Sergeant Warner retired, on my first day commanding this station.'

'Only 'cos you'd kept them hidden in the storeroom for three years,' muttered Constable Pigeon.

'What was that, what was that? You'll recall, Pigeon, that you've already received seventeen verbal warnings and five formal reprimands for insubordination. This week. I hope I don't have to remind you that – oh.'

The voice, accompanied by large and appropriate footfalls, had been drawing nearer for the past few words and now their speaker emerged from behind the screen.

'Constable Booking!' cried Ophelia in genuine

surprise. The last time that she had seen Brian Booking, he had been a subordinate himself, still nervously brooding on his wife's possible infidelities at the annual Police Ball. He had put on a considerable amount of weight since then, and his ineffectual garrulity had been overlaid by this unconvincing authoritarianism.

'*Sergeant* Booking, if you don't mind.'

'Congratulations,' said Ophelia blandly. 'Your wife must be very pleased.'

Sergeant Booking's eyes narrowed and his jaw set beneath its new fleshy covering. His wife's predilection (had he imagined it, after all?) for higher ranking officers had been the cause of many a sleepless dawn for the hapless Constable Booking.

'Can we *help* you, madam, or is this merely a social call?'

Ophelia explained.

'Oooh,' breathed Constable Pigeon. 'A murder, in Rambleton? We've not had one of them before, have we, Sergeant?'

'Not since *I've* been in command,' said Booking, suggesting that, under the jurisdiction of the hapless Sergeant Warner, the town's homicide rate would have made the Chicago Police Department gasp and reach for their smelling salts. 'And there certainly isn't one now. You weren't on duty yesterday afternoon, were you, Pigeon?'

'Afternoon off, sir. I went down the funfair with my sister's kiddies. Dead good, it was. Ee, I won a coconut! You ever won a coconut, sir?'

'No, only worked with them. But this client of Mrs O's – what was his name, again?'

'Mr Zhukovsky.'

'Zoo – cough – ski. Exactly. Now, what does that say to you, Pigeon? Zoo. Cough. Ski.'

'One of them aptitude tests, is it, sir? Ooh, you've got me there. I'm too young to've done the Eleven Plus. Zoo is to Cough as Ski is to . . . Oh I know! Broken leg, sir.'

'Imbecile. What I'm trying to say, Pigeon— By the way, were you always called that, or did your mother choose it when she realized the size of your brain?'

'What, Pigeon? It's me surname, isn't it, sir? Me dad, me granddad, we've all been Pigeons.'

'Exactly.' It had obviously become a favourite word with Sergeant Booking, frustrated by the general inexactitude of life. 'But as regards Mr Zoo-Cough-Ski, well, just listen to it. Zoo-*Cough*-Ski!' Booking pronounced the central syllable with a wild Slavic grimace, like an electrocuted Alexi Sayle, but Constable Pigeon still failed to get the point. 'He's a *foreigner*, isn't he?'

'You mean he's not from Rambleton?' Constable Pigeon was aghast. As a cadet, he had once had to travel as far as Leeds himself, but had assumed that the great wide world would not be callous enough to pursue him back to his own police station. He glanced across at the turquoise chairs with sudden trepidation.

'Not from Rambleton, lad, not from Mid-Yorkshire, not from ruddy England!' Sergeant Booking was enjoying his subordinate's discomfiture. 'He's a Russky.'

'Ah.'

'Aye.'

The two men seemed content to collapse into one of

the monosyllabic conversations much enjoyed by York-
shiremen, especially between long draughts of bitter.

'Hmm.'

'Aye.'

Drastic measures, Ophelia realized, were necessary, if
she was ever to break through this somnolent dialogue.

'You've passed it on to Scorsdale C.I.D., then, I
assume?'

'What?!' The dislike and mistrust of the uniformed
policeman for his plain-clothes colleagues was surpassed
only by the chip which wobbled on Rambleton's collective shoulder at the mention of its neighbouring county
town. 'That bunch of leather-jacketed layabouts? I'd not
trust them to clean up a baby.'

'Nor me,' said Constable Pigeon loyally.

'No, I'd not trust them to clean up you, either. And,
like I've been trying to say for the past ten minutes,
there's no case here for them to clean up, or anyone else.
That Hilda died nice and quiet over her boiled egg, just
like I'd hope to go myself, when the time comes.' His
face darkened, perhaps thinking of the opportunities that
would be opened for the widow Booking and for the
death-in-service benefits squandered on cheap perfume,
Cinzano and Acting Chief Inspectors. 'Any talk otherwise is just the fevered imagination of that Communist
husband. Deranged by grief, I shouldn't wonder, and
they've all been a bit excitable since the Berlin Wall
came down. I mean, just look at that Boris Yeltsin.
Dancing in the street. Wouldn't catch Mr Major behav-
ing like that, would you? Mind you, he's always struck
me as a nice cup of tea man, and you don't get the

hystericals from them, do you? Now the trouble with your vodka – you want to listen to this, Pigeon, this is good police information – the trouble with your vodka is that it doesn't smell. Stands to reason, you won't catch your Englishman sozzled in the afternoon (I don't speak for the Scots, mind) because he knows you'd whiff it a mile away. But these Russkies, they can wolf down the vodka and still come up smelling like a toothpaste factory. That's National Character for you, you see.'

Constable Pigeon looked duly impressed, or perhaps he was just reading his horoscope in the opened copy of the *Sun*.

'So you're not treating it as murder?'

'We are *not*,' said Sergeant Booking decisively, his exegesis cut short by the realization that it was nearly eleven and that he had not yet had his mid-morning cup of coffee. There were only four chocolate biscuits left, and he had no intention of sharing them with either Pigeon or Ophelia. 'My own granny's death was more suspicious, and she was turned ninety-seven.' Ophelia showed no signs of leaving, so he added, with bad grace, 'I suppose you can see the death certificate if you really want to. He left us a copy.'

Ophelia peered with interest at the cheap photocopy, its grainy blackness making the doctor's handwriting more difficult than ever to read. She could make out almost nothing of the details, but the signature at the bottom was familiar. From her purse she took a prescription for Malachi's skin cream, which she had forgotten to take to the chemist. Yes, the two large Hs, separated by a mass of tight squiggles, were unmistakable. The certifying doctor was their own family G.P. and Malachi's best friend, Dr Horatio Hale.

Ophelia quickly left the police station, having gained Sergeant Booking's grudging acknowledgement that she would not be committing any criminal offence, were she to investigate the matter herself, and walked down Church Lane to the surgery. Behind her, the sounds of recrimination alternated with the chink of teaspoons. Horatio was busy 'with a patient', as the imperturbable receptionist put it, although the thumping and bouncing noises from his room suggested rather that he was practising his drop kicks. Ophelia knew that it was of no use to argue, and so she made an appointment to see him on Thursday, with Dodie as her excuse.

By now her stomach, tantalized but unsated by a half-slice of Innocent's breakfast toast, with the butter already licked off, was making ferocious growling sounds, which had made the receptionist wonder whether she ought, after all, to disturb Dr Hale. There was no way, Ophelia told herself, that she could concentrate on Mrs McMurdo's Deed of Gift without some more substantial nourishment. And, in any case, she had been on client's business throughout. That gave her an idea.

Rambo's, read the coffee-coloured italics over the side entrance to the Grand Hotel. The sign had apparently not been up for long, for its neon was still comparatively free of flies, and no schoolchildren had yet worked out a way to manipulate the letters into something humorously obscene. It could, of course, be that the very existence of this – wine bar, was it? – was so inappropriate to

Rambleton that no further comment was necessary. It certainly contrasted effectively, with its smart cream canopy and smoked glass doors, with the main entrance to the hotel, which suggested, by its broken handle and drifts of dirty litter, that no one had passed its portal for several months. In any case, Ophelia was more concerned at the moment with the welcome *Open* sign in Rambo's window, and the slightly precious menu stuck up beside it.

'I'll have, er, a Brie and black grape baguette,' she said, choosing at random from the laminated copy of the menu at her table. Close up, it looked even more pretentious, even if, to the rest of the country, salade niçoise and sun-dried tomatoes were now distinctly passé.

'And to drink, *madame*? *Café au lait*?' asked the irritatingly efficient waiter in what, she was pleased to note, was an extremely bad French accent.

'A cup of tea,' she said, just to annoy him.

'Earl Grey? Lapsang Souchong?'

'Yorkshire.'

Having got rid of the now contemptuous waiter, she looked around the room. It was dimly lit by red and green lamps in what was presumably supposed to create a mysterious evening ambience but, on a dull November morning, was merely dismal. The place was fuller than she would have expected, with late morning coffees and early lunches, but, considering that Rambleton's only alternative was the grease-soaked Patty's Pantry, perhaps it was not so surprising after all. Six or eight middle-aged ladies sat in pairs, fur coats hunched over their Danish pastries, and talked in loud adenoidal voices about the others. Behind them, in the corners, lurked teenage couples, furtively smoking and eking out a shared Coke, and the occasional solitary man. For two men to have lunch together, never mind coffee, would be deeply suspicious to the Rambleton mentality.

The waiter returned with her cup of tea, flouncing with such bad grace that most of the tea slopped into the saucer and most of the lunchers looked up with curiosity.

'Why, it is Ophelia!' cried a voice from the farthest corner, and Zuke, his cappuccino held aloft, wove his way, with surprising dexterity considering his girth, past the other tables to join her. Having attracted the attention of the whole room, he proceeded to ensure that he kept it by lifting a menu histrionically to his cheek and whispering loudly behind it.

'Haf you yet uncovered the criminal?'

Ophelia looked nervously around the room before replying. The fur-coated ladies stared back at her and then turned away, convinced that nothing of real importance could involve such a nondescript heroine. 'Those *fingernails*!' she heard one of them scoff to her friend. One couple, however, whom she had not noticed before, continued to watch her with unusual attention. The man was only a few years younger than Ophelia, but with the unfinished, undercooked look of the late developer. A stamp collector, perhaps, Ophelia thought, or a model railway enthusiast. His companion, by contrast, seemed only too experienced. She was probably twenty years older than him, though it was impossible to be sure without peeling off the iridescent mask of foundation, blusher, and unspecified sparkle. Her hair was worn up, and her neckline low, leaving, between them, vast billows of throat and cleavage. One ring-encrusted hand was tucked cosily into the crook of the man's elbow while the other toyed with a voluptuous meringue.

'You have news?' persisted Zuke.

'Not really, I'm afraid.' She recounted the fiasco of the police interview.

Zuke was neither surprised nor disappointed. 'But you are finding him yourself? Or her, I mean.'

Something in that last comment made Ophelia look across the room again at the curious couple. Yes, they were both still watching intently, although the young man had the grace to redden and lower his head as he caught Ophelia's eye.

'I, um, well . . .' Ophelia had no great estimation of her investigative abilities, but after her experiences that morning, had to admit that they were probably greater than those of Messrs Booking and Pigeon. After all, if she did discover anything suspicious, she could always go back to the police and let them take over. Also, she had to admit, the discovery of Horatio Hale's signature on the death certificate had not exactly reassured her as to the cause of Hilda's death. Horatio was a charming and generous friend, with an alluring bedside manner all the more seductive for being entirely unconscious, but his diagnostic skills and general medical knowledge were those of the average corncrake. It would do no harm to try to find out what he had actually seen of his brief patient, rather than what his ever-suggestible brain had been skimming through in last month's BMJ.

'I'm looking into it.' She could not resist a brief

glance back at their spectators. Yes, there they still were, the woman's hand tightened on her companion's arm, her meringue now abandoned, untouched except for a crumbled crust. The waiter minced across to them.

'Would monsieur and madame care for the bill?'

'Mademoiselle. And we're *residents*, sweetie. Room seventeen.'

On her way out, having regretfully declined to join Zuke in a pair of chocolate eclairs, Ophelia was unobtrusively halted by a hand on her arm. Another young man stood beside her, a slightly older version of the waiter, with the same expensive air of discomfort, like a professional footballer in a business suit. He wore a gold name badge on his lapel: *JASON SPIKEWORT – EXECUTIVE MANAGER*. The name was familiar to Ophelia from somewhere, though she could not think for the moment where she had heard it.

'Do excuse me for bothering you,' he said, in a voice so cultivated that it could only have been purchased by mail-order from the Sunday supplements. 'I'm a little concerned. Are you a friend of Mr Zhukovsky?'

'I'm his solicitor,' said Ophelia, unable to think either of a lie or of a good reason why she should tell one.

'Ah. Ah *good*. I'm glad he's got somebody.' A solicitor, he implied, while not as good as a friend, would suffice for the friendless. Ophelia was inclined to agree. 'I have been worried about him, Mrs . . .'

'O.' Was it the wedding ring, the Weetabix tide-mark on her shoulder or just her general air of fatigue and complacence that made her married status so obvious?

'Most apprehensive, Mrs O. I'm afraid that this poor business of his wife has had a terrible effect on him. Quite unbalancing, of course, for anyone, even if they weren't—'

'A foreigner?' suggested Ophelia, anticipating a reprise of the policemen's parochialism, dancing Boris Yeltsin and all.

'—in a strange place, I was going to say. We can't afford stereotypes in the tourism business, you know. Not with all the overseas visitors we see.'

In Rambleton? Ophelia wanted to protest. There had once been an exchange visit with some Finnish school-children, she believed, but the Finns had rebelled at the tedium of Mid-Yorkshire and pined for the relative thrills of wood pulp manufacture and sixty thousand lakes. But Jason might not always have worked in Rambleton.

'I think he blames himself, poor dear.'

'For Hilda's death?'

'Not *directly* of course.' Jason sounded reproving at the crudity of Ophelia's implication. 'I've rarely seen a man so devoted. But bringing her so far, in her fragile state of health . . .' His pale grey eyes grew alarmingly moist. 'Not that he had any choice, as far as I can gather. At least she died quickly, in comfort.'

Apart from the coffee and eggs, thought Ophelia.

'Instead of slowly starving in a Moscow garret.'

Ophelia had never been quite sure what a garret was, apart from an Irish politician. Did they really have them in Moscow? She realized, too late, that Jason had asked her a question.

'Oh, sorry?'

'I can see that you're as concerned as I am. I just said, do take care of him, won't you? I'll keep an eye out here, of course, but you can imagine what it's like with a whole hotel to run. Chaos, my dear!'

The flicking efficiency of Rambo's was nothing like chaos, and Ophelia said so.

'How kind of you. Yes, it is taking off, isn't it? The owners said there was no call for that sort of thing in Rambleton, but as I've always believed, there's a market everywhere for the exclusive.' This seemed like a contradiction in terms, but Ophelia could not be bothered to work it out. 'I've got a long way to go with the hotel itself, of course.' He gave a deprecating little shrug and a shy smile.

He was probably right, thought Ophelia on her way, unable to postpone it any longer, back to the office. No doubt Zuke's conviction that Hilda had been murdered was just a displacement of his own guilt. Men did not expect their wives to die before them, particularly if the husband was older. She would just check things out with Horatio on Thursday and then try to persuade Zuke to forget it. There was still Trotter's Bottom to find, after all. And that, she told herself more cheerfully, taking an instinctive detour into the cake shop, was a much more suitable case for a respectable solicitor.

Chapter Four

The Knight's Tour

'By the way,' bellowed Ophelia over the uproar of the evening's supper table, 'does anyone know if we've got a book about chess in the house?' Before they had parted, Zuke had expressed interest in the progress of her chess-playing child and his wish to meet him. Or was it her? Ophelia had succeeded in changing the subject, but knew that she could not do so for ever. Sooner or later the sacrificial lamb – or should it be pawn? – would have to be chosen.

Hygenus and Urban paused briefly in their efforts to capture the world land-speed mashed potato record.

'We've got a set,' said Hygenus, wrinkling his freckled nose judiciously, 'but Urban lost the rules.'

'I didn't! Honussly, I didn't, Mummy!' Urban's large blue eyes, exactly matching his father's, blinked ominously and his lower lip began to wobble.

'We know you didn't,' interrupted Pius, conscious, as ever, that, as the eldest, he was encumbered with compensating for his parents' inadequacies. 'It was Hygenus who made a paper boat out of them and sailed it on the stream. I did *tell* him but of course he never listens.'

'Yawn, yawn,' said Hygenus, investigating the aerodynamic properties of bisected sausages.

Ophelia gave up. 'Hygenus, stop messing about with your food.'

'Me do't!' cried Innocent, noticing his brother's activities for the first time. 'Innie do't!' He flung a sausage, liberally daubed with tomato ketchup, across the table. It bounced off Malachi's thinly covered scalp and fell to the floor where it was rapidly swallowed by one of the lurking Labradors.

'Now look what you've done! Honestly, I don't know why I don't just give all of your meals straight to the dogs, since that's where they invariably end up. Good boy, Urban, you eat up nicely. And I thought I told you not to play in the stream, Pius.'

'Oh, did I say stream?' Pius raised his sandy eyebrows in utter ingenuousness. 'I think I must have meant bath.'

'I know where there's one.' Joan looked up from the copy of *Jennings in Trouble* propped up against her empty plate.

'Oh, Joan, do you have to read at the table?'

Joan considered the question carefully. 'I think I do, really, yes. All these boys, I can't stand it otherwise. I'm just waiting for Dodie to get big enough to be on my side.'

'I wish you didn't have to have these gender battles all the time,' said Ophelia, mainly to herself. 'When you were all tiny, I imagined that you'd just be, well, *children*, together.'

'We are, mostly, Mum,' Pius reassured her. 'But we're naturally different, aren't we? We've been doing it at school, all about hairy armpits and monthly prods. At least, I think it was prods. Did you know that ladies . . .?'

'Very likely,' said Ophelia quickly, noticing Urban's apprehensive interest. 'You know where there's what, Joan?'

'A book about chess. At least, I thought I saw one. It came in that box of books from Auntie Agnes. We'll have a look after tea.'

'Auntie Agnes?' said Hygenus, rolling a baked bean lugubriously around his mouth. 'Is she the one that was dead for three days then Grandpa found her? I wonder what she looked like. Was there any *rats*, d'ye know?'

Ophelia hastily fetched the chocolate mousse.

It was a quarter-past ten by the time all the children had been packed off to the rising damp of their bedrooms. Ophelia and Malachi sat opposite one another in front of the single functioning electric bar and clutched their mugs of Madeira.

'Had a good day, love?' asked Malachi, patting her knee with clumsy tenderness.

'Oh, not bad.' Some solicitors, Ophelia knew, were able to combine the requirements of client confidentiality with cosy night time chats with their spouses. Unfortunately, Malachi had never grasped the concept of reticence and she had learned not to tell him anything that should not, by the following lunchtime, be common currency in St Barnabas' playground and the Ram's Leg. 'Quite interesting, really. How about you?'

'Well, the baby woke up as soon as you went, and screamed all day. Wouldn't take anything, not even the rest of my Curly-Wurly. Eventually she just bawled herself to sleep. Honestly, Oaf, I wish you hadn't gone back to work.'

'I've got to, Mal. At least, someone has.' Ophelia was too tired to discuss the shortcomings of Wet Nose Solutions. She picked up the book that Joan had found for her and made a few conciliatory noises into her Madeira for Malachi's benefit. He reciprocated and buried himself in his 1973 Boys' Rugby Annual.

The book was more advanced than she had hoped, full of opening variations and end-game studies, but by a process of elimination she managed to deduce from these how the pieces actually moved. After twenty minutes of this, Ophelia stopped to wonder how her aunt had got hold of the book in the first place. Great-Aunt Agnes, who had never been persuaded in life even to take her turn at Beggar My Neighbour, could scarcely have been interested in the relative merits of the Evans and Blackmar-Diemer Gambits. The answer was to be found, as she turned the book over, on a dirty sticker on the back cover. *Reduced – 12½p*. Auntie Agnes could never resist a bargain.

She turned back to Chapter Three: *Mating in the Middlegame* and wondered whether she could bear any more that evening. A deep, shuddering snore aroused her, and she looked up to find Malachi fast asleep, clutching a photograph of J. P. R. Williams to his sticky chest.

Ophelia closed her book, uncurled her cramped legs and kissed her husband on his pinkish scalp.

'Come along, sweetheart,' she whispered. 'Time for bed.'

Malachi stretched, dropping the rugby annual on the floor and wrapped his arms sleepily around her. A drop of milk squeezed itself around the edge of her bra and fell on to his upper lip.

'Yum,' he murmured, opening one eye. 'Time indeed.'

His amorousness lasted all of fifty-five seconds, until the discovery that Gigabyte had eaten the toothpaste cast out all more trivial thoughts. Grunting with annoyance, for though Malachi might dispense, for a fortnight at a time, with either bath or shower, his teeth were solemnly scoured after each meal, he scrambled, head first, beneath the duvet, and, once his feet were neatly tucked under his pillow, fell asleep again. Ophelia stayed awake for a little longer, listening to the low murmur from the boys' room next door, but within minutes she too was sleeping.

The murmur was in fact Pius' elucidation of the principles of Applied Christian Numerology.

'It's all in this book that Joan found next to the chess one,' he explained, waving a garish paperback, obviously rapidly remaindered, above his head. 'It's all about how, if you choose symbolic numbers from the Bible, you'll have good luck.'

'Good luck in what?' asked Hygenus sceptically. 'D'ye mean lucky like grownups say you're lucky, having school dinners and jumpers without many holes? 'Cos if that's all, then I think I'll just play Mucous Turtles.'

'Good luck in things that use *numbers*.'

'You mean getting your sums right? I always do that anyway. Mrs Spencer says I'm a genius. Or something like a genius. Is gargoyle the same thing?'

Joan was beginning to get the idea. 'Like lotteries?'

'I'm glad someone's got some sense, even if it is only a girl. Yes, of course lotteries. We just need to get Dad to buy us some tickets. He won't mind, long as we don't tell Mum.' Pius gave the younger ones a warning stare.

'What are the numbers, then?'

'Well, there are lots, really. Thirty-three – how old Jesus was when he died. Four – Evangle-something – people that wrote the Gospels. Seven – the Holy Spirit. Don't know why it's that.'

'Just his favourite number, I 'spect.'

'S'pose so.'

''Wenty-two!' called Innocent, with the ebullience of a natural bingo-caller.

'Yes, that's one, Innie. Er, letters of the Hebrew alphabet and how many books there are in the Old Testament. You see?'

'Umm,' said Joan. 'But how do you know which ones to use. I mean, the lottery ticket only takes six numbers, doesn't it?'

'You have to tailor it to your, er, Personal Devotional Programme.'

'My what?'

'Personal Devotional Programme. It's like spiritual

60

life that Sister Hedwig talks about in Children's Liturgy.'

'But what's the difference between that and just saying our prayers?'

'It *is* saying your prayers,' said Pius, with a frustrated kick of the bunk bed ladder. 'It *is* saying your prayers, but deciding who you're going to say them to.'

'God,' said Urban promptly.

'Yes but Who? God the Father, God the Son, or God the Holy Spirit?'

'I didn't know there was three Gods,' said Hygenus, looking up from his jammed Turtle Flying Pizza Wagon, which had never recovered from being loaded with Innocent's discarded scrambled egg. 'I don't think Father Jim knows that. He always says, "We believe in one God." Has he got it wrong?'

Pius looked at him pityingly. 'Haven't you even *heard* of the Trinity?'

'No.'

'I have,' said Urban. 'Isn't it a sort of fossil?' His two-year-long fascination with dinosaurs was now leading him even further back into prehistory.

'I think that's a trilobite,' whispered Joan.

Pius perched on a pile of pillows, his legs drawn up under him like a small Buddha, and set about the instruction of his heathen brothers and sister.

'The Trinity,' he announced, looking sternly at little Innocent, who was pulling the feathers out of the only remaining pillow, 'is Three Persons in One.'

'One what?' asked Hygenus truculently.

'Bed,' giggled Urban, before he could stop himself, and plunged his mortified face into the duvet which he was sharing with Joan and Innocent.

'Oh, *honestly*! One God, of course. At least, I think so.'

'Shouldn't it be three people?' asked Joan, who was the best at English. 'The plural of person is people.'

'So there's one God and he's got two helpers with him?' clarified Hygenus. 'Sort of like the Three Musketeers?'

'Da da *da*!' chorused the three younger boys, and the instruction session collapsed in a tangle of pyjama cords, flying egg pellets and theological confusion.

For the rest of that week, Adeodata cried. She woke early in the morning, before anyone else in the family, and lay sobbing quietly in the white wood cot next to her parents' bed. Ophelia would wake, roll herself wearily on to the splintered floor and whisper, at which the baby's tears would stop in mid-roll to be replaced by smiles, kicks and triumphant cries of 'Cooee-coo-coo!'

Then Ophelia would lift Dodie out of the cot, guide her impatiently sucking mouth to the feeding slits in her Mothercare nightdress and return to the warm, sagging comfort of her bed. Those were the happiest half-hours of that difficult week; the baby a damp, clinging bundle, the smells of milk and talcum powder mingling with the ammonia of an overnight nappy, a paperback precariously balanced on a ridge of the duvet and, eventually, a cup of weak tea placed just out of reach on the bedside table. Finally, when Dodie's vacuuming desire had dwindled to the occasional absent-minded swallow, and her angry pummelling of Ophelia's breast had been replaced by the sharp tickle of tiny, never quite smooth finger-nails, just when Ophelia was glancing nervously at the unreliable alarm clock, the baby's mouth would, with a little pop, pull away and its puckered O stretch into a crescent of happiness, unattributable to either reflexes or wind.

But as soon as Ophelia swung her legs wearily over the side of the bed, Dodie, with the instinct for impend-ing desertion common to small children and animals, would clench her minuscule fists, draw her damp knees up to her chest, and let out a long wail, anger mixed with a keening note of betrayal. Ophelia could scarcely bear it and nothing short of total immersion in her tights drawer could keep her from fitting herself back into the warm hollow and taking the mourning child in her arms.

Despite her long experience of motherhood, this attachment was a new phenomenon to Ophelia, whose previous five children, with the exception of a brief period of clinginess by Innocent, in the few days follow-ing Adeodata's conception, had always been only too happy to be abandoned, whether by arrangement or accident, and had invariably preferred to be under the charge of their father, to whom nutrition, homework and personal hygiene were unfamiliar concepts, than that of their intermittently conscientious mother. Ophelia's own mother pointed out, with her customary sensitivity, that she had never left any of the other children so early, certainly not before they were fully weaned.

'In any case,' she said, while on one of her regular missions from Macclesfield, 'as I've told you with the other five, this, er, *bosom*-feeding isn't at all a good idea.

Your father wanted me to try it with you and Laertes, but I told him, "I'm not having any of that." '

'Any of what, Ma?'

'You know perfectly well what I mean. Peculiar *undercover dealings*. It only encourages them, exposing one's chest at all hours of the day and night. Don't be cheeky. And don't call me Ma. It's *desperately* common.'

Despite such cheering encounters, Ophelia felt no better. Demoralized by her maternal inadequacies, dishevelled by last-minute caresses and the regurgitation of 7-Grain Cereal and groggy from intermittent sleep and the constant dialectic between her contending responsibilities, she practically fell into Dr Hale's consulting room on Thursday afternoon.

'Ophelia!' he beamed, coming out to meet her and colliding with the sleeping Adeodata. 'Looking as lovely as ever, I see.'

'I hardly think so.'

He paused, his smooth brown hands still resting on her shoulders, and leaned forward. 'No, you're not really, are you? A bit tired, perhaps?'

'A bit.' To her horror, Ophelia felt an ominous pricking around her sinuses. She blinked rapidly and tried to stare at Horatio's ear. It really was a very nice ear, like the rest of him, classically built, but with a certain quirky humour.

'Ophelia, don't cry. Please don't cry, I never know what to do. You haven't fallen out with old Mal, have you?'

Ophelia managed, with difficulty, to laugh and sniff at

the same time. Despite his undoubted capacity to infuriate, no one, so far as she knew, had ever managed to have an actual argument with Malachi. At the first glimmer of hostility, he would melt into apology so abject and disproportionate to his crime that even hardened Jesuit schoolmasters had relented and told each other, slightly shamefacedly behind the staff-room door, that the lad meant no harm, and had no doubt bred fishing maggots in his inkwell solely out of a spirit of zoological curiosity.

'No, Malachi's fine. So am I, really.'

Horatio sighed with relief. His knowledge of postnatal depression was scarcely encyclopaedic, despite the fact that Pat, the community midwife, on vacation from her management fast-track, had recently persuaded him to attend a course on the subject in Twickenham. It really wasn't his fault that the date coincided with the Varsity match. After all, there was only a certain amount of temptation a man could bear.

'It's about Dodie.'

Horatio's fears returned. He was very fond of children, but found it difficult to see the point of them before they could master a good dummy scissors. Babies were a particular hazard, especially when wrapped up, and he had more than once been slapped by an angry mother as he tried to demonstrate a dive pass with her newborn infant. One had even been called Gilbert which was surely an inducement too far. 'It looks all right,' he said hopefully.

'She's asleep at the moment. That's because I'm here. When I leave her with Mal, she just screams all the time.'

'Don't blame her, really.' Malachi was Horatio's best friend, and a jolly good chap at that, despite his unorthodox opinions on the loose forward trio, but his nursery nursing skills were probably little better than Horatio's own. 'Why don't you stay at home and look after her?' That was what Horatio's mother had done, wasn't it, at least until he went away to prep school at six-and-a-half? And he'd grown up perfectly well adjusted.

'And send Malachi out to work?' Ah. There was the flaw. Malachi and work, somehow there was something incongruous about the mere juxtaposition of the words. Work and Malachi. No, that was no better.

'I see what you mean,' he said ruefully, glancing at his own patient list, the last five entries of which had been scored out and replaced with GOLF in large red letters. 'Some people just aren't cut out for a life of endless toil. There's only one thing for it then.'

Ophelia waited with a hope which she should have known better than to entertain. Intravenous Calpol, absinthe, the implantation of artificial mammary glands in Malachi's chest?

'You'll have to take her to work with you. Now, was there anything else?' He picked up the sphygmomanometer from his desk and began to practise putting.

'Er yes, one other thing.' Ophelia was marvelling at the simplicity of the male mind. Would Horatio, who achieved about as much work in eighteen months as she in a morning, consider minding a baby in his consulting rooms? Probably not, but then he wasn't a woman. 'You've got the *instinct*, you see,' he would insist, if she demurred. 'It's one of those female *things*, isn't it, doing lots of different jobs at the same time. Multi-tasking, Mal calls it. I'm sure you're an absolute expert.' It would all be very charming, but hardly worth while, and she dared not tell him about the problem of Oliver in case he had been reading about transvestitism and decided to recommend her for psycho-sexual counselling. The trouble with Horatio was that one never knew quite what he had discovered that week. So, instead, she asked him about Hilda.

'What, old Mrs Cough-Medicine? Yes, terrible thing that. She died, did you know that? Oh yes, you would. Funny thing, you know, she hardly sounded Russian at all. Not like that husband of hers. Oh, was she? From Rambleton? That explains it, I suppose. Yes, young Jason called me out. Met Jason, have you? Bright young chap, lots of ideas, just what we want round here. Not a rugby player, I thought, bit girly, but not what I'd call a real poof. A medical man knows these things. Something about the jawline, that's the really vital difference. What? Oh, Mrs Cough. Yes, well the really good thing was – great coincidence this, makes you think perhaps there is Someone Up There after all, oh, you think so anyway don't you, being R.C.s? – well, let's give him the benefit of the doubt, then. Long as I needn't miss Sunday morning training, eh? Eh? Yes, I'm telling you. You'll never believe it, but just as he called me, the very *second* the phone rang, I was reading this article in the BMJ – you know that, *British Medical Journal*? No, no, Ophelia, I must tell you the truth, what with my new-found faith, eh? I wasn't reading it that very second. Fact was, I'd skimmed through it, through the first page, anyway, got the gist, then had a quick look at the sport in the *Telegraph*. But, like I said, I'd got the basic idea.'

'And the article was about heart problems?'

'Murmurs, Ophelia, murmurs.' His rather long lower lip trembled in and out as he spoke, so that she felt a little wobbly and had to distract herself with a three-day-old coffee cup which was quietly fermenting on the floor. 'Sounds rather seductive, actually, put like that, doesn't it?'

'N-not particularly.'

'No? Sweet nothings? Pillow talk? I've always thought you might be rather good at that sort of thing, what with all that pleading before judges.'

'It's not at all the same. Addressing the court and . . .'

'Courting without a dress. I know it's not *supposed* to be, that's what makes it so erotic. You, Ophelia, in black lace, on your knees in front of the hanging judge—'

'I think you're getting a bit sadistic, now,' said Ophelia, wriggling uncomfortably. The picture, with Horatio as the judge, and herself, in very little black lace, clinging to his knees, was all too vivid. Was he doing it deliberately? The receptionist always claimed that he had no idea of his effect on women, but she was famously loyal and hardly immune herself to his charms.

'Yes, you're right. Must be my public school education. Flogged too often or not enough, I never know which. I'll be a good boy and tell you all about poor old Hilda. Not much of the voluptuous about her murmuring heart, I'm afraid.'

'So that's what it was, a heart murmur?'

'Oh yes, not much doubt about it. It was young Jason

that suggested it first, mind. Credit where it's due. Had an aunt or some such with the same, apparently. Come to think of it, he might make a doctor, you know. Some of the medical schools have soccer teams. D'ye think he'd make a decent forward?'

'I've absolutely no idea. Hilda?'

'As a forward? Wouldn't think so. Bit too broad on the beam. No, Hilda's your classic prop, basically. Wasted in a soccer team. Besides, the wench is dead. Hey, that's Shakespeare, isn't it? I must be getting cultured. Expect it's your influence, Ophelia.'

'I doubt it.' Ophelia looked ostentatiously at her watch, but hints had no effect on Horatio. Fortunately, he meandered back to the subject of his own accord.

'Trouble was, you see, as I said, I'd got the gist of this article, but what I hadn't quite got to was the treatment.'

'So you prescribed aspirin?'

Horatio looked startled. 'Did you know, or was it a lucky guess?'

'I knew. Mind you, I think I could have predicted it. Aspirin does seem to be your general panacea.'

'Only my second choice, though. Gin's always better, in my experience, but poor Hilda was quite adamant that she didn't want any spirits. Shame. She might have still been alive if she'd followed my advice.'

'Why? Was there something wrong with the aspirin?'

'Not that I know of. Mind you, it was her own that she took, from her handbag; some Russian packet with Cyrillic writing all over it. I mean, she said it was aspirin but I've no way of knowing. No, all I meant was she missed out on all those healing properties of juniper.'

'Has juniper got healing properties?'

'I've absolutely no idea. That reminds me, I've got a bottle of Gilbey's in my bottom drawer. Care for a nip?'

Ophelia doubted whether it was orthodox medical practice to drink gin during a consultation, especially when the tonic bottle proved to be almost empty. However the prescription was in her case, she had to admit, exactly what she needed, and by the time the tumbler was half empty her problems seemed considerably less intense.

'There was something else I meant to ask,' she said vaguely, waving her arms in the air. The sleeping baby had, thankfully, been tucked up on top of the examination couch. 'Oh yes. Next morning. When she died.'

'She died,' echoed Horatio lugubriously. 'Awfully sad. Heart attack, you know. Young Jason helped on that one, too. Said his Mum went the shame way. Old bat.'

'Who?'

'What?'

'Never mind. So you gave a certificate?'

'Oh yes. People like it, you know. They don't like all these postmen – postmore—'

'Post-mortems?'

'That's it. All that cutting up of loved ones. I mean, it's not nice, is it? Not shivilized.'

'Not shivilized at all,' agreed Ophelia. 'Wha'bout the odd couple?'

'The Odd Couple?'

'Mm. Mutton dressed as lamb, and the toyboy. Not a very exciting toy. Educational. Stamp album. Don't think she's his mother. Residents.'

Horatio, with commendable navigation, managed to follow her stream of consciousness.

'Did see a bloke like that. Wearing his granddad's zip up cardigan. He was in the corridor when I left. Just outside the door. Sort of sidled off as I came out. Oh, and I saw the bird, too, further down. I walked past this open door and a voice said, "Sweetie, that you?" Husky, you know. So I poked my head round and said, "'Fraid not," and there was this bimbo in a silky thing, bit past it, like you said, but not bad. "Ooh," she said, "why don't you come in anyway?" so I sort of made my excuses and buggered off. I've seen that type before. Bloody petrifying. More gin?'

Ophelia woke up early the next morning and lay in bed for a few seconds, trying to work out what was so odd. Then she realized. She had woken up of her own accord, and, what was more, Dodie had not cried in the night.

'Oh God!' she cried, forgetting how to get out of bed and wrapping the duvet cover around her ankles. 'She's dead. I've killed her.' Dragging yards of flowered cotton with her, she shuffled over to the baby's cot. She gripped the wooden rail, struggling to focus through the six o'clock gloom, and tried to remember the events of the night before. She and Horatio had finished the gin bottle, she was pretty sure of that, and gone on to the cough mixture which a pharmaceutical rep had conveniently left that afternoon. Then Dodie had woken and Ophelia had fed her, in front of Horatio, who had shown a distinctly unmedical interest in the proceedings. The trickle of milk down the front of her nightdress ran faster at the memory. They had changed the baby's nappy, with the assistance of a roll of Sellotape, and emerged into the dark foyer, the receptionist having gone home hours before. Ophelia's Volvo and Horatio's little Morgan stood patiently in the car park, but they had, thankfully, retained enough sense to know not to drive them. How, then, had she got home? She had no idea, but that hardly mattered now. It was still too dark to see the baby clearly, and Malachi's snores were loud enough to obliterate any sound of her breathing. Ophelia reached out a tentative hand to Dodie's back, uncovered except by the towelling Babygro. There was another thing. She, or perhaps Malachi, or even Horatio, had laid the baby on her stomach instead of her back, as the authorities now advised. She was a thoroughly unworthy mother. But the child, beneath the slight dampness of the terry, was undeniably warm, and the little spine rose and fell in regular contentment.

'Congratulations,' said a bleary voice behind her. 'You've got her to sleep right through. I told you that you ought to drink more. My mother always swore by half a bottle of whiskey before the night-time feed.'

'Oh, Mal.' Ophelia turned with insufficient regard for the tender state of her head. 'Ow. Mal, was I terrible last night?'

'How d'ye mean, terrible? You nagged us a bit, but we're quite used to that. No, we had a bit of trouble finding any cash to pay the taxi driver – he got a bit sniffy when I suggested American Express – but Joan came up with the dosh in the end. Then you and the kids toddled off to bed while Horatio and I had a few beers.

I'm afraid we got a bit rowdy, trying to remember the words to "Sospan Fach" – the Llanelli song, you know – and that's when you came through and shouted at us, but nothing worse than that. Look, Oaf, if I were you I'd sneak off to work now, before she wakes. Have a nice fry-up breakfast in Patty's Pantry or something. Bacon, black pudding, fried bread, just what you need.'

The room, which had been only a cold grey, turned black, with a shower of shooting stars.

'I think I'll stick to orange juice.'

'Whatever you like. But off you go. Don't worry about Dodie. After all, we have got a medic in the house.'

'What, Horatio?'

'Well, you couldn't expect him to walk home at four in the morning, could you? He's on the sofa with the dogs. Fella ought to have been a vet, you know. They really take to him, especially Gigs.'

'Perhaps you're right. The walk down to the main road will do me good and there's bound to be a bus eventually.' Ophelia bent, not without a certain nausea, to the chest of drawers and began pulling clothes out at random. She had no desire, however innocuous her behaviour back at Moorwind Farm had been, to face Horatio this morning. Never, in all the detective novels that she and Joan exchanged, had the hero made the elementary mistake of getting drunk with the principal medical witness. Glimmerings of their conference about Hilda were coming and going, like fragments of newsprint in a fire, together with other shreds of conversation, about which she would rather not think. The principal problem, apart from her searing headache and the feeling that her

73

stomach was filled with quick-drying concrete, from getting dressed this morning, was that no ordinary breast pads could possibly deal with the flow of a night's unused milk. Eventually, hearing faint groans from the sitting room that could be Megabyte's dreams or Horatio's waking, she stuffed a couple of muslin nappies down the front of a sweater and slipped out of the front door.

The walk along the rutted drive, as she had hoped, cleared her head, and by the time that she reached the main road she felt almost hungry. A watery sun was trying to coax its way through the clouds, the sheep were in full-throated dawn bleating and two magpies were quarrelling in the dusty hedge. A bus came along after half an hour or so, bearing taciturn men to work in Rambleton, their sandwich boxes and flasks protruding from army surplus shoulder bags. Ophelia sat at the back, where the sun was making optimistic pawings at the window and she could indulge in a little invigorating passive smoking. By the time the bus, after a circuitous route through half a dozen ugly dormitory villages, arrived in Rambleton, she felt well enough to buy a hot dog from the van in the market square and to sit on a chilly bench and eat it, watching the stall-holders prepare for the cornucopia of consumerism that was Rambleton's market day.

Polly, despite the smell of fried onions and traces of French mustard that clung to Ophelia's coat, read the situation immediately. Nineteen years of experience of Mid-Yorkshire rural life, in which the pub was not merely the focal point but the entire *raison d'être* of cultural existence, had taught her both to recognize and treat a hangover.

'Gently now,' she cautioned, leading Ophelia into her room and wedging her into the chair with a couple of cheap pillows. 'I'll leave off the typewriter for this morning. Now, if you just rest your head on this pile of blotting paper you should be able to nod off for a bit.'

To her surprise, Ophelia found that Polly was right, and it was past eleven, with the sun making gallant attempts to go so far as to shine, when she was woken.

'Oo-oh-ee,' Polly was saying, with enormous stretchings of her incarnadine lips and gestures towards the desk drawer.

'What?'

'Ooh-a-oo-oo-oo. Eee.'

'It's all right. My head's better now. You can talk normally.'

'Oh good. It's that Mr Bottleponce. He's here to see you.'

'Pottlebonce,' corrected Ophelia. 'Right-oh. You can show him . . . in,' she finished redundantly, as Edgar Pottlebonce bounced into the room like an old leather football and shot a red hand out in greeting.

'Mrs O.!' he bawled, as if calling to some far distant herd of deaf sheep across miles of moorland. 'Good to see you. Bairns well?'

'Apart from the foot and mouth,' muttered Ophelia, but Edgar, who had inherited a slight deafness from generations of recalcitrant cowmen, did not hear.

The door opened again and Mrs Pottlebonce, whose sight was no better than Edgar's hearing, stumbled through it, knocking her six foot frame simultaneously on the filing cabinet, the window and her husband.

'Monica!' cried Ophelia, as much to guide her towards the desk as in a spirit of welcome. 'How nice to see you. Do sit down.' She was surprised to see Mrs Pottlebonce here, for the older woman, shy and awkward in company, had never previously been known to accompany her husband on his trips into Rambleton, preferring to stay at home and ruminate upon the evils of female priesthood. She would say nothing now, staring down at the floor between her widely separated knees, as Edgar spoke.

'We're not here for, like, a *consultitiation*, tha knows. Nay, it's in the nature of a social visit.'

'Really?'

'Aye.' He paused for a long time, staring at the Will Power poster, and Ophelia thought that she could catch a twinkle in his watery eyes. 'Well,' he said at last, 'suppose a might as well take t'bull by t'horns. Fact is, I'm to be dubbed.'

'Dubbed?' An agricultural video, perhaps, intended for an audience unfamiliar with Mid-Yorkshire dialect. Or was it something to do with fishing?

'Aye. Sir Edgar. What dost think o' that, then?'

'I think . . . I think I'd better offer my congratulations. So you,' she desperately tried to establish eye contact with the still bowed Monica, 'will be Lady Monica. No, Lady Pottlebonce, isn't it?'

That was the trouble with these long established country firms, thought Ophelia, there always seemed to be such a lot of etiquette to master. She would have to

ring her mother and ask her to bring that copy of
Debrett's on her next descent from Macclesfield. It was
quite a new edition as well, bought in the heady days of
Ophelia's first term at Cambridge when her mother had
discovered that the dim-looking Natural Scientist down
the corridor, who never seemed to remove his blue
kagoul, was actually the Earl of Something-or-other. It
had all 'come to nothing' for Ophelia had never even
spoken to the Earl, except to warn him when the lavatories were blocked, and had met Malachi at the end of her
second term, but it was another perpetual reproach of
filial ingratitude.

'You could be a Countess by now, darling, instead of
stuck out in this hovel, and I'd be . . .'

'Nothing whatsoever, Ma, so don't be so silly, there's
a love.'

'There must be something. Dowager-in-law, perhaps.
And don't call me Ma!'

Monica spoke, so unexpectedly that Ophelia gave a
start and knocked over her cold cup of coffee.

'Load o' rubbish. I'll just stick with plain Monica,
thanks. Mind you, it might be useful on Narcof's letter-
head.'

NARCOF, Ophelia remembered, was Monica's pet
society, the acronym standing for *No Anglican or Roman
Catholic Ordination of Females*. Its successes to date
were not notable, for within weeks of its inception the
first women vicars were ordained, but it was rumoured
that one of the 'flying bishops' had sent a note of
encouragement.

'Aye, that's right,' agreed Edgar, giving his wife's

gargantuan thigh a reassuring pat, as if she were a nervous heifer waiting to be milked. 'Big day fer us both. So, thing is, we're having a bit of a get-together up at t'house tonight. Just a few close friends, like, and we'd be honoured if you'd come along.'

'Why yes, I'd be delighted. That's very kind of you.'

Edgar became brisk. 'No need fer fuss. Half-seven, then. Come along, Monica.'

They were halfway out of the door, Monica groping ahead and Edgar steering her from behind, when Ophelia asked the question.

'By the way, er, what exactly is the knighthood for?'

'Services to agriculture,' chuckled Edgar, and disappeared.

Tartleton Court, thought Ophelia, as the Volvo's disintegrating tyres slid on the wet cobbles, had scarcely changed in the year since it had been owned by the eponymous Lady. Not that there was very much that could change about its low, dark Yorkshire stone, the kind that looks wet even on rare sunny days, or about the persistent moss that grew in every crevice. The cars already parked in the courtyard, too, were the same as those of Lady Tartleton's erstwhile guests, solid Mercedes and muddy Land Rovers, the uniform transport of Mid-Yorkshire's approximation to a county set. The only thing missing, as she hung the same Barbour, its waxproofing now completely worn off, on the same institutional aluminium pegs, were Lady Tartleton's three adult male Labradors, Horace, Virgil and Caesar, from their old spot in front of the enormous fireplace. Edgar and

Monica Pottlebonce, strangely, or perhaps not so strangely, considering their history, had no animals, and the precincts of Tartleton Court were silent of mew, bark or whinny.

Edgar Pottlebonce had begun his adult life as a farmer, inheriting a dairy herd from his father, but, owing to a peculiar financial astuteness, sharp enough to penetrate the accumulated layers of Mid-Yorkshire orthodoxy and suspicion, had been one of the first farmers in the North to take full advantage of the complex system of EC subsidies, quotas and allowances. He had done little conventional farming after the late 1970s, depending instead upon the exotic cash crops of llamas and aubergines, and claiming gargantuan sums for unused fields and quotas. Eventually, even these profitable activities had been superseded, and he had set himself up as an agricultural consultant, providing advice, at extortionate rates per hour, to other farmers anxious to milk the CAP cow while she was still productive. Finally, a year ago, inspired by Ophelia's other mortgage bandits, he had sold Greenhaigh Farm to Stewart Saggers and had moved into Tartleton Court.

The great hall was filling up now, with little groups of tweed and cashmere, sipping suspiciously at their sherry. They need not have worried. Lady Tartleton had taken her stocks of *Wearside Cream* away to Yardley Farm with her, and the Pottlebonces' replacement, if not adventurous, was at least drinkable. Monica herself stood in a dark corner, glowering through her new spectacles at a mousy girl whom Ophelia recognized as Rambleton's new curate. From time to time, Monica's principles were to be overcome by her hospitable duty and she would blunder forward with the decanter and pour sherry over some unsuspecting guest, who was driving home anyway and looking for the orange juice. There was no sign of Edgar.

To Ophelia's left, Nick Bottomley, who never missed a likely client-gathering occasion, was advancing upon the lady curate, the coals behind his black eyes rekindled in anticipation of a conquest. On her other side was a little group of middle-aged Rambletonians, among them Major Lamb and his wife Letitia. Ophelia joined the group and was warmly welcomed by the Major.

'Why, it's young Mrs O. again! Now there's a coincidence. I was just saying, wasn't I, Charlie, that it must have been here, in Lady Tartleton's time, that we first met. Plenty of water under the bridge since then, eh?'

'That's right,' agreed Ophelia in a low tone, aware of Nick's presence behind her. They had called a truce after Dodie's birth, but she was uneasy, and unwilling for him to discover any more about the forgotten Mortgage Bandits. 'I'm glad you're here. I was wanting to ask . . .'

'Best thing I ever did, coming in with you on that business. Wouldn't have met old Porridge otherwise.' He addressed the man called Charlie. 'Know old Porridge, do you, my business partner? Marvellous chap. Brown as a burnt chapati, isn't that right, Letty, but salt of the earth, salt of the earth.'

Letitia, who, during the day, as Rambleton's Chief Assistant Librarian, was fierce and half-moon spectacled, merely simpered and gazed up at her husband in adoration. 'Mm-hmm,' she nodded, filigree earrings tinkling.

'Fact is,' continued the Major, 'business is going so well that we— What the blazes?'

Edgar had entered the room, portly and dapper in a tight-fitting suit of yellow tweed and a burnished mahogany walking-stick. But it was not at this rather Mr Toadish ensemble that the Major was staring, vermilion with fury, but at a small enamel badge on Edgar's lapel. It was a brass disc, about an inch in diameter, upon which was painted a plump and very pink pig.

'Evening, Major,' called the unusually jovial Mr Pottlebonce. 'Pleased to see you. Anything more I can get you? A whisky, perhaps?'

'You . . . you . . .' stammered Major Lamb, advancing too quickly for his limp and losing his balance momentarily. 'You . . . *bounder*!'

It was then that Ophelia realized she was wearing Malachi's trousers.

Chapter Five

The Zonal Tournament

The trouble had started that morning, as soon as the Pottlebonces had left the office. Invigorated by the half-pound of broken biscuits which Polly had wheedled from her mum on the sweet stall, Ophelia began, for the first time since leaving the house, to worry again about Adeodata. She reached for the telephone.

'Wet Nose Oh my God Dodie don't roll off there Solutions no Innocent I meant a *clean* nappy no get your fingers out just a moment the baby . . . Aarrghhh!'

The line tailed off into a harmonic scream with Adeodata taking the soprano, Innocent the alto and Malachi the bass parts. Eventually, after some more thumps, rustles and sobs, Malachi retrieved the receiver.

'Coping all right, are you, love?' asked Ophelia sweetly.

'Oh fine, fine, of course. Just having our usual morning sing-song. So important to develop the children's musical abilities at an early age, don't you agree?'

'Absolutely. So you don't want me to have Dodie here at the office with me, then?'

There was a silence of awe and joyful yearning, a pause of such exquisite ecstasy that only the buzzing of Rambleton's still analogue telephone system was able to contain it.

'You mean it?' gasped Malachi, when the power of speech was restored to him. 'You could really take her? Just this afternoon or . . .?' The concept was almost too much for him.

'Well,' said Ophelia, wondering what aberrant impulse of the maternal gene had made her telephone at all, 'for as long as Mr Snodsworth doesn't find out, anyway. If he does, then I'll really lose my job, so we won't have all this to worry about, just little things like how to pay the mortgage and live on a diet of nettles and those peculiar pink things that grow behind the hen-house.'

'I'll bring her right over, shall I?' said Malachi, making the fumbling sounds of a man trying to insert his arm, telephone and all, into the wrong sleeve of his overcoat.

'Yes, you might as well. But you'd better disguise her as something.'

'Disguise Dodie? As what, exactly? Orson Welles? A soft-boiled egg?'

'No, no, just don't parade in here triumphantly bearing a carry-cot. Try to be a bit subtle about it.'

Even as she said this, Ophelia thought it was probably a mistake. Subtlety, other than as applied to the habit of New Zealand forwards sneaking tries around the backs of their opponents' knees, was not a concept of great importance in Malachi's quotidian existence.

'Subtle. Right-oh, got the message. I'll be as subtle as a . . . remarkably subtle thing.' There was a gentle tinkle and a plop, as the car keys fell into something soft and yielding. 'Oh no, that bloody nappy, I forgot . . . See you soon then, Oaf. Bye.'

Half an hour later, as Ophelia was once again corresponding with the Legal Aid Area Office in an attempt to extract payment for a case concluded in 1973, she heard the front door of the office open and several unco-ordinated feet negotiate the doorstep.

'Ah, Malachi.'

But it was not Malachi. To her horror, hardly had she honed her final delicate irony when Polly appeared in the doorway, gesticulating desperately and overshadowed by an outsized Stetson. The Stetson was removed, flourished and flung extravagantly towards the hat stand in the corner. It fell short by some four feet and knocked over the bottle of ink which Ophelia had bought in the hope of impressing her clients.

'Oh, darn!' said the Stetson's owner, an immensely tall and thin man whose brown, rangy joints protruded from collar and socks. 'There was me a-thinkin' I'd have a chance against Huddersfield Hal in this year's Yorkshire Ten Gallon Hat Derby. Looks like I'll have to stick to the freestyle lasso after all. Howdy, Ophelia. Rib-munchin' good to see you back. Up in the saddle, that's the thing, show them thar cattle who's in charge.'

'Morning, Mr Ranger. Yes, it's nice to be here again. Was there anything special?'

'Oh no, nothing to fret about. Just a good ol' welcome

back to the ranch. And say—' He fumbled in the pocket of his fringed leather waistcoat. 'The missiz made these for your li'l tyke. Think she'll like 'em?' He drew out a pair of pink mittens, of a size likely to fit a small squirrel. 'She was in something of a fritfly's fuzzle with the tension, but I told her not to tiz herself.'

'You did quite right. Tell Dorothy they're lovely. But right now—'

She broke off as another figure appeared in the doorway. This time it was Malachi, with Innocent clinging to one trouserleg and carrying a large cardboard box.

'Hello, Oaf. Sorry to break up the party. I just brought along those urgent files that you wanted.' His pale blue eyes stared into Ophelia's with great intensity. 'Those very important files. The ones that you said you wanted to have with you. All the time.'

Ophelia looked down with some trepidation at the box, which seemed, upon close inspection, to be vibrating very gently with a distant snuffling sound. 'Oh, lovely,' she said hastily, raising her eyebrows up and down in an attempt to signal her comprehension. 'Fantastic. Just what I needed. Are there any, um, spare . . . pads of paper in there?'

'Pads of paper?' Malachi was mystified.

'Yes, you know, for when one gets filled up. The kind with a waterproof cover and a nice *nap*. The sort that feel like soft skin, or, as they say in France, *peau douce*.'

Malachi's mouth was hanging open.

'Oh no!' cried Ophelia, grabbing her arm in wild improvisation. 'I think I've got a touch of crampers. *Pampers*,' she hissed.

Malachi's face cleared like a newly wiped blackboard. 'Oh yes!' he boomed. 'Yes, you've got plenty of those.'

At the resonance of his voice, there came an alarming little creak from inside the box.

'And it's well ventilated,' thundered Malachi. 'No danger of the poor little files' not being able to breathe properly.'

A louder and distinctly unpapery sound was issuing from the depths of the cardboard box. Ophelia acted quickly.

'Bother!' she said loudly. 'I think Innocent's got a dirty nappy. I'll have to change him in here. Quick, Polly, take Mr Ranger through. This isn't a suitable experience for a hat-hurler in serious training.'

'I not smelly!' cried Innocent, deeply affronted, for he had been fully potty-trained for the past six months.

But Deputy District Judge Ranger was already on the other side of a firmly closed door. As Ophelia had suspected, he found the whole business of procreation, childbirth and infant development deeply disturbing, having only recently obtained any experience even of the preliminaries. He had been rather nervous even of handing over the mittens, afraid that they might involve him, at some unknown point in the future, in actually touching one of the squalling little creatures, holding it, perhaps, or tickling its unnaturally small and pink toes. As for the processes whereby matter was introduced to, and expelled from the infant, even the vaguest contemplation filled him with a ghastly horror.

'Never mind, sir,' commiserated Polly with a dimpled smile. 'At least she hasn't got the baby in there as well.'

Her expression was one that Ophelia would have recognized, with a mixture of elation and foreboding. Polly was in her conspiratorial mode, which, in Ophelia's experience, combined immense complications, desperate secrecy and a hearty dollop of illegality. It inevitably led to disaster.

'Tarnation!' replied Mr Ranger, unexpectedly. 'I've just remembered why I came over here in the first place. Ole Pardner Snodsworth wants to see some guy called Oliver – I guess he means our Miz O.?'

'Bound to,' agreed Polly. 'But I, er, wouldn't disturb her now.'

Mr Ranger's hand jumped off the door handle as though it had been electrified. 'No, no, you're right there, li'l Poll. Guess I should just holler, hey?'

'Oh no!' whispered Ophelia to Malachi, beneath the cover of Innocent's *Baa, baa black sheep*. She was feeding Dodie at last, the milk cascading in grateful torrents over the Legal Aid Board's most recent correspondence. In her hungover hurry to get dressed that morning, she had combined the large sweater with a long and rather exotic black lace skirt. It was unlikely that Mr Snodsworth would fail to notice it, or that Oliver would be allowed to get away with such blatant cross-dressing.

Mr Ranger was tapping on the door now, his squeamishness vying with his fear of the senior partner. 'Please, Ophelia. He'll have my liver for a lanyard if we don't get our but – I mean speed up a bit.'

'It's no good, Malachi,' said Ophelia. 'I'll just have to borrow your trousers.'

Thankfully, the interview with Mr Snodsworth was

not too onerous. Ophelia's hair managed to stay tucked in the polo neck of her jumper, which the old man evidently took to be some archaic form of wing collar. Malachi's trousers, an old pair of army fatigues, were baggy enough to fasten even over her post-natal folds and needed only a couple of extra turn-ups. She had to wear them long, in any case, to cover up the gold satin bows on her pretty little pumps, the only complete pair of shoes she had managed to find that morning. She could have borrowed Malachi's footwear as well, for he was willing enough, but she had doubted her ability to cross the cobbles in size ten rugby boots. No, her impersonation of Oliver was, if anything, only too successful. Mr Snodsworth had evidently taken a great liking to the boy, and regaled him with longer and longer stories of his days in the Law, of frankalmoign and ultimogeniture, of *jus primae noctis* and John Doe, while the bruised sky darkened and, across the Square, Malachi shivered in his Y-fronts.

Finally, as Mr Snodsworth reached the dramatic conclusion of *In Re Monkton's Trusts*, in which he, as a humble articled clerk, had noticed the fatal ambiguity which had destroyed the Lord Chancellor and nearly brought the Government down, Malachi could wait no longer. Innocent was agitating for tea, haunted by the vision of fish fingers and custard creams, Dodie whimpered and the older children would be stamping their feet as they stood, a solitary huddle outside St Barnabas R.C. Primary School. He opened Ophelia's door an inch or so, to see Polly in the outer office talking to a couple of stout women. He looked down at his uncovered legs and shut the door again. It would have to be the window. Fortunately it was growing dark and the window opened only into a quiet alley, a quick sprint from the surgery car park and the safety of the Volvo.

Innocent came out first, solemn and silent with the gravity of the endeavour. He stood, sturdy on a grating and held his arms out to take the baby.

'Good boy,' whispered his father, and Innocent held on tight to the faintly shivering bundle. For the first time he was truly a big brother.

Next came Malachi himself, more awkwardly than the children, with elbows and knees unaccountably wedged in the corners of the frame. Finally all was extricated, and he jumped down, the studs of his boots reverberating on the paving slabs.

'Made it!' he triumphed, and 'Really, sir?' came a sardonic echo from the darkness. Malachi blinked, rubbed a hand across his forehead and came face to face with the quietly smiling Sergeant Booking.

It was Ophelia who came to his rescue some half an hour later, as she strode, in as masculine a manner as she could muster, back across the Square. Innocent, who was torn between the excitement of seeing a real policeman so close at hand and the vicarious humiliation of seeing his father ridiculed, spotted her first.

'Mummy! P'liceman got us!'

Sergeant Booking was enjoying himself, and was not inclined to desist upon finding out that his suspicious character was Ophelia's husband. He had not forgiven her for her mild-sounding enquiries after his wife. She, in turn, had no intention of telling him the real reason why Malachi was wearing no trousers.

'I expect the baby was sick,' she improvised wildly, 'and Mal had to use them to clean it up.'

'That's right!' said Malachi, rather too quickly, and then, over-egging the pudding somewhat, 'Innie was sick too. And then I was.'

Sergeant Booking took a step backwards. He was pretty sure that they were lying, but it did not do to take any chances. To succumb to a gastric epidemic would not be the ideal way to improve the Rambleton force's clear-up rate.

'Very well then,' he condescended. 'We'll take no further action at present. But listen here.'

Malachi's eyes widened in the pantomime of innocence that Ophelia knew so well.

'I'll be keeping an eye on you. And the next time I catch you loitering in my town centre . . .'

'Yes, sir. Of course, sir. Thank you very much, sir.'

Sergeant Booking suspected irony, but could do nothing about it, though he contemplated a call at the next Police Conference upon the Home Secretary to make Sarcasm Towards A Senior Officer an indictable offence, so he marched off to persecute a couple of teenage canoodlers on the other side of the Square.

The older O. children had, by the time that their parents collected them, been waiting outside the school for an hour and a half.

'We might have been *inducted*,' said Pius severely.

'Yes,' agreed Hygenus. 'Or kidnapped.'

Ophelia and Malachi expressed contrition, but only fish and chips, they could see, would constitute real restitution. Ophelia gave Dodie a quick feed in the car while Pius and Joan queued for seven times haddock, chips and extra mushy peas, and Malachi desperately tried to hide his goose-pimples with the dog blanket. Back at Moorwind Farm she let them out, called them back for the front door key and turned around immediately for Tartleton Court, completely forgetting her unusual attire.

But when, following Edgar Pottlebonce's outburst, she did look down at the faded fatigues, everyone else was too excited to notice. It had been thirty years since the last disturbance at a Tartleton Court cocktail party, when Sir Lionel's nephew had turned up in bare feet and offered a joint to the Chief Constable. On that occasion, it was recalled, the entertainment had continued for some time, as it transpired that at least twenty members of the Rambleton Hunt had already succumbed and were holding a love-in under the hay loft. Major Lamb, however, somewhat unsportingly, declined to insult his host further, but stomped out of the room, his limp forgotten, and into his waiting Range Rover. Ophelia was as disappointed as the others, for she had just learned from the jovial Charlie that the Major, 'bloody clever chap' was the president of Rambleton Chess Club. She had also noticed, in her new found detective role, that the lapel badge worn by Edgar depicted exactly the same pink and rounded pig as appeared on the corner of Hilda's map. A flush of investigative enthusiasm welled up in Ophelia, and once again she forgot the trousers. But the Major showed no signs of returning, and no one else, not even Monica, seemed to know anything about the badge, so she decided to leave, and fulfil a long-standing assignation with the ironing-board. On the way out she met Lady Tartleton.

'Missed anything, have I?' she called, as though across three fences and a pack of bellowing hounds. Ophelia tried to tell her, but Lady Tartleton, certain that nothing in Rambleton would dare happen without her, gave a dismissive whinny and proceeded forth, followed by a train of muddy Labradors.

'Oh-ahh!' she barked suddenly, turning on her heel so that the following dogs fell over one another's rumps. 'Sprogs haven't got school in the morning, have they? Saturday. Bring 'em over, then. Fella's deliverin' the stock. Y'know, for the Hydro-Porcine thingummy. Should be a bit of excitement for the poor beasts.'

Ophelia did not dare to ask whether she meant the children or the pigs.

'Very wiggley,' was Innocent's considered verdict on the piglets and indeed they were, squirming joyously in a great heap on the back of the pick-up truck. They had surprisingly large, triangular ears and very bright, intelligent little eyes. A young man in overalls scooped each piglet up in turn and gave it a cursory check, his large fingers spread across its belly, before dropping it unceremoniously into the nearest of the two blue plastic paddling pools.

'Fancy wallows y'got.' He addressed Pius, presuming that he, as the eldest male present, was the source of local authority.

'They're not *wallows*,' objected Lady Tartleton.

'They're hygienic porcine habitation units.'

'Oh aye?' He continued to scoop up the piglets with only the faintest twitch of amusement across his large bland face.

Unfortunately, the pools, purchased the day before from a toyshop in Scorsdale and so like those at Innocent's playgroup that he had already had to be lifted out twice, were becoming less hygienic by the minute. Not every piglet, but certainly every other one, reacted to its unexpected landfall in four or five inches of warm water by raising its stubby tail slightly, emitting a couple of mild eructations and sending forth a stream of khaki-coloured liquid.

'Never mind,' said Lady Tartleton, through only slightly tightened lips, for she was not fastidious, only mean, and the water supply was not yet metered. 'Albert can clean them out when he gets here. All the same, I can't understand it. In all the photographs the water was perfectly clear. Perhaps Canadian pigs are better house-trained.'

'Albert?' asked Ophelia, rescuing Urban's glove from the jaws of a small pig. 'Not . . .?'

'Skate, yes. You'll remember him of course.'

Ophelia had hardly had the chance to forget. Already, in her first week back at work, she had come across seven current files dealing with the various litigious activities, all legally-aided, of Albert and his son Darren.

'He ought to be here by now, actually. I've taken him on as pig-man, since he's been sacked by the Council.'

This was scarcely a surprise. Even a body so inefficient and petty-minded as Scorsdale District Council could hardly fail to realize, eventually, that Albert Skate, dirty alike in body and soul, illiterate, generally drunk and an inveterate scrounger of some forty years' standing, was ill-fitted for the dynamic role of Rambleton's Chief Planning Officer. He was barely more appropriate as a Hygienic Porcine Operative, but it was unlikely that anyone else would do the job at the wages Lady Tartleton was offering.

Lady Tartleton's thoughts were evidently moving along the same tracks, for she continued, 'I needn't pay him much, you see, because he's still "on the sick". What is it now. Incapacity Benefit?'

'Which I suppose he was claiming all the time he worked for the Council? No, don't tell me, I don't want to know.' Ophelia looked around anxiously to make sure that Pius, who had a tendency to live up to his name, had not overheard. But the children, with the apparent connivance of the phlegmatic driver, had scrambled up into the back of the pick-up truck and were helping to pass out the last few delighted piglets.

'Dunna forget to separate 'em,' he said, when all were happily splashing in the pool, its water now a uniform dark green.

'Separate them? Into what?'

'Boars 'n' gilts. Males and females, y'know.'

'Of course I know,' said Lady Tartleton, whose androgynous tweeds sometimes made one wonder. 'But they're all just piglets, aren't they?'

'Weaners,' corrected the young man. 'Grow up fast, pigs do.'

'Oh, very well then. We've got two pools, anyway. I

suppose Albert can sort them out, if his limited intelligence stretches that far.'

'It'll be quite easy, I think,' said Pius. 'If you look at them from behind then you can tell the male ones. Look, there, hanging down, its little test . . .'

'Quite,' interrupted Ophelia, wondering whether it was too late to withdraw him from the fascinating sex education lessons. 'Unfortunately we have to get home. It's time for lunch and then we've got the family chess tournament.'

On their way over to Yardley Farm that morning, the children had called at the library for their weekly assault on the Roald Dahl and Dick King-Smith shelves, and Ophelia had taken the opportunity to ask Letitia Lamb about Rambleton's chess club. Letitia was more flustered than usual, something of her feather-brained domestic persona overlapping with the professional one, and was obviously unwilling to speak to a witness of her husband's recent behaviour. She could not, however, refuse a legitimate request from a council tax payer, and pointed, though with bad grace, to a fading poster at the corner of the noticeboard.

RAMBLETON CHESS CLUB
Novices welcome
Weds 8pm
Ratchet-Crampers' Social Club, Brack Street

As she mused over what a ratchet-cramper could be, and recalled, with a sinking heart, some of the less than savoury businesses from Brack Street for whom Parrishes had acted, her eye was caught by a poster advertising the local dramatic society's production of *Rosencrantz and Guildenstern are Dead*. Her mind boggling only a little, she remembered, by a comparatively straightforward process of association, that her elder brother Laertes had played chess as a schoolboy.

'He'll know how to run a tournament,' she said aloud, attracting a hard stare from Letitia, 'and he's bound to be at home for lunch, in between Sainsbury's and golf.' Laertes, despite, or perhaps because of his name, was a man of habit and precept, who combined perfectly his mother's social ambition with his father's golfing perseverance, so that his arrival on the links at precisely two-thirty, with the correct socks, was a point of tranquil immutability in a wild and wandering world.

'But I can't talk any Swiss!' wailed Hygenus, drumming a headless knight impatiently on the table.

'There's no such thing, is there?' said Malachi, wandering past, festooned with baby blankets and small pink nappies. 'They all speak other people's languages, don't they: Frog and all that? And then Cantonese in the cantons, I suppose.'

'But I can't talk those ones *either*!'

Ophelia was sorting through a button collection bequeathed to her by a great-aunt. She picked out two knobbly cream buttons and placed them thoughtfully on the home-made chess board in front of her.

'Bishops, perhaps,' she mused. 'Oh, Hygenus. A Swiss tournament's got nothing to do with Switzerland. At least, Uncle Laertes didn't say that it did. Perhaps it was invented there or something. It means that . . . Oh well, we'll just start playing and you'll see.'

By dint of excavating toy-boxes, drawers and Innocent's secret cache of treasures stashed away in the hen-house, they managed to put together one and a half extant chess sets and were creating a further one and a half using household objects and the last of Pius' model aeroplane paint.

'There we are!' he said triumphantly indicating two black enamelled cotton reels drying stickily before him. 'Now let's get started.'

In the first round, Ophelia played against Urban, hissing the rules to him across the table, and lost, not altogether intentionally, when she forgot about the leaping facility of the knight. Malachi also lost, due, he suspected, to Hygenus' dexterous rearrangement of the pieces while Malachi went out to fetch Innocent's Ribena. Nothing, however, could be proven. Pius, the only child to have played the game before, was paired against Joan, and was mortified to be checkmated in twelve moves.

'You should have guarded that pawn in front of the bishop,' she explained kindly. 'And your king hadn't got anywhere to go. Perhaps you should have done that, you know, swapping over thing with your tower.'

'Castling,' growled Pius. 'And it's called a rook.' He disappeared into the kitchen with Reredorter.

For the second round, following Laertes' instructions, Ophelia put two of the winners, Joan and Hygenus, together on what he had called the 'top board', and two losers, herself and Pius, on the third. The middle did not work out so neatly, but she paired Malachi and Urban. Pius, smarting from his feminine defeat in the first round, beat her easily, while Malachi and Urban, their blond heads conspiratorially close over the chess board, agreed a quick draw and sidled off to raid the pantry. On the first board there was more of a struggle, as Joan, inspired by her success and suddenly motivated by an unprecedented instinct for victory, watched the board intently, noticing every one of Hygenus' subtle nudges of a pawn, so that her brother was eventually, and much to his disgust, forced to play by the rules.

'I assign!' he shouted furiously, upon losing his queen, and stomped off to join his father and younger brother amidst last week's jam tarts.

The tournament controller, with her badly depleted flock, calculated the scores at the end of the second round. Joan was easily leading with two points, Urban following her with one and a half, Hygenus and Pius had one point each, Malachi a half, and Ophelia herself had yet to score.

'Come on, you lot!' she called. 'We've got a third round to play.' But she was greeted only with bulging mouths and strawberry-smeared chins. Joan was therefore declared the winner and awarded a rather hairy bar of Turkish Delight, together with the honour of accompanying her mother to Rambleton Chess Club on the following Wednesday evening.

'And the first ball,' announced the television presenter, with an excellent simulation of excitement, 'is number . . . thirty-three!'

'Years of Our Lord's life,' recited Malachi, as though to the catechism. 'Any of you got that one, kids?'

He looked around him at the five elder children who were sitting cross-legged on the lino, each staring intently at a National Lottery ticket. As Pius had predicted, he had made no objections to buying the tickets and, when apprised of the secrets of Spiritual Numerology, had entered enthusiastically into the scheme.

'Actually,' he had confided to Joan, the most sceptical member of the syndicate, 'my auntie Siobhan in Kerry used to do more-or-less the same thing. She'd go to Confession, and however many Hail Marys the priests gave her, that would be her first number for the week. She never won, mind, not that I knew of, but I expect her numerology wasn't quite scientific enough.'

The children drew their forefingers across the lines of numbers.

'Yes!' shouted Pius, and, after a nudge from Joan, Innocent. Urban burst into tears.

'Never mind, darling,' said Ophelia, who was struggling with a book about chess which she had found in the library. 'Nobody's actually going to win.'

The next pastel-coloured ball was rumbling through the digestive system of the machine.

'Seventeen.'

'Apostles plus the Evangelists. Anyone got seventeen?'

Hygenus had, and Innocent again.

'He's too young to have a Personal Devotional Programme anyway,' complained Pius. 'It would've been much better if you'd given two tickets to me. After all, I *am* going to be a priest.'

'Well you can't win it, then,' said Joan. 'Priests aren't supposed to have any money.'

'I'd give it to the poor, of course, which means Mum and Dad, so it wouldn't make any difference.'

'Forty.'

'Days in the wilderness.'

'Yayy!' shouted Hygenus, punching the air in a manner which Ophelia found rather distasteful. Meanwhile, Urban had broken his duck.

'Seven.'

'Creation of the world.'

None of the children had chosen seven, convinced by Pius' assertion that it was essentially a pagan number.

'Nine.'

'The Trinity, squared?' suggested Malachi, without much conviction. The children looked at him coldly.

'And . . .' A drum roll from the background of the studio. '. . . The final number, the sixth ball, number . . . Two!'

'Second Person of the Trinity,' said Malachi with smug triumph, then doubled up in pain as a turbo-charged six-year-old shot into his stomach. 'Oh, you've won, have you, Hugeness?'

'And Innie,' came a proud voice from his sister's knee. It was the only number he could recognize, but it was unmistakably there. 'Two. Innie's number.'

The bonus ball was twenty-nine, to which even Malachi's ingenuity could not ascribe a theological significance. 'Bugger the bonus ball. You two are in the money, anyway. Ten quid each, isn't it? What are you going to spend it on?'

Through Hygenus' mind passed visions of football cards, chocolate bars and jumbo packs of lollipops. But he remembered, at least, he remembered once Pius had kicked him a couple of times, the original purpose of their endeavour.

'We're going to buy something for Mum, aren't we, Innie? What would you like, Mummy?'

Ophelia, who had not been listening, abandoned her book with exasperation. The few lines in it that were not composed of incomprehensible chess analysis were full of thirty-year-old stories of skullduggery from the Cold War; psychological bombardment and colour-coded yoghurts. It all helped to explain Zuke's apparent paranoia but was not of much practical assistance now. What she needed was something to tell her about the current chess world, its characters and motivations.

'I wish I had a chess magazine,' she said to the room in general. 'Does anyone know if such a thing actually exists?'

Chapter Six

The Modern Bishop's Opening

'But we went last week, and the one before!' wailed the children next morning when Ophelia broke up the cartoons with the suggestion of Mass. 'We can't be s'posed to go *every* week. We'll know it all by the time we're grown up and then we won't want to go any more.'

'We'll be *lapsed*,' said Joan in a catastrophic whisper. 'If you force us to go to church now, against our incler, inclon, when we don't really want to, then we'll just rebel when we're old, and become atheists or single mothers or those people who go to car boot sales.'

'Not all three, then?' asked Ophelia. 'Come on, kids, you were keen enough on your Personal Devotional Programmes when you were doing the lottery.'

'Well, Huge and Innie can go then, since they're the only ones that won.'

'Defiantly not,' said Hygenus. 'That Lady Tartyton's always there and she pokes me in the back. She absolutely *must* be a witch.'

Ophelia sighed and resorted to her last weapon. 'If you come along now, then we'll call at the sweet shop on the way back and you can each choose something.'

'Out of your money,' warned Hygenus, turning grudgingly from the screen. 'We need our ten poundses, don't we, Innie? For what *she* asked for.'

Ophelia, missing the last sentence, wondered once again how two such financial incompetents as she and Malachi had managed to produce children with the bargaining acumen of Shylock on a wet Venetian Monday.

It was evident as soon as they arrived at the small church of Our Lady and Saint Barnabas, comparatively early, at only two minutes past ten, that something unusual was happening. The large pot-holed car park, usually three-quarters empty, was jammed with vehicles and more cars were jammed together along the narrow streets of terraced houses, with an unworldly disregard for bumpers and wing-mirrors. The children cheered up and Ophelia, with a sense of foreboding, found a hairy comb in the gluey recesses of her handbag and set about grooming all those within reach.

They trailed into the church, dripping holy water behind them, during the second verse of the opening hymn, and Urban, lost, as usual, in some fantastical kingdom of his own, became entangled in the middle of the procession. Uncommonly, for an ordinary Sunday, this consisted of all the available altar-boys, several of them rather too obviously on their way to football practice, with garish Premier League shirts obtruding from wrists and neck-lines, and imperfectly cleaned studs making muddy indentations in the carpet. There were also several altar-girls, an innovation which Father Jim, the parish priest, had seized upon with enthusiasm, their voluminous white surplices unflatteringly bunched at the waist by firm cords, waddling after the boys like liturgical potato-sacks. But it was towards the rear of the procession, behind the recently promoted senior altar-boy, bearing the silver crucifix, and behind Fr Jim himself, bouncing nervously on his schoolboy soles that all eyes were turned, to a slight, stooped figure, his face pale and tremulous between the stiff cope and heavy mitre. He reached the altar steps, turned, and, with a visible relaxation of his shoulders, removed the mitre to reveal a small skull cap. Without his headdress he suddenly seemed very short, although he must still have been a head taller than Fr Jim, and oddly vulnerable, as he gazed out across the ranks of scrutinizing faces.

Malachi disentangled Urban from the smallest altar-girl and they squeezed into the end of a pew.

The reason for the uncharacteristic congestion outside was at once evident. The first three or four pews, normally remaining empty but for the very latest, most dishevelled families, were full on either side of the aisle, right up to the bishop's nervously tapping brogues. On the left hand side, in demure undulations of navy blue and grey, sat the fifteen sisters of Saint Wilgefortis' Convent. Few were under seventy, and all sat silently, rheumy eyes patiently resting upon the poor bishop, with only the occasional shifting of an arthritic knee to indicate that they were still alive at all. The only exception was Sister Hedwig, the youngest sister at forty-seven, who was crooning out of tune and swaying her solid little body from side to side. As Fr Jim's Parish Sister, she was accustomed to the informality of a family mass, whereas the other sisters, who generally heard daily Mass only in their own chapel, were a little too stiff for the tuning guitars and dying strains of Taizé rhythms.

On the right hand side, however, discomfort of quite a different sort could be observed. Straggled along the pews, some couples and friends sitting close together for protection, some leaving exaggeratedly generous spaces, were some twelve or thirteen persons, mostly women, aged between about thirty and sixty. A few were dressed with painful formality, the women uncomfortable in Mrs Thatcher-style floppy neck bows and the men in suits tight about the paunch and riding high on their drooped shoulders. Others were aggressively casual, in jeans and sweatshirts with faded slogans, tapping their feet to the music of the Taizé chants while showing in their resolute faces that they had no intention of listening to the words, which, in any case, were largely in the elitist formulations of Latin. Ophelia recognized one or two of these, from personal injury or employment law consultations, as teachers at the Alderman Penbury Comprehensive School, and identified the tight cluster of pinstriped grey and royal blue hats behind them as the school's headmaster and senior governors.

The two camps gave sidelong glances at each other across the aisle, as though at some morganatic marriage.

The bishop looked from one side to the other, unsure

of where to fix his gaze. He settled on the door at the back of the church, bit his lip momentarily, and began.

'In the name of the Father, and of the Son, and of the Holy Spirit. The Lord be with you.'

The teachers shuffled uncomfortably, as though making room for an over-proximate Deity, while the sisters settled back in their pews, crossing themselves with only a hint of smugness. The Mass proceeded as usual until the end of the Gospel, when Fr Jim, in place of the customary rambling inconsequentialities which made up his weekly homily, came up to the very edge of the altar steps and peered engagingly at his flock.

'Moi friends,' he began, his Irish accent intensified by the weight of the occasion, 'my friends, I think most of you know all about the talks which the, er, Diocesan Finance Comm-committee,' he stumbled over the words slightly, 'have been havin' about the future of Saint Wilgefortis' Convent, home of our darlin' sisters over here.' He permitted himself a tiny nod in the direction of the Reverend Mother.

Ophelia felt a little peeved. Despite being privy to the legal secrets of half of Rambleton, she always seemed to be the last to hear any real gossip. She supposed that it was because she did not collect the children from school, or accompany Innocent to Mums & Toddlers in the church hall. Meanwhile the children, who were great frequenters of the convent, attracted equally by the hedgehog sanctuary and constant baking, had abandoned their evangelical colouring books and were perched on the edge of the pew with horrified faces.

'And s-so,' Fr Jim was stammering, 'in the view of

the . . .' He squinted down at the crumpled paper in his paw. 'Can't read me bluddy writing. In view of . . . things . . . our dear bishop has very kindly come to speak to us himself to tell us that . . . to . . . to . . .' He trailed of. Instantly the bishop was beside him.

'Thank you, Father Jim,' he said inaudibly, being accustomed to the cathedral's microphone. 'Thank you.'

Avoiding both the tremulous hope in the sisters' faces and the sceptical stares of the teachers, he focused on the far end of the aisle, into which Innocent was just escaping.

'Hello, little boy,' said the bishop to the approaching toddler, seizing the excuse for procrastination. 'That's all right, Mum and Dad.' Ophelia and Malachi had become wedged together in the entrance to the pew, in their simultaneous efforts to recapture the child. 'Suffer little children, remember? He's not doing any harm, are you, young chap?'

Gradually, however, as the paschal candle rocked precariously, the bishop's shoelaces were untied and Innocent grabbed the altar-cloth, it became evident that children could be suffered no longer and that the bishop must return to his reluctant task. Malachi disappeared through the back door with his crimson flailing charge as the bishop coughed his way to an announcement.

'As Father Jim says, they . . . the diocesan finance . . . that is, all of us who were involved in the decision, with which, of course, I entirely concur, that is to say that despite my personal feelings . . .' He began to rub the palm of his hand over his jaw, as though the faint pinpricks of stubble beneath the skin might at any moment burst into a bushy beard like that of the frowning schoolmaster before him. 'The facts, in case any of you are unfamiliar with them, are as follows. The house and grounds of Saint Wilgefortis' Convent belong to the Scorsdale Diocese and were, of course, originally known as Rambleton Convent School. In 1978, when the school became the new Alderman Penbury Comprehensive,' a few of the teachers gave guttural grunts of approval, as though at a union conference, 'most of the land and buildings were sold to the Mid-Yorkshire Education Authority. The diocese retained only the convent house itself and a strip of land behind it.' He glanced at the ancient Reverend Mother who smiled, remembering the bishop as a small boy with a passion for Sister Mary-Joseph's gingerbread. 'Now, however, the diocese has received a proposal from the Education Authority, that they be permitted to purchase the strip of land and the convent house, which they propose to turn into a,' he paused to concentrate, 'a Gender Redefining Resource.' Two women in the second pew gave simultaneous bounces of excitement. 'And I understand,' continued the bishop innocently, 'that it is particularly important to the school that this matter be dealt with quickly, as the governors are considering applying for grant-maintained status.'

'Shame!' cried the bushy-bearded gentleman, who had previously appeared to be asleep.

'Quite. Now, obviously, foremost in all our minds was the best interests of both the children.'

'Young persons,' corrected one of the school-mistresses.

'And the sisters currently residing at Saint Wilgefortis.'

At that 'currently' a few laughter lines sagged beneath the row of veils and Sister Hedwig's blue eyes darkened.

'It would be true to say, however,' the bishop inclined his head slightly to the left in order to avoid the gaze of Mother Thérèse, 'that the number of sisters at the convent is, over the long term, diminishing.' He could think of no more tactful way to say that most would be dead within ten years, 'and that there are no significant indications of new vocations.'

Sister Hedwig gave an audible sigh. It was quite true. The last postulant, little Mary McClaverty, the first since Hedwig's own clothing in 1967, had, after some unfortunate tabloid publicity earlier in the year, gone home to Wigan to rethink her calling.

'And so,' the bishop was concluding, 'it is with some personal regret that I have to announce that the proposal has been accepted. The building is to be available to the Alderman Penbury Comprehensive from January the first, and the sisters are to amalgamate with the Little Daughters of the Shroud in Scorsdale, with whom I am sure that they will establish a happy and fruitful community life. Now, let us stand to profess our faith. We believe in one God . . .'

But Sister Hedwig was already on her feet. Devout and gentle as she was, Father Jim's devotion to the cause of a female priesthood, combined with her own comfortable Old Catholic background, had given her a confidence which no mere bishop could curtail.

'Excuse me, Bishop,' she called, to the consternation of the other sisters, who had by now reached 'maker of heaven and earth'. 'If I could just ask a question?'

'Er-wum,' said the bishop.

'In coming to your decision, did you bear in mind my, I mean our, suggestion that a Third World Study Centre could be established within the existing convent?'

'Er, yes, that was considered,' said the bishop uncomfortably, remembering the rather unholy haste with which the finance committee had dismissed the suggestion.

The teachers, however, feeling themselves to be now on familiar debating ground, began to clamour all together.

'Just like to emphasize our shared commitment.'

'If I could clarify.'

'Woman is still, in a very real sense, the nigger of the world . . .'

'The swindle of grant-maintained . . .'

Several of the deafer sisters had not even noticed Sister Hedwig's original interruption and were chuntering through the Creed in a rapid monotone.

'One holy, catholic and apostolic Church . . .'

Innocent reappeared at the vestry door with a panting Malachi behind him. He caught sight of the dish of unconsecrated hosts waiting for the Offertory and cried out in delight, 'Bit-gits!'

The bishop forgot his pastoral duties, forgot his role as reconciliator and peace-maker, forgot his silent meditations before the eucharistic liturgy. Placing his mitre back upon his head he took a great breath and bellowed, louder than he had ever done since the age of four months, 'Will you dreadful people just BE QUIET!!!'

★ ★ ★

Later that day, at about four o'clock, the four elder O. children were again gathered together, this time in the little herb garden at the back of Saint Wilgefortis' Convent, scuffing the heels of their school shoes against the low stone wall upon which they sat.

'What is a gender fining sauce, anyway?' asked Urban. 'Ow! I thought you said these leaves were nice to chew, Joan?'

'Lemon balm, I told you. That's a nettle. Sister Hedwig said that this Resource place is to study the differences between men and women.'

'Ah . . .' interrupted Pius, anxious for another opportunity to demonstrate his pubertal learning. 'You mean wet . . .'

'No, I don't,' said Joan quickly. Among the many gifts which she had inherited from her mother was an instinct as to when a conversation was heading the wrong way. 'I mean like boys being good at football.'

'And rugby and cricket and sums and science and running and having adventures and just about everything else,' said Hygenus, who would not have recognized diplomacy if it had leaped out of the nearby clump of oregano and tweaked his grimy and freckled nose.

'Girls are good at lots of things,' retorted Joan.

'Like?'

Joan was silent for a couple of seconds. 'Chess?' she suggested, with a tentative sidelong glance at her elder brother. But she need not have worried. The smart of the day before had left no scar.

'Oh, *chess*.' He dismissed the subject with a contemptuous wave which nearly propelled him into a sage bush. 'We were talking about important things.'

'Yeah,' said Hygenus. 'Like making a plan to stop the sisters from having to go to smelly Scorsdale.'

'*Another* plan?'

'Course. We've got to have a plan, haven't we?' Hygenus shook his head in eternal male disbelief at the obtuseness of women. 'And Pius is always the best at making plans. You've got to emit that.'

'S'pose so,' said Joan, trying to remember what 'emit' meant and wishing she could be slightly more certain that it couldn't possibly be the right word. 'Yes, even if they never quite do what they're supposed to. Anyway, it's going to take more than one of our plans to make those teachers and the bishop change their minds. I don't expect they'd do it even if Saint Wilgefortis himself told them to.'

'There you are!' cried Hygenus. 'See? Girls can think of plans, after all. Well, only if they've got very clever brothers to learn from.'

'What are you wittering about?'

'One of us can pretend to be Saint Wilbur-fort's ghost, can't we, and haunt them until they change their minds? Oh, go on. It'll be ginormous fun. Woooo! Woooo!' Hygenus, manifesting not wisely but too well, fell off the wall.

'You awight, Hy?' Urban gazed at his brother's grazed knees with trepidation.

'Course. So what d'ye think?'

Pius was unenthusiastic. 'All this about ghosts and stuff, it's not very Christian, is it?'

'But we're not Christians,' said Hygenus. 'We're Cafolics.'

'It's the same thing,' hissed the scandalized Pius.

'Is it? I thought Christians were the ones on television.'

'So did I,' whispered Urban, 'but Pius is mostly right.'

'Well,' said Joan into the faintly Jacobin atmosphere. 'I think it might be a good idea. We certainly can't think of anything better. And I think it's probably all right about being Christians. I mean, in the olden days everyone was a Christian, weren't they?'

'Um, s'pose so. Except Moors and Red Indians.'

'And they had lots of ghosts then, didn't they? So they must go together. Let's go and ask the sisters about Saint Wilgefortis so that we know what to do.'

Her proposal was acted upon with alacrity, for beckoning smells of baking had been issuing from the kitchen window for some time. The children clattered across the stone-flagged floor and took their accustomed seats around the table.

'Sister Eulalia,' said Pius, putting on his most winsome expression. 'Tell us about Saint Wilgefortis, please?'

But Sister Eulalia, a solid, taciturn woman in her early sixties, merely ruffled his hair and placed an enormous slice of jam sponge cake in front of each child.

'But we really need to know!' protested Hygenus, although, through his mouthful of cake, nothing was produced but a shower of crumbs.

Presently two more sisters joined them, identical in

114

their tiny, wrinkled brownness and looking themselves rather like the hedgehogs to whose comfort and safety their long retirement had been devoted.

'Hello, Sister F'licity! Hello, Sister 'Petua!' said the children randomly, having, in common with most of Rambleton, no idea, until the two old ladies spoke, which of them was which.

'Good afternoon, dears,' said one, in a low rumble which identified her as Sister Felicity. 'I hope Sister Eulalia is feeding you properly.'

The children nodded, their mouths being now crammed with lemon curd tarts, chocolate Swiss roll and Dundee cake. The best thing about the convent, at least, the best thing while the hedgehogs were hibernating, was the fact that there was never any nonsense about sandwiches first or only three kinds of cake. As soon as there was sufficient space for her tongue to move, Joan asked again about Saint Wilgefortis.

'We were wondering whether you could tell us a bit about him.'

'Him?' squeaked Sister Perpetua in her drilling falsetto. 'Oh, not *him*, my darlings. Saint Wilgefortis was a woman.'

'A girl saint?' said Hygenus in dubious disgust.

'Saint Joan was a girl saint,' pointed out her namesake.

'Yes, but she was nearly like a boy, wasn't she? Fighting and all that.'

'Saint Wilgefortis went further than that,' began Sister Felicity, and then broke off in confusion. 'Or perhaps it's . . . *unsuitable*.' She mouthed the final word in Sister

Perpetua's direction. 'Maybe we should wait for Sister Hedwig.'

'Oh, it'll be all right,' chirped her friend. 'They know about all sorts these days. Saint Wilgefortis, you see, dears, or Saint Uncumber, as they used to call her in England . . .'

'Saint Cucumber!' cried Urban in delight, and, horrified at his boldness, cringed beneath the table.

'. . . was the daughter of the King of Portugal.'

'So she was a princess as well as a saint?'

'Yes, I suppose she was.'

Hygenus was doubtful again. 'Are you allowed to be both?'

'Oh yes, dear, think of Saint Edmund. Anyway, Wilgefortis had made a vow of virginity.'

'What's that?'

'It means that she wouldn't, that she couldn't . . .'

Sister Felicity came to her rescue. 'That she wanted to be a nun, like us. Instead of getting married.'

'Pius is going to do that,' confided Urban, his chin resting on what had been his chair. 'Not get married, I mean, and be a priest instead. We don't want to get married too, do we, Hy, 'cos we don't like girls, but we don't want to be priests either. What's it called, if you don't do both?'

'New Laddism, I believe,' said Sister Perpetua, who was an avid reader of the Sunday papers. 'So, getting back to Wilgefortis, she didn't want to get married, but her father wanted her to marry the King of Sicily.'

'So she'd be a queen, too. Lucky thing.'

'Well, she didn't think she was very lucky. So she

prayed to God that He would find a way to help her.'

'A Plan, like ours . . .' began Hygenus, and was silenced by Pius' putting another lemon curd tart into his open mouth.

'And God answered her prayers. What do you think He did?'

'Made the King of Sicily fall down dead?'

'Made the King of Portugal fall down dead?'

'Made her be able to run very quickly?'

'No. He didn't do any of those. What He did, and it may be just a story, mind, but what the old books say He did, was . . .'

'Go on.' The plate of chocolate slices lay untouched.

'He made her grow a beard.'

Pius' doctrinal objections to ghosts vanished in a moment. His mouth opened and little laughter lines creased at the corners of his eyes.

'Ace one,' he breathed.

Chapter Seven

Zugzwang!

The only way, Ophelia had decided, that she was going to be able to smuggle Adeodata and all her essential paraphernalia into the office on Monday morning, was to arrive at least three-quarters of an hour before anyone else. It would mean being very early indeed, for although Polly's adolescent metabolism kept her firmly asleep until three minutes before the last possible bus, Mr Ranger had been known to go straight to work after a sunrise coyote hunt and Mr Snodsworth, confused by the concept of British Summer Time and by his ebbing fob-watch, might arrive at any time between eight and midday. Accordingly, she set her alarm for six o'clock, and, after the first disbelieving moments, resisted the snooze button and flung the duvet back, so that the full force of the bitter morning smote her bare legs and impelled her out of bed.

'Rarumph,' complained Malachi, and pulled the

discarded portion of duvet over his head so that there was no going back.

So it was that at half-past seven on that chilly Monday morning, a dark not-quite-slim figure could be seen tiptoeing across the cobbles of Rambleton Market Square, carrying an old Adidas sports bag. It held the bag carefully, with one hand on the handles and the other supporting its weight, and seemed to be whispering something soothing through its unfastened zip. The figure had almost reached the bottom of Parrish's steps, lit by a single flickering street-light, when it suddenly stopped abruptly, so that the bag swung forward and a faint moan of irritation came from its interior.

'Ssssh now. Zuke? It is you again, isn't it? Unless this is a particularly chronic form of *déjà vu*. Or perhaps I've slipped through a hole in the space-time continuum and got back to last Monday. I hope not. I could do without that week again.'

'Is Zuke, indeed,' replied the fur hat from its customary position at the top of the steps. 'And is another week. But I think you are mistaken about space-time continua if you will pardon me. My brother is astrophysicist and he says is quite, quite impossible. Only romantic English still believe. But I come now to be sure that I am before all your other customers. You say customers?'

'Clients, usually,' said Ophelia, choosing the politest of the possible epithets. 'But they're not usually queuing before sunrise. Anyway, come in and have some coffee.'

Ophelia had been counting on an undisturbed hour at

her desk, to feed, change and gaze at Dodie, and to think about the convent. The bishop's announcement had shaken her, for, over the past year, the sisters had become friends and their cool quiet house a haven from the complexities of work and life at Moorwind Farm. She had been tempted to join the children as they rushed out, ice-cream still melting in their mouths, after Sunday lunch, but could think of nothing practical that she could do. At least the children had been cheerful on their return, although Urban had cried later on as they told her that the hedgehog sanctuary had been closed.

'Sister 'Petua said it wasn't fair on the hedgehogs, giving them a home when they might be convicted any minute.'

'Who, the sisters or the hedgehogs?' Either sounded equally implausible.

'Both, of course.'

'He means *e*victed,' explained Joan. 'But Sister Felicity said she was sure God had some other work for them to do.'

'What sort of work?'

'I don't think they know yet. Anyway, we couldn't ask any more because Mrs Pottlebonce came in.'

'*Monica?* Are you sure?' Monica Pottlebonce generally avoided Saint Wilgefortis, polluted as it was by the presence of Sister Hedwig, whose parish activities represented everything NARCOF was sworn to oppose.

'Mm. She said they had to forget their differences and fight together against the common enemy. I suppose that must be the bishop, mustn't it?'

'Not the *bishop* exactly,' protested Ophelia, mindful of the respect owed to the Apostolic Succession. 'The forces of secularization, perhaps. The new orthodoxy of political correctness.'

'Okay then. Oh, and she had this brilliant pig badge on. Hy wanted it, for when we go and see Lady Tartleton's again, but she said it was too precious. Anyway, she ate the rest of the cake, so we went home.'

'Altruistic to the last,' muttered Ophelia, remembering this as she unlocked the door of the office for Zuke.

'I am begging your pardon?'

'Oh, nothing. Would you mind filling the kettle?' There was no possibility of hiding Dodie's presence from Zuke, as full-throated roars were now emanating from the bag. She would just have to brazen it out, pretending that it was normal for English solicitors to breast-feed their babies in front of their recently bereaved clients. If it seemed banal enough, perhaps he wouldn't mention it to anyone else. Never apologize, never explain. Fortunately, it seemed to work, for after a few avuncular chuckles, he returned to the subject of Hilda.

'You have found the murderer? And Trotter's Bottom?'

'Not yet, I'm afraid. But I've spoken to the doctor, that is, I think I did.' Zuke nodded encouragingly, perhaps taking this as English modesty rather than alcoholic amnesia. 'And I've contacted the Land Registry, Ordnance Survey and the Yorkshire Deeds Registry and they're all looking into it.'

'Is excellent. All these great British institutions. Tell

me, Ordnance Survey, they are also making the guns, yes? This may be of great use to us in apprehending the villain.'

'I d-don't actually think it's the same people. Besides,' she tried a lop-sided drawl in an effort to sound like Humphrey Bogart but only succeeded in pulling a muscle at the back of her tongue, 'I guess we can dispense with the shooters on this one.'

'As you wish. In fact I have also another request to make. This morning I am visiting the body of my poor Hilda at the,' he took a card from his pocket and read from it with evident disbelief, 'the funeral *parlour* of Mr Marrow. This is right, *parlour*? I think that Hilda was telling me it is quite outdated. Not at all good modern English.'

'Well, this *is* Rambleton. I'd be delighted to come. What time were you thinking of?' She wasn't sure that this light social tone was quite right for replying to an invitation to view a corpse, but could hardly think of an alternative. In any case, she ought to go and see it, if she was going to be any sort of detective at all. Even the squeamish Inspector Morse, she remembered, managed to make a token appearance at the post-mortem. Polly professed herself delighted at the prospect of taking charge of the Adidas bag and its contents, especially since she was going through one of her periodic troughs of despair at Gary's paternal prospects, so Ophelia could dismiss any qualms as to the effect of embalming fluid upon the infant psyche.

Ten o'clock until eleven o'clock was Mr Marrow's preferred time for conducting the bereaved into his hushed chamber of repose, sufficiently distant from both breakfast and lunch, and too early in the day for most to have begun drowning their sorrows. He was waiting for them in the little reception room, slight and pale in his three-piece suit, once black, now rubbed to a shiny holly-leaf green.

'Mr Zhukovsky.' He had evidently taken pains to perfect the pronunciation. 'And my dear Mrs O.' Mr Marrow had been a contemporary, friend and client of the late Wilfred Parrish, whom he had despatched with great spectacle, and in the past year Ophelia had continued the association, exchanging her distraught widows for his unpaid invoices to mutual advantage. 'If you would care – this way, please.' He pushed at a panel of the baize-covered wall, which revealed itself to be a door, and ushered them through.

Inside it was so dark that Ophelia's eyes took some moments to adjust. The room appeared to be entirely covered in crimson velvet, on the floor, walls and ceiling, making it seem, itself, like some oversized casket. Electric imitation candles, with red-orange bulbs, provided the inadequate lighting. The room contained three chairs, carefully chosen to compromise between comfort and grief, an elaborate sideboard, and the coffin itself. Ophelia wandered, with what she hoped was tact, about the edges of the room for a while, as Zuke clutched the edge of the coffin and let large tears fall, staining its pink satin.

'Hilda, Hilda,' he murmured, with low Russian endearments. 'Hilda.'

Ophelia examined the carving of the sideboard and

tried not to speculate on its contents. Spare light bulbs, probably. Finally, she could put it off no longer, and approached the body.

Her first thought was that, English as the dead woman undeniably was, there was also something Slavic about her, in the broad smooth face and the body, still sturdy, beneath the white nightgown. Her second thought was that Hilda was startlingly like someone Ophelia knew, someone she saw regularly and had never before thought much about. For a tantalizing quarter-second she saw this person in her mind, but as she groped for the thought it was gone, leaving no clue, not even as to whether the person was male or female. Ophelia looked intently at the body, searching the exposed face and hands for clues, but could discover nothing. Hilda, in death, reminded her now only of her own grandmother, lying, like this, in patient peace, untroubled by speculation or regret. Zuke was holding the coffin still tighter, his plump knuckles white, crying without restraint. Ophelia turned, feeling superfluous, and found Mr Marrow, soundless on crepe soles, standing behind her. With a scarcely discernible gesture he indicated the door and they returned to the little vestibule.

'You are ... acting in this matter?' The long lines across Mr Marrow's face had deepened.

'Yes, to some extent.'

'Then I think I should speak to you. I must tell you, I am not happy with this death.' It was unusual for him to use the stark word. 'I have great respect for Dr Hale, but something – I am not medically qualified, of course, I speak only from experience – something tells me that this was no heart attack. Would that surprise you?'

'Not entirely. Mr Zhukovsky himself is of the same opinion.'

'Ah.' He seemed, if anything, even more troubled. 'Then I must tell you what I think, and you must do as you think fit. Again, as I say, I have no evidence, only my lifetime's work. I have buried close to two generations of Rambleton folk, you know. You see most things, in all that time. But there was something about this body, as soon as it was brought to me, that made me say to myself, "Logward, nineteen-fifty-six." You have heard of the case?'

'No, I don't think so.'

'Strange. Wilfred and I would often speak of it. It was the old story, you know, adultery, jealousy, poisoning. Mind you, in that case it was the husband who died, and the wife who did it.' He looked towards the green baize panels and the inference was clear.

'But I'm sure . . .'

'Hush.'

The two panels separated and Zuke appeared, stumbling through the doorway. His cheeks, collar and lapels were wet but his voice was clear and steady.

'I think that I wish to go now. I have said goodbye.'

Ophelia drove home unusually slowly that evening, through the muffling dusk. Dodie slept in her car seat, tranquil as she had been all day, but Ophelia could not relax to enjoy the baby's contentment. There could be no doubting Mr Marrow's implication. If Hilda had been murdered, and the undertaker clearly suspected foul play, then her husband was, naturally, the principal suspect. That much, of course, was simple statistical probability, and Ophelia felt foolish at not having considered it earlier. But, if Zuke had really killed his wife, why had he come to Parrish Snodsworth Ranger in the first place? Why not simply accept Horatio's diagnosis and say no more? He might have anticipated, prodded by guilt, that someone might raise objections, but this was surely a dangerous way of forearming himself? Nevertheless, the suspicion, once raised, could scarcely be buried again. She would have to keep as close an eye on her client as upon his supposed enemies, and, should she find any tangible evidence, face Sergeant Booking once more in his newly upholstered lair.

'See Dogie, see Dogie!' clamoured Innocent, as soon as she opened the front door. He was closely followed by three more children and a cluster of leaping Labradors.

'She's in the car, sweetheart. I'll bring her in as soon as these canine hordes have subsided a bit.' She looked sternly at the dogs but they continued to prance about her like demented carousel horses. 'They seem unusually pleased to see me tonight. Has your father forgotten to feed them?'

'Oh, er . . .' came an apologetic murmur from the back of the group. 'Might have just slipped my mind today. And yesterday, come to think of it. But come quickly, will you, Oaf? I'm a bit worried about Hygenus.'

Ophelia, like a mother hen, had sensed that one of her chicks was missing, but had not yet worked out which one. 'Oh no. He hasn't fallen off the tractor again, has he?'

'No, nothing like that. I think it might be worse. He's
– *writing a letter.*'

'A letter?' The O.s were not, as a family, great ben-
efactors of the Royal Mail. After a day of legal correspondence, the last thing Ophelia wanted to do in the
evening was to start again, while Malachi had convinced
himself that all his business communications would be
far more efficient carried out by e-mail. This would
probably have been so, had he not still been relying on
the lorry-load of faulty modems which he had bought a
year earlier and distributed to Mid-Yorkshire's legal
firms with such disastrous results. Despite extensive
tinkering, and modifications including the use of milk
bottle tops as miniature satellite dishes, Malachi's carefully prepared messages got no further than the parallel
port on the back of his computer. The children had
inherited their parents' epistolary reluctance and had
refined it to a fine art, so that even Santa Claus had to be
content with last-minute requests shouted up the flue
behind the ailing boiler.

'A letter?' she repeated. 'But who is it to?'

'Don't worry, Mum,' said Pius, and if she had not
been worried before, then she was now. Pius and
Hygenus rarely formed alliances, and when they did it
generally meant trouble. But by the time that she got
inside, to find Hygenus sitting demurely at the kitchen
table with felt pen smeared across his forehead and
school shirt, the envelope had been sealed and he was
laboriously copying out the address from a note in
Pius' handwriting on the back of a chocolate wrapper.
If she had read the letter, then perhaps Ophelia would

have been reassured, or perhaps not. It ran:

Deir Mrr ZUGZwANg chess magazine,

We want to by yoor chess magazine. We have got £20o00, I thinck this is moor than enuph. (thats me and my brofer)

yooors sisterly

Hygenus n Innocent (o).

Chapter Eight

Les Eschez amoureux

Dodie's good nature continued through the night, during which she woke only once, and into the morning, so that Ophelia, despite her worries about Zuke, felt quite elated as she made her way to work, the baby strapped in an intricate sling beneath her duffel coat. Malachi was taking the car to a little man on the other side of town, whose periodic proddings of the bodywork and tut-tutting over the state of the gearbox was described by both men as a service. For some complex reason which Ophelia suspected she was not supposed to understand fully, but was probably something to do with the cut-price sweet shop, he would not drive into the Market Square but dropped her off at the bottom of Church Street. It was a beautiful morning, though, crisp and sunny, so she made no objection. As she started up Church Street, past the plate-glass of Nick Bottomley's offices, she realized that it would be only a small detour to go via the Grand Hotel. She was much later than she had been on the previous morning, having resolved simply to toggle up the duffel coat and claim post-partum obesity if challenged, but she still had plenty of time before her first appointment.

As she approached the hotel she saw Zuke coming out of the front door. His shoulders, beneath the large overcoat, were hunched, as if against the cold, although Ophelia doubted whether Rambleton's chill could compare with a Russian winter. He did not look in her direction but turned towards the town centre and set off briskly. Ophelia followed, a little breathless at his pace and with mingled hope and fear lest he incriminate himself. But he took none of the seedy side streets inhabited by Rambleton's criminal classes, foraged in no dustbins for unconsidered evidence and met with no potential accomplice, unless one counted the postman. As he grew closer to the Market Square it occurred to her that he might simply have been coming to see her again, as he had the previous morning. At this her heart fell, and she almost wished that he might be the murderer, if he would only leave her alone. For it is the ubiquitous client, however respectable and beneficent, who fills the solicitor's nights with dread, and not the merely mal-odorous or criminal.

Thinking about this, and about how, if it should prove to be the case, she could explain her presence barely five yards behind him, Ophelia suddenly realized that Zuke was no longer in front of her. They were passing a row of rather shabby shops behind the Ram's Leg. There was a barber, a second-hand book shop specializing in third-rate erotica, a bookmaker and, indicated by the clouds of greasy steam billowing from the open doorway, Patty's Pantry. She could think of no excuse for visiting the barber, a well-known misogynist who believed women's hair to be intrinsically unclean and, what was more, refused to allow any boys under fourteen into his shop. The book shop keeper, on the other hand, would be delighted to see her, as she had discovered during her first few weeks in Rambleton, when she had unwisely called in search of *Tristram Shandy* and had been lucky to escape with only a smeared handprint on the bosom of her blouse. She thought that she could have coped with the bookie, parted with a pound each way on the favourite at Beverley, but it was closed until ten o'clock. Patty's Pantry it would have to be, then, and if he was not there then a window seat would at least allow her to observe the other doorways. As she stood dithering, Ophelia was overtaken by two more customers who passed impatiently on either side of her and into the steamy café. Ophelia glanced at them in mild annoyance, then looked again more closely. But the second inspection had not been necessary. No one else in Rambleton owned a fake fur with quite so much shabby chic as the woman's, nor a blazer so expensive and yet ill-fitting that it could only be the uniform of a minor public school, as worn by her companion. Ophelia hesitated no longer, but followed them in, discretion forgotten in the excitement of cornering her three principal suspects in a single room.

Patty's Pantry was, considering its unpleasantness, surprisingly full. However, it was, Ophelia remembered, the only place in Rambleton, unless one included the

Friday hot dog van in the Market Square, where breakfast could be purchased, since Rambo's did not open until the genteel hour of ten o'clock. There was only one table available, conveniently compressed behind the sinister couple but on the other side of the room from Zuke. Ophelia sat down, trying not to notice the flaccid bubble of dried tomato ketchup which decorated the menu.

'Toast and, er, cold milk, please,' she murmured to the sullen waitress, remembering previous encounters with the coffee.

'Why yer whisperin'?'

'Sore throat.'

'Oh aye?' The waitress backed away contemptuously, knocking the fake fur to the floor.

'Honestly!' The coat's owner picked it up, with a contemptuous look at the waitress, Ophelia, and anyone else within the orbit of her flashing eyes. She turned back to her companion. 'Why on *earth* did you have to bring us here, Marcus?'

'You wanted us to follow him,' said the young man in a dejected monotone. 'And I don't expect there is anywhere else for breakfast.'

'You're probably right. *God*-forsaken hole. And why the hotel had to refurbish its kitchens *this* morning, when I'd finally got that man to understand what I meant by a properly poached egg, I shall never know. Such a shame. We were building up quite a *rrrapport*.'

'So I noticed.'

'Oh, Markie, can you really be jealous? What a little sweetheart you are sometimes. But seriously, darling, I don't see the point in following him all the way to this

134

ghastly place and then sitting on the opposite side of the room. You know, you shouldn't let dreadful people like that waitress *bully* you. I've noticed that in you, Marcus, especially where women are concerned.'

Ophelia could not resist turning to look at Marcus' expression, but he was evidently too disconsolate to recognize the irony.

'Oh, Arabella. I don't think I'm really cut out for this sort of thing. I'm not sure I can go through with it, not with all the poor chap's suffered already. Couldn't we just leave him alone and forget the whole scheme?'

'Forget the whole scheme!' The woman's voice, which had been huskily lowered, rose to a muted shriek. 'I don't know what you're thinking of, Marcus. Don't you realize, you've burned your bridges now? There's no going back. If you lose your nerve now, then you'll lose everything: your job, your reputation, me . . .'

'You?'

'Darling.' Her voice had recovered its throatiness, assisted by an untipped cigarette. 'Darling, you can't really expect me to, what is the phrase, "stand by my man", just because you've got a sudden fit of conscience? I'm not, not *quite* as young as you, you know. I can't afford to wait all those years.'

'I don't know. Maybe they wouldn't treat me too harshly if I told them everything.'

'You're a fool, Marcus. A very sweet fool, but a fool. Tell them now, and you'll just end up—'

At that point Dodie woke up, and, finding herself wedged uncomfortably between Ophelia's chest and the edge of the table, gave out a furious cry. Zuke looked up from his untouched 'English breakfast'.

'Why, Ophelia! We meet again so soon, so pleasantly!' He rose, without a backward glance at the breakfast, which was obviously not so pleasant, and came towards her. Marcus and Arabella slipped away, with surprising alacrity and without paying their bill.

'Oi!' shouted the waitress and set off in pursuit.

'Do you know that couple?' Ophelia asked Zuke.

'What is couple?' He might, indeed, not have known the word, but something in his sideways glance made Ophelia think that he was playing for time.

'Those two people who just left. They've been staying at your hotel.'

'No . . . no, I think not.'

'A young man, rather shy, and an older woman. Rather striking, the woman. Dark curly hair and very high heels. Arabella, she's called, and he's Marcus.'

'This Marcus I do not know, certainly.'

'But Arabella?'

'I think so. I was not sure, was trying to keep away from her. But now you say the name, yes, it must be she. Miss Arabella Springfield, unless she has married, but somehow I think not. Is not the marrying type.'

'And how do you know her?'

'How to put it in politeness? In English, I think you have a word for a girl who follows the pop groups about, hopes to have love with them?'

'A groupie, yes.'

'Gropie. Arabella, she is chess gropie.'

'I see. Including you? Has she groped – I mean had an affair with you?'

'Sadly, yes. Is long ago. Arabella, she was very beautiful, very high in her spirits, very hard to say no. But it is not good for married man, and so I say "No more".'

'And she was upset?'

'Arabella? Oh, never, never!' Zuke smiled for the first time that morning. 'There are many more chess players, many more funs to be enjoyed.'

'I see. But you don't know who this Marcus is?'

'Alas, no. It used to be said that Arabella would never give her loves to any man less than International Master. But now it may be that she has less to choose from. I do not know. But why these questions? Certainly Arabella is no enemy, nor mistress of one. These people can have nothing to do with my poor Hilda's death.'

'I'm not so sure about that.' Ophelia was about to tell him about the overheard conversation but changed her mind quickly. Given Zuke's excitable temperament, it was probably best not to point his suspicions too unequivocally in any one direction. He might decide to take retribution into his own hands – a sort of Russian lex talionis – and then she would be practically an accessory. What was more, as he had admitted, he and Arabella had been lovers once, and might, despite appearances, have conspired together to do away with an inconvenient wife. She contented herself by telling him to be very careful, especially of what he ate, and to bolt his bedroom door securely, or as securely as the droop-ing joinery of the Grand Hotel would allow.

'Naturally,' smiled Zuke, with an indulgent bow. 'I am much obliged, my most assiduous Ophelia.'

Chapter Nine

The Queen's Gambit Accepted

The Ratchet-Crampers' Social Club on Brack Street, the meeting-place of Rambleton Chess Club, was the last remnant of the town's never very flourishing industrial base. Rambleton was really too small, and its menfolk insufficiently libidinous, to have much of a red light district, but, such as it was, Ophelia realized, upon slowing down outside the club, Brack Street was it.

She parked the Volvo as inconspicuously as possible, its balding tyres wedged against the broken kerbstones, locked the doors, more out of superstition than any real expectation that this would deter the hovering clumps of youths, took Joan firmly by the hand and looked about her.

The Ratchet-Crampers' sign had long since deteriorated into a few unconnected letters, but the smell of stale beer and cigarette smoke and the roar of unfocused male aggression which came from a half-open doorway was sufficient indication of their quarry. Ophelia took a deep breath and went in, pushing past a scornful girl in off-white PVC who lounged against the narrow passage wall. Inside the noise was even louder, but Ophelia was relieved to see that most of the cries and thumps came from an enormous television screen, its colour turned up to the garish maximum, upon which two men were wrestling, their vast undulations of flesh fluorescent orange against the violet floor of the ring. None of the men in the room appeared to be watching the programme; neither were they talking to each other, although the volume of the television set probably precluded any serious conversation. There were no women, except for Ophelia and Joan, and a chisel-faced barmaid whose enormous bosoms were resting on the counter next to a pile of used beer towels and an overflowing ashtray. Ophelia approached the barmaid and attempted a smile of sisterly solidarity. The woman curled her lip and Ophelia could almost imagine that the dark roots of her platinum hair stiffened a little, like a dog whose hackles rise upon the scenting of a rival.

'Members only,' she snapped, without removing her cigarette.

'Er, we're looking for the chess?'

'Members only.'

'The chess club. It said in the library "all welcome". I think Major Lamb runs it. Frederick Lamb? Do you know him?'

The woman snorted. 'That lot,' she said with a smirk

which Joan, in innocence or charity, chose to interpret as a smile. 'Bloody waste of space.' She jutted an elbow towards the end of the bar, automatically supporting her breast with the other hand as she did so. 'Out left, through Gents, fust door right.'

'Through the *Gents*? Isn't there another way? I've got my young daughter with me here.'

'Not my fault, is it?' The shoulders rolled forward in a slow shrug and the right breast knocked over a half-empty beer glass. 'Never bin no lasses afore. Go on then, if you're going, or I'll have to get Ernie to chuck youse out.'

At the mention of his name, Ernie, a large blank-looking man in a shrunken polo shirt, rose slowly to his feet.

'Left, Gents, right,' squeaked Ophelia, pushing Joan before her. 'Lovely, so kind.'

Once in the corridor they paused outside a grimy door, its bottom half pocked with rubber kick-marks, upon which the word 'Menn' had been scrawled in black felt tip pen. Ophelia placed her ear against the door, listening for plashy sounds, then covered Joan's eyes firmly with her hands and marched her through.

'Eh!' cried a little man at the urinals, and Ophelia, despite her best efforts to look straight ahead, could not help but catch a glimpse of mottled flesh against the front of his brown nylon trousers.

'Seen it all before,' she said airily and propelled Joan rapidly through the end door and into a half-full bucket of disinfectant.

Another door, more substantial than any they had

yet seen in the club, stood before them. It bore a neat sign in scholarly handwriting.

Silence please.

and, in more emphatic capitals,

THIS MEANS YOU!

'Come on, Mum, this must be it. The chess club. Oh come on, Mummy, hurry up!'

Feeling rather as she had when hovering on the stone staircase before her first Cambridge interview, Ophelia followed her daughter into the precincts of Rambleton Chess Club.

Here, in contrast to the stultified roar of the bar, still audible, in muted form, through the mediation of the lavatories, was an atmosphere of serenity and wisdom. Two long rows of tables filled the small room, upon which seven or eight chess boards had been set up, each flanked by a pair of studiously bowed heads. Only a few were raised as the newcomers quietly closed the door, among them the familiar red face and twitching moustache of Major Frederick Lamb.

'Bless my soul, it's Mrs O.!' he spluttered, in the nearest thing he knew to a whisper. 'Looking for me, were you? Don't tell me old Porridge has got us into a pickle. Mango pickle, what?' His barrel chest constricted with a series of snorting laughs, and a couple of the chess players looked up reproachfully.

'Who's Porridge?' murmured Joan.

'Mr Puri. You know, Major Lamb's partner in the bowling alley.'

'Oh yes,' said Joan, then turned to the Major. 'I don't think you ought to call him that, you know. People might think you were one of those recasts. We did about it at school.'

'What's the little filly blethering on about now?' He seemed to have recovered from his outburst at Tartleton Court, for his tone was still bluff and jovial. 'Gave the finest years of my life to the natives, you know. British Empire was the best thing that ever happened to them. Look at 'em now, fighting between themselves, bad as the fuzzy-wuzzies.'

Joan opened her culturally sensitive mouth to complain again but her mother was too quick for her.

'I'm sure you're right, Major. But we weren't actually looking for you. Not specifically, I mean. The thing is, Joan's very interested in chess, and we were wondering whether she could join the club here?'

The Major bent slowly, and creasing his faded blue eyes into tight little corrugations, peered into Joan's face.

'Interested in *chess*? A pretty girl like you? No, no, you should be out in the fresh air, keeping those rosy little cheeks aglow.' He pinched her with surprising force. 'Or why not pop into the library if you'd rather be indoors. My good lady runs a charming little poetry club for the kiddies. Just the thing, I'd have thought.'

Joan, up to now, had not been at all sure that she wanted to join the chess club. It had been fun beating Pius, and she loved the shapes of the pieces and the smooth way they fitted into the palm of her hand, but she could not honestly say that the progress of the game excited her very much. She did not know why on earth Mum was making such a fuss about it, especially as she herself had hardly even looked at the board during her own two tournament games, but it was nice to get away for the evening, just the two of them, leaving the horde of boys to its own devices. If they had to go somewhere, however, Mrs Lamb's poetry club would normally be much more to Joan's taste, and, she thought, to her mother's as well. But all that had changed with the Major's first condescending little clearings of his throat. Joan was suddenly determined, not just to play chess, but to enjoy playing it, and to play it better than this room full of variegated men, all now looking at her, albeit with, on the whole, quite kindly expressions.

'Chess,' she said, staring firmly at the embossed pewter buttons of Major Lamb's waistcoat.

'Very well then, little girl, we'd better find you an opponent. Now, let me see . . . Hah!' he snorted suddenly, and strode off towards a table at the far end of the room, his slight limp causing his left leg to jog each chess board that he passed.

'Forced draw, there,' he boomed. 'No point in playing on.'

The two men looked, perplexed, between the chess pieces and the speaker.

'I don't think so, Fred,' said one, a slight middle-aged man with well-groomed silver hair and delicate fingers which caressed his opponent's captured queen as he spoke. 'The rooks are still on, and it's a knight for a bishop. There's plenty of play here.'

'It's a draw, old chap. Take my word for it. And I want young Giles to give this little girl a game.'

The second player, a boy in his late teens, turned around, and Ophelia recognized him for the first time. Giles Glade-Rivers, in the Upper Sixth of the Alderman Penbury Comprehensive School, had become a friend of the whole O. family and a hero to the children since the events of the summer, when he had rescued Innocent from the uppermost sail of a becalmed windmill and had utilized fifteen redundant dot-matrix printers to restore electricity to a powerless Rambleton.

Joan suddenly felt the assertion of feminine equality need not be such a penitential experience after all.

'Hello, Giles!' she called, and the room full of chess players, unable to object to the Major's barrack-room volume, exercised their pent-up frustration in a communal '*Shh!*'

'Sorry,' whispered Joan to the company in general, and contented herself with an enthusiastic wave.

Giles, too, would have liked to have continued the game, for he sensed that, although the pieces taken on either side were even, his pawn structure was superior and might have led to his first ever victory over Simon, the silver-haired man. But it was useless, he knew, to argue against the Major, and, in any case, he liked little Joan, whose wry stoicism in the face of her brothers' incorrigible maleness he took as a model for his own attitude, whilst awaiting his reception into the Catholic Church, towards his eccentrically atheistic parents.

'Come on then, Jo,' he said, collecting another board and pieces from the cupboard, while Simon and Major

Lamb continued their twenty-five-year-long discussion of variations in the King's Indian.

'Have you had your mocks yet, Giles?' asked Ophelia.

Joan, anxious to be of help, took the board and chess pieces from him, wondering, incidentally, why they were packed in a plastic lunchbox, and set them up on an empty table.

Giles extricated himself from Ophelia's fumbling attempts to sympathize with differential calculus and came over.

'Well done,' he said, and then his face changed. 'Er . . .'

'What's the matter?'

'Oh, you've just got the bishop and knight the wrong way around. Easy mistake to make.'

Joan, reddening, switched the pieces about.

'And, um, the queen . . .'

'Next to the king, I thought,' said Joan, with an undertow of sulkiness.

'Yes, yes, but er, *Queen on her own colour*, we say, you know.'

'Don't see how she can be, when the board's green and white. There, can we start now?'

'Well it *is* customary . . .' began Giles looking more closely at the board. '*White on the right*, and that. But never mind. We'll keep it as it is for now. Silly rules anyway, I expect.' He smiled and Joan was mollified.

Then, to her astonishment, Giles seemed to snatch something from the board and thrust two clenched fists in front of her.

'What's the matter?'

'Choose.'

'What?'

'Choose one of my hands. One's got a black pawn in it and the other one a white. It's the usual way, in friendly games, to decide who'll play which colour.'

'Oh, I see. But I don't really mind.'

'So choose.'

Joan put out an inky forefinger and touched the back of Giles' brown left hand.

'Black. Hard luck, Joan.'

'Does it make much difference?'

He grinned again. 'Not at our level, I shouldn't think.'

He pushed his first pawn forward and Joan stared at it for a few seconds.

'Do you want a hint?'

'No!'

'Sorry. You can play almost anything against this, anyway.'

'Shh, I'm thinking.'

Joan became aware of her mother's amused smile from a judicious position a few yards from the board. Suddenly embarrassed, she moved a pawn at random.

'Oooh, no,' came Major Lamb's low growl. 'Shouldn't have done that, m'dear. Not unless you want to gambit it, of course.'

But Giles, rather than taking the offered pawn, moved one of his knights, and Joan followed his example.

'Please go and watch someone else, Mum,' she said, emboldened by her development, and sounding almost as though she did not normally say 'Mummy'. 'I can't concentrate with you hanging over me.'

Ophelia disappeared.

After nine or ten moves, things seemed to be going well. One pawn on each side had been taken and Joan's pieces were apparently moving out nicely. She castled kingside, looking cautiously at Giles before taking her hand off the rook.

'That's right. Do you know how to do it queenside?'

She shook her hand.

'Like this,' he demonstrated. 'There. Your move again.'

Joan was definitely enjoying the game, although not in quite the way she had imagined when she had first surveyed the masculine stronghold. There was something about Giles' long brown fingers as he moved the pieces, about his knees that occasionally brushed hers under the cramped table and about the inexorable merging of the white and black pieces that made her tingle pleasantly beneath her pink and white leggings. He was awfully handsome, rather as she had imagined Sindy's boyfriend to be, before the primitive delights of Moorwind Farm had put an end to such feminine pastimes. She looked fixedly at his king, statuesque yet vulnerable behind its broken line of pawns and began to manoeuvre her queen and bishop on to the long diagonal. He moved again, a pointless-looking pawn move, scarcely seeming to notice what she was doing. Her heart beat faster. Another move. She calculated: one, two three. She would win, wouldn't she? Suddenly, she was not sure whether she wanted to. The game seemed very grown up now, disquieting and overripe, like the films which Mummy would quickly switch over when she came through to the sitting-room late at night, or the time she had half-opened her parents' door to hear Daddy, in a voice quite unlike his usual ineffectual burr, shout at her to go away. Then she remembered that the honour of the female sex was at stake, and, taking care to keep her eyes away from his languid smile, she made her penultimate move. But it was too late.

'Check,' he announced, without triumph, but with an infinitely more mortifying thread of sympathy.

Ophelia joined them. 'Hard luck, Joannie.'

Joan stared furiously at the chess board, and at the green and white squares which would, despite her obstinate blinking, persist in dissolving around the edges and blurring into one another. A tear splashed on to her queen, filling the tiny black crown with liquid crystal. She turned to her mother. 'I *told* you not to watch.'

'I didn't,' began Ophelia. 'I only came along at the e—' She broke off, belatedly recognizing Joan's need for a scapegoat. 'Yes, I'm sorry, darling. I must have put you off.'

But Joan was not listening. 'Just a moment,' she said to the uncomfortable Giles. 'You only said "check", didn't you? Not "checkmate"?'

'Yes, of course. There are lots of things you can do now. Block it with that bishop, move your king . . .'

'All right, all right.' Joan's small face was set sharply. 'Just let me work this out.' All was not lost, after all. It had been foolish of her not to have considered his attack, but she would not make that mistake again. If she moved her king along by one square, then he would not be able to check her on his next move. Then, surely, she could deliver the fatal blow.

He didn't check her, that much she had been right about, but he moved a pawn to block the diagonal line between her queen and bishop. Now, the move that she had planned would simply condemn the unguarded queen. She would have to think of another way around.

It was another hour before the game ended, and the table was surrounded by onlookers, gently jostling for a sight of the little girl. She sat very still, her eyes darting along the rows and files of the board, her lips tightly pressed and jaw line set firm. Ophelia hovered on the edge of the group, not daring to disobey Joan's injunction but acutely conscious of the child's vulnerability in the midst of the throng.

But Joan, when she finally emerged, shouldering her way through the thicket of elbows, looked anything but vulnerable.

'I won, Mum,' she said with rehearsed nonchalance. 'Shall we go home now?'

Ophelia would have been happy to go, but Simon, Giles' former opponent, had approached them with a little bow and asked whether Joan would do him the honour of a game. Ophelia consented, and took Giles into a corner to ask his opinion about Zuke.

'Zhukovsky here? Honestly? Wow, that's brilliant! No, I don't suppose he's in what you'd call the first rank of grandmasters, but he's better than anyone we've ever had in Rambleton before. Quite an exciting player, you know, quicker than most Russians. Careless, but he's had some brilliant victories when it's gone right for him. What's he doing here, then?'

Ophelia explained.

'No kidding? Poor old chap. Sounds like standard grandmaster paranoia to me, though, this stuff about chess enemies. I mean, even Bobby Fischer never accused anyone of actual *murder*, did he? And certainly not in Rambleton, even if we have had our share of feuds. Take Major Lamb and Mr Bradley, for example.'

'Mr Bradley?'

'Mortimer Bradley, yes. He organizes the Humbert Havelock Memorial Tournament in Rambleton. That reminds me, it's on in a couple of weeks and Joan really ought to play in it.'

Humbert Havelock, it transpired, had been the original founder of Rambleton Chess Club in 1884, when Joseph Henry Blackburne, the 'Black Death', had dominated the English chess scene and a knowledge of the Queen's Gambit had been as essential an accomplishment of the Victorian gentleman as stashing pornographic lithographs in his waistcoat pocket or bullying the maidservants. Mortimer Bradley, who rather modelled himself on Blackburne, with his enormous black beard and uncertain temper, had uncovered the memory of Humbert Havelock ten years earlier and had started the series of tournaments which bore his name.

'Not that Bradley ever comes to the chess club now,' explained Giles. 'He and Major Lamb had a row about the adjournment rules six years ago and he's not set foot in the Ratchet-Crampers' since. But pop along to see him, he'd like to hear about Joan, especially if you can persuade Zhukovsky to play.'

'Oh. Right then,' agreed Ophelia. The prospect was scarcely tempting, but, after all, a potentially violent chess player was exactly what Zuke expected her to find. And if Joan really was going to be good at this game, then she deserved her chance to show off. She got little enough chance at home, dominated by all those brothers. Ophelia looked around to make sure that Joan wasn't hovering, ready to go, but Simon's place had been taken by another opponent, and there seemed to be a queue after him.

'I'd better go now, if you don't mind,' said Giles. 'It's my "A" levels this year, you know, and Dad starts muttering if I take too much time off. What with my instruction from Father Jim and giving the sisters a hand down at the convent, I don't seem to have an awful lot of time left.'

'What? Oh yes, of course. Thanks for your help, Giles.' Ophelia was distracted by the stranger who had just come through the door, flustered from the passage through the Gents. It was, yes, it certainly was, Arabella from the Grand Hotel.

Arabella stood poised for a few moments on the threshold of the room, her magnificent chest puffed out like a winter pigeon, waiting to be admired, her rather round eyes flickering about the gathering. But no one, except Ophelia, and Giles, who was on his way out, seemed to see her at all. She stepped subtly back into the doorway, so that he would have to squeeze past her, but Giles, courteous and also wise beyond his years, stood aside for her to enter the room.

Once he had gone, Arabella condescended to notice Ophelia.

'Oh! I keep seeing you about the place, don't I?' The tone was that of a titled lady, mildly exasperated at finding, once again, that the housemaid had left the dustpan on the stairs. 'Are you working for Lex in some way?'

'Lex? Oh, you mean Mr Zhukovsky? He asked me to call him Zuke.'

'Hmmm. Yes. That's what his *male* cronies call him. He and I were a little more, *intimate*.'

'So he told me.'

Arabella looked annoyed. 'Possibly. So who are you, then?'

'I'm Mr Zhukovsky's solicitor.' Ophelia stood on tiptoe to try to appear more formidable. 'I'm investigating the circumstances of Mrs Zhukovsky's death.'

Arabella gave a little scream. 'Oh, goodness me! And you are trying to tell me that I'm a *suspect*? Do you want to know what I was doing on the night of the murder?'

'How do you know it was a murder?'

'I don't, silly. But why else would you be investigating it?' Arabella gave a great sigh, wobbling her tight blouse so that at least one chess player glanced up at last, and reflected on how impossible it was to have a conversation with another woman. Now a male solicitor, she was sure, would have played along beautifully, with none of this boring literalism.

'Plenty of reasons,' said Ophelia, unable, for the moment, to think of any. 'But murder is certainly one of the possibilities. I can't say that I've ruled it out at this stage.' She realized with horror that she was starting to talk like a policeman. Any moment now she might whip out a notebook and start talking about 'proceeding in a westerly direction'. 'So yes, I will want to know what you and your, *young friend*, were doing in the hours leading up to Mrs Zhukovsky's—' She broke off, remembering that Hilda had died first thing in the morning and that she would really prefer not to hear the details of Arabella's night with Marcus. Arabella smiled, with either glee at Ophelia's discomfiture or pleasure at the memory. '*And*,' continued Ophelia, 'why you followed him to Patty's Pantry yesterday morning and what you were plotting there.'

'Oh,' said Arabella. 'Oh, you were there, weren't you?' Her manner changed abruptly, her shoulders sagged a little and the chess players who had been assessing her now turned back to their games. 'Okay, I'd better explain. I suppose it all sounded rather sinister in the circumstances. Marcus Fry, my, er, friend, as you put it, is the editor of *Zugzwang!* magazine. Have you heard of it?' Ophelia frowned. She had seen the name on the front of Hygenus' envelope as she provided him with a stamp and had assumed that it was a children's television programme. This detection work was all very well in the office, but she certainly didn't want the children to be involved. Perhaps she should not even have brought Joan here tonight. Arabella misinterpreted the frown. 'Don't worry, I wouldn't expect you to. It used to be called *The Weekend Chess Players' Review*, but last year one of the big media groups bought it and decided to go for the youth market. I've done what I can to help, an agony column and so on, but basically, yob culture and amateur chess don't really fuse into a commercial success. The "yoof" writers have run out of double entendres and the old *Weekend* contributors don't like their neat little studies of the Fleissig Variation being livened up with "kin ells" and deliberate spelling mistakes.'

'Sounds ghastly.'

'It is, absolutely, but it's Marcus' life. He's been editor for fifteen years, since he left school almost, and he'd fall apart without it. He and I, well, it won't last long, but he's a nice lad and I don't like to see him messed about.'

'So, what's this got to do with Zuke?'

'I heard, a few weeks ago, that he was planning to come over to Britain more-or-less permanently. As you know, he and I were once – and I generally keep in touch with what my old flames are doing. There've been a few, as you might imagine, all of them chess players. I was pretty good myself, once, might have made Women's International Master, but I guess I got side-tracked. Which is what I'm doing now. Anyway, the only hope I could think of for *Zugzwang!* was to try to get a scoop with Lex. You know the sort of thing, why he's come to Britain, what he thinks of the current top players, all that. And then, more importantly, there are a lot of questions about the Soviet chess system that people want answers to. Most of the defectors left too long ago to be able to tell us much, and the others are still too loyal. What I hoped was, if Lex had left because he was disillusioned, he'd spill the beans.'

'So you came here to interview him?'

'That was the idea. What I hadn't realized – I hadn't actually seen him since we split up all those years ago – was quite what a devoted husband he'd become. I tried to say hello when he first arrived on the Saturday afternoon, but he just ignored me. Then, of course, his wife died, and Marcus wanted to forget the whole thing and go back to Nottinghamshire. That's where the magazine offices are, you see. But he's done nothing at all for next month's issue, we'd pretty well burned our boats so far as that was concerned, so if he went back without the Zhukovsky story, he might as well just hand his notice straight in. So we've been trying to corner him somewhere and get him to say something, anything, just so that there's a few lines of copy for poor Marcus. That's why I'm here tonight, on the off-chance that Lex fancied a game with the local talent.'

'But surely Marcus could find something else if he lost this job? I mean, I assume he's a pretty good chess player himself. Couldn't he do coaching or something?'

Arabella shook her head, so that her filigree earrings tinkled. 'No confidence. You're right, he was very good as a boy. Then he played in his first really big tournament when he was seventeen and got slaughtered. He never played again. He'll write about chess, but never his own opinions and he won't even comment on someone else's game. Is this your little girl? It looks as though she's ready to be off.'

'Oh yes. Well done, Joannie. By the way, Arabella, where was this big tournament?'

'What, Markie's? In Russia, I think. And I only meant big in importance, not numbers. Six player all-play-all, I think. Lex was probably there himself. See you around, then. Good luck with the detective work.'

Joan's euphoria had evaporated abruptly upon their re-emergence in the cold night, and after a few sharp replies to Ophelia's questions, she had fallen defiantly asleep. Ophelia was perplexed at Joan's uncharacteristic petulance but put it down, with the complacency of permanently fatigued adulthood, simply to tiredness. She had forgotten, of course, her own meteoric crush, at about Joan's age, upon a spotty undergraduate cousin, overtaken, as it had been, by the messier and less single-minded infatuations of adolescence. All the same, she was quite relieved when Pius made his announcement at breakfast the next morning.

'We'll be back late today.'

'Who's we?' asked his mother suspiciously.

'Us schoolchildren. Me, Joan, Hygieneless and Urbs.'

'I do wish you wouldn't call him that.'

'Who me?' asked Hygenus, raising a jammy face from his toast. 'Hygieneless means dirty, and I always is, so it's all right. We wanted to call Urban Burps, but he cried, so we couldn't.'

Urban looked fixedly into his Weetabix.

'And we call Joan the old Moan, essept she . . . hits us.' Hygenus ducked upon saying this, but Joan, gazing out of the grimy window, her yoghurt untouched, made no move.

'And what do you call Pius?' asked Malachi.

'They can't think of anything,' said Pius triumphantly. 'It's me that's the best at nicknames.'

'Only 'cos you're the oldest,' growled the others in unison. 'Anyway, where are we going?'

'Oh, just to Saint Wilgies.'

'The convent? Again?' Ophelia was simultaneously

helping Innocent with his Ready Brek and breast-feeding the baby, and the two were getting rather confused, with nasty smears down both sleeves of her last remaining jacket. 'Isn't that the second time this week? I don't want you being a trouble to the sisters.'

'It's all right,' said Hygenus airily. 'We cheer them up, really.'

Such was the saintliness of the sisters, reflected Ophelia, that this was probably true. 'All right then. I'll come round and pick you all up at half-past five.'

Despite all the anguished Sunday-supplement articles, Ophelia had no qualms about letting the children wander across Rambleton in the charge of Pius, who was considerably more responsible than his father. He had apparently been born with an instinctive knowledge of the Green Cross Code and a sense of responsibility which would credit many a grammar school headmaster.

'That's all right then, darling,' she murmured, and reached for the baby wipes.

If Ophelia had seen Pius' leadership in action that afternoon then she might have had her faith in the intrinsic mischief of small boys restored, and her peace of mind correspondingly shaken. He led the others through the wrought iron side gate of Saint Wilgefortis, through the sharply-scented herb garden and through the green painted door into the field beyond.

'O-oh,' moaned Hygenus, as they passed the kitchen door without pausing. 'Aren't we having any tea?'

'Later on. Come on, now, this is important.'

Pius strode on ahead, his school shoes squelching

satisfyingly into the damp ground, down the full length of
the long narrow strip of land which had been retained by
the sisters after the establishment of the Alderman Penbury Comprehensive. At the end of the field, where the
ground sloped down towards the disused railway line,
was a small copse of beech trees, and, through the trees'
undressing branches, a low grey structure could be seen.

'What's that.'

'It's what I've discovered. Our new place. It's a
medieval castle.'

'Wow!'

Hygenus and Urban raced through the fallen leaves
and began to scramble up the building.

Joan turned to her brother. 'Is it really a castle?'

Pius jammed his hands deeper into his pockets, pulling the stitching out of either seam. 'Well, it's something
like that. It might just as well be a castle as anything
else. At least I found it.'

Joan nodded in pacific agreement and followed the
others through the copse.

What the 'castle' really was, no one quite knew, but it
was certainly not medieval, having been built in the early
months of the Second World War by some public-
spirited Rambletonians, apparently anxious to secure the
sisters' protection from the invading Hun. It was a
circular structure, turreted about the top, with thick rusty
veins exposed through the crumbling concrete. Around
its base lay lumps of concrete, upon some of which wiry
tufts of grass had begun to grow. 'The Fort' had been
well known to the girls of Rambleton Convent School,
many of whom were now themselves mothers of teenage

daughters, and might not care to remember the uses to which it had been put. At the creation of the Alderman Penbury Comprehensive, however, since the structure fell within the strip retained by the sisters, its usefulness as a base for illegal activity had ceased and it had been wholly forgotten.

'Yay!' shouted Hygenus, reaching the shaky summit first. 'Yay, we can play knights and soldiers and battle-ships and spacestations and Robin Hood and *everything*.'

'And dinosaur battles,' added Urban.

'And Henry VIII cutting off his wives' heads in the Tower of London,' said Pius, a little peeved at being outrun. 'Come on, Joan, can't you think of anything?'

Joan was still several yards from the tower, trudging slowly with her head bent.

'She doesn't want to play any boys' games,' said Hygenus. 'I 'spect she wants to play Sindies.'

'I *don't*. I'm just thinking, that's all. Seems to me that you boys might do better thinking a bit instead of running about all the time. Don't you ever want any peace and quiet?'

'She must be tired from last night,' said Pius, who, however much he affected to despise chess, was madly jealous of Joan's expedition. 'After all, it must be 'zaust-ing, being beaten by everyone.'

Joan awoke from her romantic torpor and Pius found himself rapidly ejected from the top of his discovery.

When Ophelia arrived at Saint Wilgefortis, as promised, at half-past five, she found only Sister Eulalia in the kitchen, and no sign of the children.

'Nay,' was all that the taciturn sister would reply. 'Nay, not bin here today.'

Sisters Perpetua and Felicity entered, arm in arm, their button noses twinkling appreciatively at the smell of Sister Eulalia's ginger cake. Ophelia noticed that they had abandoned their usual grey dresses and navy cardigans for rather striking pastel-coloured jogging suits and that they were somewhat out of breath.

'Dear me, the darlings,' twittered Perpetua. 'No, no, we've not seen them for weeks. Such very well-behaved children and so charming. A credit to you, Ophelia dear.'

Ophelia assumed that Perpetua must be thinking of a quite different set of children.

'No, no, mine are the three boys and a girl. And the babies, of course. Scruffy lot, never brush their hair, always eating sweets and trampling through the herb garden.'

'Yes, we know them. Little Joan and her brothers. But they don't trample the herbs, dear. They're always awfully good about using the path. Except little Innocent, of course, but we couldn't expect him to know.'

'But it's been weeks since you've seen them? They weren't here the other day?'

'Of course they were, Perpetua!' boomed out the firmer tones of Sister Felicity. 'Don't you remember them asking about Saint Wilgefortis? We haven't seen them today, mind, but I did catch a glimpse of something red at the bottom of the field. Could that be . . .?'

'Urban's jumper, yes. He was sick down his navy school one. Thanks. I'll walk down and fetch them.'

As Ophelia plodded up the field, impeded somewhat

by the slipping straps of Dodie's sling, she was feeling uncharacteristically glum. Arabella's story sounded plausible, and she could check up on the *Zugzwang!* angle – what *could* Hygenus have to do with it? – but it did not preclude Arabella's having done away with Hilda as well, to facilitate the interview, perhaps, or simply out of pique or unrequited love. And as for Marcus, he too had the perfect motive. A sensitive young man, his career ruined by his humiliating defeat. Surely that was the kind of injury that could fester over fifteen years, finally, when all seemed to be lost, exploding into violence? And, if Marcus was the murderer, what about Zuke himself, and the other four players? Would their lives too not be in danger? From having no suspects, Ophelia suddenly seemed to have a surfeit, and that was even before she braved Mortimer Bradley.

And there was Dodie to worry about, as well. Not, she trusted, as a potential murder suspect, but she couldn't go on taking her into the office for much longer. Already, that afternoon, on a snooping visit from T'other Side, Mr Snodsworth had noticed small squeaking noises coming from beneath Ophelia's desk. The quick-witted Polly had been there and had extemporized a story about their taking custody of a new-born lamb, the subject of a custody dispute between two farmers from the hamlet of Shedd. Ophelia had gestured desperately at the calendar, and mouthed 'Autumn' but neither Polly nor Mr Snodsworth had taken the point and the matter had rested, albeit with a warning from the old gentleman of the effect of sheep-droppings upon parchment. There was no doubt about it, something, somewhere, would have to give.

'Mummy!' called Urban, always the most observant, and her spirits rose. 'Are you going to have tea with us and the sisters?'

'Do you think they've got enough for us all?'

'Course they have.'

And Urban, as usual, was right. Ophelia insisted that she and the children should do the washing-up, which led to the loss of only two tea-cups and a side plate, and the discovery by Hygenus of something, he would not tell her what, wedged under the kitchen table drawer where the long knives were kept. She thought that he had put it back, but was diverted, as they left, by a sudden eruption in Dodie's nappy, so that she neither saw Pius stuff the paper into his blazer pocket nor heard Urban breathe, with delighted awe, 'Secret Treasure Map!'

Chapter Ten

Progressive Twins

Ophelia spread the newspaper out on the library table, accidentally nudging a sleeping tramp who opened his pink eyes, said something unintelligible and tried to go back to sleep on her shoulder. Ophelia knew how he felt. It was half-past three in the afternoon, and she had been at the table since ten o'clock that morning. Even the tramp had gone out for lunch, after vainly trying to eat his distressed chicken leg under Letitia Lamb's gimlet gaze.

In the morning's post had been replies from the Land Registry, Ordnance Survey and the Yorkshire Deeds Registry in Northallerton. All had concerned Trotter's Bottom, and all had the same message: nothing. Neither the map nor the name meant anything to anyone and Ophelia had been reduced to scanning old copies of the *Rambleton Courier* in search of a clue. Rambleton library, of course, had not yet discovered microfiche, and CD-ROM was a terrifyingly futuristic concept, so that the newspapers had to be brought up from the basement in crates, from which the grey bobbled dust floated into Dodie's eyes and throat. Ophelia was working backwards from 1945, when Hilda left Rambleton for good to marry the dashing Russian major she had met in France while she was working in the Ambulance Corps. Zuke had described the meeting to her, the confusion as he took a brief nap with his men in a barn, only to wake and find his leg being bandaged by an earnest young Englishwoman, who, for a long time, refused to believe that it was the sergeant beside him who had actually been injured. Once convinced, however, she had been mortified with embarrassment, and it had taken several suppers and the best wine he could cadge from the locals before she was willing to laugh about it.

Oh, why did these newspapers have to be so long, and so dense? Surely paper and ink must have been rationed? Perhaps it was a way of keeping up morale, all the recipes for meatless steak-and-kidney pie, sugarless marmalade and powdered egg omelettes, together with the two mile queue which had formed from Rambleton Market Square on the rumour that the greengrocer had a punnet of strawberries. They were obsessed with food, poor creatures, and Ophelia could sympathize, having had nothing since breakfast herself. Any moment now, she would be tempted to purloin the hamburger, left over since Friday's van, which hung precariously from the tramp's trouser pocket.

1944, 1943, 1942. The years passed, in smudged newsprint, as the sky outside the library darkened and the baby mewed in her sling. Ophelia's eyes were beginning to swim, reading the same headlines again and again with no idea of what they said. When she finally found what she was looking for, amongst the tremulous brides of June 1941 in their barrage balloon wedding dresses, she had to say the words out loud before she could believe in them.

'*Trotter's Bottom for Birthday Girls!*'

'Eh?' The tramp jerked himself awake and looked around fearfully. 'Whose bottom? Whose birthday?'

'Sshhh!' hissed Letitia, scandalized at such lewd talk in her library.

'Sorry,' said Ophelia. 'Look, could I photocopy this?'

'Photocopy what?'

'This art— Oh no!' Lifting the page away from the one beneath, Ophelia realized for the first time that the paragraph beneath the headline had been neatly cut out. What was more, to judge from the neat, crisp edges, the article had been removed recently.

'I trust,' said Letitia in a voice of petrifying authority, 'that you have not been vandalizing the archives, Mrs O.?'

'Of course I haven't!' Ophelia, affronted, forgot to keep to a library pitch. 'It was like that before I found it. You can search me for scissors if you like.'

The tramp looked happily from one woman to the other. This was better than a punch-up outside the Ram's Leg. Nice ringside seat, too, and it was warm. But he was to be disappointed.

'Oh,' said Letitia, capitulating as quickly as a punctured dinghy. 'Oh dear.'

'Who did it, then? It looks pretty recent to me. Come

on, there can't be that many people asking for old copies of the *Courier*.'

'Oh, you'd be surprised,' said Letitia vaguely. 'The anniversary of D-Day, you know. Quite a throng there's been.'

'D-Day was nineteen-forty-five. Or 'forty-six or something.' Ophelia's modern history was shaky. 'Whichever, it certainly wasn't nineteen-forty-one. Come on, Mrs Lamb, please. This is important.'

'I don't know. And if I did I couldn't tell you. People expect privacy in a library. I consider it a sacred trust to keep their confidence.'

'Honestly, it's not the confessional.'

'As far as I am concerned,' said the librarian loftily, 'it might as well be. And if you're so anxious to see that article I suggest that you try the *Courier*'s own offices. They should still be open. And you can take your unwashed friend with you. I'm closing in five minutes.'

The tramp grinned and gathered up his carrier bags.

The offices of the *Rambleton Courier* were perched at the top of one of the town's older buildings and reached via a narrow staircase pinched between a fish and chip shop and a rather seedy newsagent. The stairs were steep, as well as cramped, and by the time Ophelia reached the top she was breathless with the weight of Adeodata and the smell of the tramp who had persisted in following her.

The two telesales girls who sprawled on either side of the doorway were combing their hair and retouching their lipstick in preparation for going home. They greeted Dodie with little coos and ripples, which died away abruptly as the tramp heaved his way to the summit.

'Yeaaas?' drawled the blonde as she reapplied purple mascara to an unlikely pair of eyelashes. 'You're too late for this week, unless you're going in *Under a Fiver.*'

Ophelia explained what she had come for, and tried to indicate, without hurting his feelings, that the tramp was nothing to do with her.

'Oh aye? You'd best see old Seamus – t'editor, then. Back copies got nothing to do with us.'

The brunette, who had a kindly heart beneath her leopard print crop top, offered to make the tramp a cup of tea. 'Have a biscuit, too,' she advised. 'We mustn't, 'cos we're dieting, and we don't see why old Seamus should have them all.'

Old Seamus, who was in fact a thirty-three-year-old from Croydon called Philip, had been nicknamed thus because, in the dark glasses he invariably wore, he was supposed to look like an IRA hitman. He had in fact intended to wear the glasses only on his first day, while recuperating from the farewell party hosted by his Surrey friends. Unfortunately, when he had arrived on his second morning without them, no one had recognized him and he had been forced into making them a permanent accessory. Actually, they came in rather handy, in providing a second line of defence against the irate farmers and mothers of misspelled brides which made up his experience of his readership.

Philip was sitting, as usual, in the improvised office, rather too obviously a converted garden shed, which stood in the centre of the room and constituted his inner sanctum. Ophelia peered through the polythene window to see him, head in hands, staring down at an old copy of *Time Out*. She tried to tap on the window but it only gave a feeble flapping sound as a piece of the Sellotape holding it in place gave way. Ophelia lifted a corner of the polythene and called in.

'Eh? What? Uh? Oh, it's you.' He could scarcely have looked more crestfallen if Mr Marrow himself had come to take him away. 'Go on then, who is it?'

'Who is what?'

'Your client who's suing for libel. If it's Edgar Pottlebonce then we've got a defence. Once he's accepted the gong, it's all in the public domain. I've got a reliable source who can confirm that those llamas were a quarter donkey. Pensioned off from Filey beach only to get a second career as a Peruvian stud. I should be so lucky.' He gestured mournfully at his *Time Out*. 'Think I'll ever get back there?'

'T'South, lad? Come on, it could be worse. I'm not acting for Edgar and no one's suing you. Not through us, anyway. Libel's a bit sophisticated for Parrish's. If you can't get legal aid for it, then Rambleton tends not to bother. Anyway . . .'

'Anyway most of them don't bother reading the *Courier* at all?'

'Not till it wraps up the chips, no. What I'm actually after is a back copy of the paper. June nineteen-forty-one.'

Philip snorted. 'You must be bloody joking. The *Courier*'s been published weekly since eighteen-eighty-three. That's six thousand-odd crumbling issues to store, when we haven't room for next week's supply of Tippex. No, you want to try the library, that's what you want.'

Ophelia, too weary to explain, thanked him and set off for the Grand Hotel, in search of Zuke and an approximation to afternoon tea.

'Nineteen-forty-one,' mused Zuke, drawing the syllables out with his cigar smoke. 'Yes, in that year my poor Hilda she is twenty-one.'

'The headline said birthday girls. Plural.'

'Plurole, yes,' said Zuke calmly. 'Of course. It is also the birthday of Hilda's twin sister.'

'You didn't tell me she had a twin!'

'No? No, I believe not. Neither did I tell you that she was falling over a boot-scraper when a child, and so scarred forever her knee, that always she cleaned her teeth at midday, nor of her fantastical passion for watermelon. Is any of this important?'

'Her sister might be. What was her name? Is she still alive? In Rambleton?'

'Alas, I have no idea. This sister – yes, yes, I do remember her name. Dennis.'

'Denise, perhaps?'

'No, no – Dennis, Derris . . .'

'Doris?'

'Dilys! – Dilys, certainly – this Dilys, she did something so dreadful that never again could she be spoken of by the family. She was, how is it that you say – disinherited. Even my Hilda, she told me only once of this sister, never again spoke of her.'

'Not even when she remembered about Trotter's

Bottom and showed you the map?'

'Not even then. To speak the truth, my dear Ophelia, I think that then she had forgotten ever that she had such a sister. There were, I think, no other children.'

'Right. Well, I think it's going to be worthwhile checking out Dilys. I'll have a look at the registers. Perhaps she just married someone unsuitable.'

'More unsuitable than a Russian chess player?'

'If such a thing is possible. That reminds me . . .' She told Zuke the little she had understood about the Humbert Havelock Memorial Tournament.

'Yes, yes, indeed I shall play. It may, what is it, take my brain off poor Hilda. So, you have many chess-playing friends in Rambleton?'

'Mainly just Giles, really.' Mention of Giles led inevitably to the sisters and their plight, in which Zuke showed a compassionate interest.

'So these poor old ladies are to be thrown from their house? This is very bad. In Russia, now, we are welcoming the religious back. Something must be done for your friends. Yes, something certainly must be done.'

Washed away by this tide of benevolence, Ophelia was halfway out of the front doors before she realized that she had forgotten to ask Hilda's maiden name. There was not much point in looking for Dilys' marriage without that. Luckily Zuke, after some lateral thinking, managed to recall it.

'Beans. No, what is it that beans are inside?'

'Can?' asked Ophelia, who had forgotten, after twelve years of marriage to Malachi, that they were not created ready baked and swimming in tomato sauce.

'Not Can, no. Ah – stupid Zuke! It is not beans, at all, is peas. What is it that peas grow in? Long and green. I would shell them for my mother.'

'Pod!' they cried in triumphant unison.

On the way home, Ophelia was uncomfortable. Not only had she failed to collect the essential data, but something else was worrying her as well; something vital that she had overlooked about this whole business. This, she supposed, was why the great detectives were generally single and leisured, without a full-time job and six children to worry about. Ophelia was sure that she would be able to see the salient features of this case quite clearly, were she not preoccupied by Innocent's nasty cough at breakfast, the loss of Pius' fifth pair of rugby socks this term, what to buy for Malachi's birthday and the erratic functioning of the office fax machine. Sometimes she wondered why they bothered having a fax line at all. Communication seemed to have been much smoother when they only—

Aarghh! That was it, the obvious line of enquiry that she, chasing after marriage registers and chess tournaments, had completely forgotten. The old Parrish's compliment slip in Hilda's handbag – and the file on Mr Snodsworth's desk! *Podd*! So the papers relating to Trotter's Bottom had been in the firm's offices all along and Hilda's mysterious assignation on the night before her death had almost certainly been with Mr Snodsworth himself. Ophelia had been so anxious to avoid him recently, lest his faith in Oliver be shaken by the discovery of Dodie amongst the old copies of the *Law*

Society's Gazette, that she had not even thought to check his appointment book. Ophelia flushed red and narrowly missed Gigabyte, bounding down the track to meet her. Well, never mind, at least she had remembered it now. She would telephone Zuke now to ask him what he thought, then look at the file first thing next morning. After all, another day couldn't make that much difference.

Chapter Eleven

Playing Blindfold

Unfortunately, one day made quite a considerable difference.

Ophelia officially had no keys for the building on T'other Side but had decided, since her fresh incarnation as Oliver, that access to Mr Snodsworth's office might come in handy from time to time. She had once, in her cumbersome antenatal days, needed to abstract a file from his room, a manoeuvre that had required dead of night and a golf club, and had led to a sore throat and an embarrassing encounter with the then Constable Booking. She had therefore, only the week before, detailed Polly to pinch the Yale front door key and get a copy made by the drunken shoemaker behind the Ram's Leg.

As a precaution against Mr Snodsworth's arriving early, she was dressed in as androgynous a manner as possible, with her maternity leggings under Malachi's old dinner jacket and hair tucked into her collar. She felt quite dashing, actually, smarter than in her usual tweed skirt suits, recommended by Lady Tartleton, and the leggings were a welcome barrier against the frost. A slash of red lipstick (together with the loss of a couple of stone, which was inconceivable) would have really completed the Cherie Blair look, but Oliver dared not push his luck.

The key almost fitted, and with a bit of wriggling and the application of her nail file to the edges, Ophelia managed to turn it in the lock. It was still almost dark outside, and the office was a gloomy indigo, except for a band of light under Mr Snodsworth's door. Ophelia hesitated, wondering whether to tiptoe away and try again tomorrow. But that would mean another day wasted and, after all, if she (or Oliver, rather) could get Mr Snodsworth to talk about *Podd*, then she might find out even more than from the file. That was, if he was really there, and had not simply left his light on all night. He might well have found himself defeated by the complexities of an electric switch. Gingerly she knocked, then pushed the door open, feeling the familiar drag of the Persian carpet beneath the wood.

Her first thought was that her history was repeating itself. Once before, following a light left burning, she had come into a senior partner's office first thing in the morning, to find him sprawled, like this, across the expanse of his desk.

'Not again,' she whispered to the motionless body, for this time she did not even have Polly to turn to, only the warm vulnerable bundle of the baby against her chest. And the comparison was worse still, for Mr Parrish had died innocuously of a heart attack, leafing through the

Part-Time Appointments in the *Law Society's Gazette*. His room had been, like himself, neat and ordered, and in his death he had not even spilled his tray of paper clips.

Mr Snodsworth's room, by contrast, opulently untidy to begin with, had been comprehensively ransacked, so that opened files spilled on to every surface, drawers hung open and the little porcelain vases with which the old man had covered every available inch of mahogany lay in cracked splendour in the deep pile of the carpet. Worst of all, across the back of his gleaming head, was smeared a long stripe of freshly-dried blood.

Softly, wondering about fingerprints on the bald pate and annoyed with herself for wasting time, she touched the back of his neck, as she did when checking Dodie's temperature in the middle of the night. It took her brain a few seconds to process the message. He was still warm. What was more – she tried a different finger, then another, afraid to take hope from what might be only her own pulse – yes, he was breathing. She stood still for a few moments, her hand resting on his neck, in a muddle of will, prayer and physical warmth. He was such an old man, and so confused by the irrationalities of the modern world. It seemed essential that he survive this attack, to die as he had lived, in the grumbling idiosyncrasies of his own imagination.

After a while she felt his muscles tense as he tried to lift his head.

'Careful now, Mr Snodsworth. Take it gently, sir.' She moved her hand away but kept it hovering a few inches from his straightening shoulders. He looked at her, blinking his great, pale eyes like an owl in unaccustomed daylight.

'Are you all right, sir? Can you remember who did it? Shall I fetch a doctor?'

He said nothing for a long time, then, nodding his head as though in parody of the man he had been, spoke two words: 'Client confidentiality.'

'I've finished tidying his room now,' announced Polly as she came back into Ophelia's office later on that morning. 'As far as I can tell there's nothing at all missing. He won't go home, but I've tucked him up with a big rug and a cup of cocoa. I gave him our biscuits, by the way.'

'Good. Has he said anything yet?'

'Nothing at all. Except "client confidentiality", of course. He says that every few minutes. Your friend Dr Hale's with him at the moment. He says he'll pop in to see you afterwards.'

'Oh, will he?' said Ophelia weakly. She had been trying to avoid Horatio since their evening's debauchery but she did have to speak to him about the post-mortem. Mr Marrow was arranging it all with the Home Office but it would be politic to make sure Horatio had no objections.

'Yes. He seemed dead keen. Said he'd got a bottle . . .'

'When you say there's nothing missing,' Ophelia added quickly, 'have you checked *Podd*?'

'Pod? What pod?'

Ophelia explained.

'No, I haven't seen that at all. He's certainly not asked

for any typing on it. Or "fair copies" as he puts it. So, you think that it was Hilda's murderer who attacked him?'

'It's an unusual coincidence otherwise. We'll have another look later, okay? He might have hidden the *Podd* file somewhere himself. What about the police? Are they coming to have a look?'

Polly sighed, her little pierrot face, rather over-eyelined this morning, falling into a pantomime of exasperation. 'That Sergeant Booking. Remember what he was like when he was just an ordinary constple? Couldn't say boo to a chicken. Now he's turned into one of those mega—'

'Megalomaniacs,' supplied Ophelia, to save the five minutes it would take Polly to apprehend the word. 'I know. But are they going to do anything?'

'It doesn't sound like it. He says that if there's nothing valuable missing and poor Mr Snodsworth survives then it's "probably domestic".'

'That's unlikely. There's never been a Mrs Snodsworth, and his only surviving relative is a great-niece in Adelaide. I don't see why she should come halfway around the world to trash Great-Uncle William's office. Sergeant Booking just can't be bothered, I suppose.'

'Looks like it. He says he's investigating a matter of paranormal importance and he can't waste his time on trivialities. Says that this crime, whatever it is, is the biggest thing Rambleton's ever seen and that he wouldn't be surprised if he got made an Inspector, once he clears it all up. I asked him if he meant the dog-fouling problem and I'm afraid he threw me out then.'

'Uh-huh?' Ophelia was deep in thought and in the bag of iced buns she had decided on in lieu of lunch. Could the police have decided to take Hilda's death seriously after all? Presumably they had been notified about the post-mortem and had decided to investigate before the Scorsdale C.I.D. leapt into the fray. She took another bun and wondered how she would feel to give up her first murder case. After her recent blunders, it would be primarily a relief, but she was reluctant to hand it over without, at least, a strong hint as to the murderer's identity.

'Oi!' said Polly. 'You promised to share those!'

Ophelia looked shamefacedly into the empty paper bag. 'Breast-feeding,' she explained. 'My body needs extra calories to sustain me in my vital work. Effectively, by giving them to you, I'd be taking them away from Dodie. You wouldn't want that on your conscience, would you?'

'I wouldn't have minded having one on my con-science. One out of *six*.'

'It didn't seem like six. Look, have some of my emergency shortbread. Oh and, Polly, could you take some notes for me?'

Polly's face lit up, and not just at the sight of the tartan shortbread tin. 'I thought you'd never ask. Over a year I've been working for you now, and never a chance to practise my shorthand. Now, d'ye want Pitmans, Speed-writing or BAD? That's Bung Anything Down. I invented that one.'

'Sounds perfect. I just want to run through the main suspects for the Big Three.'

'The Big Three what?'

'Elements of the crime. Or crimes, I suppose now. Motive, Opportunity, Method.'

'But you know the method of Hilda's murder, don't you? At least, you will after this post-natal thing.'

'Post-*mortem*. Post-natal's what I am. Oh, hello, Horatio.'

'Hi. Aren't I supposed to examine you for that?'

'Post-natal? Don't worry, you did. Or rather, the midwife did and you signed the form. No one could really expect you to peer up a—'

'Quite. Well, I've been taking a look at that old buffer of yours across the Square and I don't think you've got anything to worry about. Bit of a bump, but no lasting damage.'

'Did he speak to you?'

'Depends what you mean by *speak* really. He said "Cly's comfy; don't rally me" or something like that once or twice, but he didn't seem anxious to elucidate. Didn't think it was my business, really. I'm sure he'll snap out of it. It isn't concussion, if that's what you're wondering.'

'Er, Horatio, are you *sure*?'

'What with my being such a bloody awful doctor, you mean? It's all right, I know about the post-mortem and I'm not offended. Cardiology's never exactly been my thing. Like obstetrics. But bashes on the bonce, they *are*, you see. The number of skulls like your Mr Snodsworth's that I see in the course of an average club rugby game . . . I've always admitted it, I'm a lousy G.P., but give me a sports injury, or anything resembling it, and I'm your man.' He gave such a deliciously ambrosial smile that Polly had to quickly stuff another piece of shortbread into her mouth to stop herself from shouting, 'And I'm your woman!'

Ophelia, less overwhelmed, was nonetheless susceptible. 'But – you do think that someone hit him?'

'I'd have thought so, yes. Very dirty tackling. Or, of course, he could just have bumped it on a shelf. Wasn't really much, you know.'

'So anyone could have done it; a woman, say, or an er – not very athletic man?'

'Bit of a wimp? Oh, yes, I should think so. Looked much worse than it was, anyway. That's the worst of these bald heads, show up every scratch, as poor old Mal will find out pretty soon, eh?'

'And when do you think that it happened?'

'This really is the third degree, isn't it? Right little Miss Marple you're turning into. Much sexier though, of course. I'd have thought that it was probably late last night. The old boy's most likely been sleeping it off since then. Best thing, too. Finest medicine there is, sleep and a good dinner. Which reminds me, Ophelia, can I whisk you off to lunch somewhere?'

'I've already eaten, I'm afraid.'

'And how!' muttered Polly. Horatio turned to her with a bow. 'Then perhaps you . . .'

'Polly's very busy,' said Ophelia firmly.

When he had gone ('see a man about a two-iron') Polly pouted. 'Just because you don't want him, there's no need to be a mangy dog about it. I could've done with that lunch.'

'And what about Gary? Remember Darren the photo-copier mechanic? I don't want a contract out on Horatio's life, thank you. Not when he's the only person in Rambleton who'll listen to Malachi's rugby stories.'

'It would've been all right. Gary's not really violent, you know. It's just all that chopping up meat all day. He sort of gets accustomed to it. But never mind. Let's get back to the Big Two. Motive and Opportunity.'

'Right. Well Arabella, first. She's got a motive, even if it's just wanting to get a good story for the magazine.'

'That's a bit feeble, isn't it?' objected Polly, who was trying to invent a shorthand symbol for 'Arabella'. 'People don't really commit murder so that they can have an interview.'

'You never know with these literary types. But that's only the surface motive. The real one would be her passion for Zuke.'

'Kept hidden for twenty years then bursting forth as she sees him across the crowded hotel lobby. Suddenly she can't bear for them to be apart any longer. Their eyes meet—'

'Quite, yes,' said Ophelia dryly, afraid that Polly was about to burst into 'Some Enchanted Evening'. 'Except that the hotel lobby was hardly likely to be crowded.'

'There's our motive, then. What about opportunity?'

'I suppose that depends on when the poison, if it was poison, was actually administered. Hopefully we'll know that after the post-mortem. In any case, she was staying in the same hotel and could probably have got into their room to tamper with the water glasses or whatever.'

'She'd have to know which glass Hilda was going to

use. Otherwise she might have killed Zuke instead.'

'Unless, of course, that's what she meant to do. You know, the woman scorned and all that. Bother, this is getting too complicated. Let's just leave it that she could easily have been wandering around the hotel at the relevant times, whatever they were.'

'But it was Marcus that Dr Hale actually saw that night, wasn't it? Arabella was just waiting for him to come to bed. D'ye think Marcus was her accomplice?'

'Oh, Polly, do be quiet and take these notes. I'm coming to Marcus in a minute. We've got to think about Mr Snodsworth's attack, too. What motive would Arabella have for that? None of the motives we've looked at have anything to do with Trotter's Bottom.'

'Perhaps she was after Zuke's money?'

'But how would stealing the file help her then? Unless the file contained definitive proof that Hilda *didn't* own the land and Arabella's going to come up with something showing that she *did*. And even then, there's Dilys to worry about. She'd have to bump off Dilys next – but no!'

'No?'

'Dilys would have to die before Hilda for it to benefit Zuke. Otherwise, if they were joint tenants in equity . . .'

'My head's beginning to hurt,' said Polly.

'. . . then when Hilda died, the whole of the property would pass to Dilys. If they were tenants in common, on the other hand, Hilda's share would go to Zuke and Dilys would keep hers. Now, if Dilys had died first and they were joint tenants in equity, then it would all go to Hilda and then to Zuke.'

'And if they were tenants in common?' Polly was beginning to get the hang of this.

'Then it depends on whether Dilys made a will, and whether she's got any closer relatives than Hilda. Husband, children, even their parents might still be around. But it's all academic, because I'm sure Dilys is still alive. I'm sure I've seen her, in the last few days even, I just can't quite remember who she is.'

'Let's think about Marcus, then.'

'Okay. The only motive he'd have for killing Hilda would be the magazine article one, which, as you've already told me, is pretty feeble.'

'It's not so feeble for Marcus, though. I mean, it was his job on the line, wasn't it? But I reckon that if it was Marcus . . .'

'Then he was really trying to kill Zuke? Yes, I'd agree. Unless he wanted to make Zuke suffer first, and that was why he murdered Hilda.'

'Hmmn.' Polly made some random marks in her notebook. 'Look, Ophelia, I know I haven't seen these people myself, but from what you've told me, this Marcus doesn't exactly sound like a murderer.'

Ophelia wished she had a pair of spectacles that she could glare over. 'Polly, great detectives do not judge by appearances. If every murderer *looked* like a murderer, then even Sergeant Booking could manage to catch them. We can't afford to lose our objectivity.'

Polly, who didn't know what an objectivity was, and hoped it wasn't the funny little calculator thing that she had given to the Scout jumble sale, said no more.

'And Marcus' opportunity is the same as Arabella's,

possibly more so, since Horatio actually saw him in the corridor. How much weight do we give to their conversation in the café and Arabella's explanation of it?'

'I wouldn't care to comment,' said Polly haughtily.

'Oh, I'm sorry, Poll. Here, have one of these.' From her bottom drawer, Ophelia took her most private desperate-circumstances-only bag of rum truffles. There were two left.

'Honestly, Ophelia, do you never stop eating?'

'I told you, it's a question of Dodie's development. It's not that I *enjoy* it. Cows eat all the time when they're in milk, and no one criticizes them. Go on then, what do you think of Arabella's story?'

'I've no idea, really. It could be true, or it could be half-true. Marcus could be helping Arabella or Arabella could be helping Marcus or they could have both wanted to get rid of Hilda for different reasons, or – anyway, he's got even less reason than Arabella to pinch the *Podd* file and bop old Snoddie. Try someone else, can't you?'

'Letitia Lamb.'

'Mrs *Lamb*? Mrs Lamb the *librarian*?'

'You're sounding like a game of Happy Families. She looked awfully guilty when I found that cut out article and she wouldn't tell me who'd been looking at it. Librarians can't really be bound by the seal of the confessional, can they?'

'Perhaps she just thought you were being nosy.'

'Just being nosy? This is my case, my investigation, my murder. It's my *job* to be nosy. Honestly, even Sherlock Holmes wouldn't get far in Rambleton. "Was that the baying of a great and fearsome hound?" "Eee, never you mind. Our hounds got nowt to do with some fiddler from t'South.'

'Finished?'

'I think so, yes.'

'What about Mrs Lamb's Motive and Opportunity, then?'

'Oh bother. Well, the motive's got to be something about Trotter's Bottom, hasn't it? Perhaps it's actually the land that the Major's bowling alley is built on.'

'But you did the conveyancing for that when he bought it from Stewart Saggers.'

'Oh, so I did. And I'm sure it was all okay. Oh, I know. Letitia might be Dilys. No, even I'm not convinced by that one. A lifetime of blinis and sour cream couldn't make a bony old thing like Letitia look like poor Hilda. Stick a question mark by motive, there.'

'And opportunity?'

'Oh dear, that needs a question mark too. But if it was her, and it's about *Trotter's Bottom*, then that explains the *Podd* file. I'll have to look into everyone's alibis for last night. Let's think of someone else, now.'

'Dead professional, I must say. Just what Inspector Morse says to poor old Lewis. "Let's think of someone else, now. Anyone, anywhere." '

'If you were Sergeant Lewis then I'd suggest that we adjourn to the Ram's Leg. But then Morse doesn't walk around Oxford with a soggy baby strapped to his chest. I'd better change her, I think.'

'Well, like Mr Marrow said, there's always Zuke himself. I mean, I know he seems really nice, but you said we mustn't judge by appearances.'

'I know, and he's by far the hottest on Opportunity. As for Motive . . .'

'Yeah, you're right. I s'pose he hasn't really got one of those.'

'Oh, Polly! Are you and Gary ever going to get married?'

'Doesn't look like it, the way he always takes the long way round to avoid the jewellers. I think his mum spoils him. Why?'

'Because, if you ever do, you'll know that husbands and wives don't need a Motive, capital M. Just their existence, some mornings, is enough.'

'Ophelia, you don't really think that. Not with your lovely Malarky.'

'No, I don't really. But it is true that most murders are committed by the victim's spouse. However devoted Zuke seems, we don't really know anything about their marriage. But I still don't see, if it was Zuke, why he bothered coming to me at all.'

'To find Trotter's Bottom?'

'Well, obviously, but he didn't need to say that she'd been murdered. He could just have come along like any other probate client. And why should he take the file from Mr Snodsworth?'

'Perhaps it gave away something about him. That he wasn't really married to Hilda or that he was a war criminal, or something. He is a Russian, after all.'

'Polly, the Russians were on our side in the war.'

'Are you sure? My dad doesn't seem to think so. Is there anyone else?'

'Not until I work out who it is that looks so much like

Hilda. I've got this funny feeling that I dreamed about her last night, but all I can remember is a biscuit tin. That reminds me, are you still hungry?'

'Not now,' said Polly. Ophelia had finally undone all the poppers holding Dodie's Babygro together and had removed the bottom half, to reveal an oozing mess quite unconfined by the small disposable nappy. 'Er, if we've finished the notes then I'll just pop out. I've just remembered, the typewriter's out of ribbon.'

If Ophelia had noticed that Polly's typewriter did not use the old-fashioned ribbons, but cartridges, of which there was a stack in the stationery cupboard, she had the grace not to point this out. There came a point, and Dodie's nappy was probably it, at which even the most loyal secretary must be allowed to waver.

Chapter Twelve

The Corkscrew Counter-Gambit

Early on Saturday morning the five elder O. children were all crammed into their favourite meeting-place, the larger of Moorwind Farm's two dilapidated pigsties. The castle, as they, under Pius' firm leadership, had agreed to call it, was too cold and too far from an insecure pantry to be of use for these morning assemblies.

'So who's going to be Saint Wilgefortis, then?' asked Pius through a mouthful of purloined Garibaldis.

'I don't know why you like eating flies,' said Hygenus smugly, showering digestive crumbs over the sleeping Labradors. 'It's got to be Joan, hasn't it? She's the only girl.'

'Essept Dodie,' said Urban clearly, being the only child without his mouth full.

'Noodle! Dodie's only a teeny-weeny tiny *blob* of a baby, isn't she? She can't do *anything* 'cept cry and drink milk and have dirty nappies. A little blob can't put on a beard and pretend to be a ghost, can it? A little blobby thing can't pretend to be a grown-up princess.'

'Neither can Joan,' broke in Pius, having chewed the last of his currants. 'She's too little as well.'

The children sat in glum silence looking at each other and recognizing the truth of their brother's words. None of them were especially tall for their age and Joan and Innocent were particularly small.

'It's Dad's fault,' said Joan gloomily. 'If he was a bit taller then we might be too.'

'Well, he didn't choose to be short, either,' pointed out Pius. 'It was 'cos of his parents in Ireland and their parents and all that, going back probably centuries.'

'But why were they all little?' asked Hygenus. 'Some of them must have been big.'

Pius looked studious. 'I think it was the Great Tomato Flaming,' he decided. 'I saw a programme about it once. But you do agree, don't you, Joan, that it wouldn't work very well with you?'

'Oh yes, of course,' said Joan casually, fluctuating between chagrin and relief. 'But have you got any idea who might do it?'

'I was thinking about Giles' girlfriend.'

Joan flushed furiously. 'I didn't think he had one. Thought he had more sense.'

'P'raps he's in *love*,' said Hygenus with blood-curdling relish. Urban shuddered.

'I daresay he is,' said Pius in a grown-up manner. 'It's that Claire, you know, the one that kept following Mum round in the summer.'

'Her!' Joan's face was thunderous. 'But she was

awful. She wouldn't leave Mum alone. You know she even went to the hospital with her when Dodie was born.'

'Yes she did!' said Innocent, with no idea what they were talking about.

'It was her job, Joan,' said Pius, disturbed at this display of outrage from his usually imperturbable sister.

'Why? She's not a midwife.'

'Not migwife,' agreed Innocent.

'No, I mean her job was asking Mum questions. She was a reporter, wasn't she?'

'Supposedly. Anyway, what do you mean, "was"? Isn't she any more?'

'No, she's gone to college in Manchester. A place came up at the last moment, so she left the *Courier* and went there.'

Joan cheered up a little. 'Well, if she's in Manchester then she can't do being Saint Wilgefortis, can she? Manchester's miles and miles away. And Giles can't see her very often either. I don't s'pose she's really his girlfriend. I expect he just says it to be nice. He *is* nice, you know.'

'No, she comes over to stay with his mum and dad every weekend. It's really quick on the Pennine Express, he told me. 'Fact, she's probably there now. Shall we ask Mum if we can go and see?'

Joan knew when she was defeated, and agreed with moderately good grace, only muttering to herself, as they trailed towards the house, 'But she must be thousands of years older than him. Twenty at least.'

Ophelia was moderately enthusiastic about the

children's plan to visit the Glade-Rivers. She sometimes wondered whether the sisters' contemplative life was really assisted by quite so many noisy invasions and was glad that they had thought of an alternative venue. 'Fine, if Tansy doesn't mind. I'll drop you off on my way.'

'Why, where are you going?' asked the children suspiciously.

'To see a man about a chess congress. Joan, just run and get Innocent some clean clothes, will you? He's soaking. He didn't fall into the cow trough again, did he?'

'Not essackly,' said Hygenus, who had pushed him.

Tansy Glade-Rivers and Claire Lamb, Giles' girlfriend and the niece of Letitia and the Major, were standing in the newly-built kitchen of the Glade-Rivers' substantial Victorian terraced house and looking out into the white-washed back yard.

'I'm afraid it's starting again,' said Tansy, absent-mindedly taking plates from the draining rack and replacing them in the sink. 'Funny, these dishes seem to be coming out dirtier than they went in.'

'Perhaps you need to change the water,' suggested Claire without looking round. 'That same potato peeling's been floating in it since last Sunday. What do you mean, "starting again"?'

'I had a dishwasher before,' mused the older woman. 'Before the cellar blew up. But I never really got the hang of it. I'm not very good with machines. Or housework.' She dropped a plate to illustrate the point.

'But what's starting again?' persisted Claire. She was

very fond of Tansy, who was completely free of that gimlet-eyed expression common among boyfriends' mothers. It had to be admitted, however, that conversation with her could be very hard work.

'Oh, Gordon's publicity mania. You remember how he was when you first came here, all that posing in his best Viyella shirt and pestering all the Sunday supplements. Then he seemed to be all right after that awful Skate man exploded half the house and all the papers finally turned up.'

Claire remembered it well. Following the detonation, caused by the synthesis of several tons of dog and sheep manure with a lighted cigarette end, Gordon and his fearful Eco-Process had achieved brief celebrity on the honourable roll of English Heroic Failures. That had seemed to sate his promotional desires, and he had settled down quite happily for a while to a sober study of rainfall in central Pontefract. Now, however, as Claire peered through the cloudy kitchen window (Tansy had never been able to resist an over-generosity with the Windolene), she could see what his wife had meant.

Giles had been set to work scrubbing the front of the garden shed, apparently with some bleaching concoction, for wherever his bundle of steel wool passed, the previously unremarkable brown of the woodwork burst into a glorious orange, and where drops fell on the boy's jeans, bright discs of white appeared like a host of variegated full moons. Gordon was prancing up and down in front of him, bland and skittish as an overgrown garden gnome, alternating heavy gesticulated commands with sudden jerks, as shoulders, stomach and posterior were remorselessly brought into line. When the front elevation of the shed was suitably ravaged, Gordon motioned Giles away and posed in front of it, head turned in magnificent profile, patrician as the engraving on a Roman coin, eyes gazing fixedly towards the distant horizons of scientific endeavour.

Giles, meanwhile, was fiddling with an expensive camera on the other side of the yard, and was slower than his watching womenfolk to respond to his father's sudden squawk of anguish. Gordon, after trying an artfully coy emergence around the edge of the shed, and a winsome perch upon a campstool in front of it, had decided upon an insouciant pose leaning against the newly stripped door. He had remained there for some seconds, wriggling his plump buttocks against the wood in an effort to find the perfectly photogenic position, when he became aware of a mildly burning sensation. Jumping away from the door and twisting painfully backwards, he discovered to his horror that the seat of his expensive corduroys had been entirely eaten away in a yellowish fraying circle, and that his cornflower blue underpants, now a muddy grey, were similarly beginning to disintegrate.

'Giles!' he cried in fury, and his son, interpreting the annoyance as being at his own delay in setting the exposure, whirled around and, aiming wildly, took a perfect photograph of his father's emerging bottom.

'Giles!' repeated Gordon, moving up the register of outrage, but Giles was now clicking prodigally, hardly noticing that the little red semicircles on the viewfinder were now centred upon a procession of small children.

'You've got a big hole in your trousers,' said Hygenus helpfully to Gordon's quivering back view. 'Our daddy's never had one that big.'

'He has nearly, though,' said Urban, with what he imagined to be sensitivity. 'And once his swimming trunks got splitted and you could see a bit of his willy.'

'Bottom,' said Innocent, catching up with his brothers and pointing with satisfaction. 'Big bottom.'

Gordon, who had once written a seminal paper on the infant's innate capacity for scientific observation, locked himself, moaning, into the garden shed.

'Hello, you lot,' said Giles, concluding his photo-montage with a poignant shot of the flapping latch. 'Been building any more dams lately? Or d'ye want a go on the bike? We'll have to be careful, though. Mum's bound to think you're too young.'

'No, that's all baby stuff,' said Pius, casting, nonetheless, a wistful glance towards the shiny little Suzuki in the corner of the yard. 'We've got something absolutely vittal (Pius' reading occasionally outmatched his pronunciation) that we need your help with. Yours and your er . . .'

'*Girlfriend*,' completed Joan with crimson scorn and took refuge in picking up the unwilling Innocent.

'What, Claire?' asked Giles, also pinkening beneath his burgeoning pimples. The conquest of Claire, four years older than he, a graduate, and, albeit briefly, a real working woman, was still rather too much to contemplate, especially in the presence of the inquisitive O.s. Luckily Claire herself, with her worries about her legs, self-deprecating humour and innocent, rather jammy embraces, was not nearly so terrifying as her *curriculum*

197

vitae. 'Course. I think she's in the house, actually, helping Mum with the washing-up. Come on up and we'll talk about it.'

The O. children followed him eagerly, with only Joan dragging her battered plimsolls through the decomposing leaves. Even she, however, was not slow enough to hear the series of high-pitched squeals which came from the mysterious interior of the shed. A low bark of annoyance came from Gordon, followed by a louder shout, as he realized that he had pulled the door rather too firmly, and was now contemplating the scuffing of his Hush Puppies in order to kick his way out again.

Ophelia, meanwhile, was shifting Dodie desperately from shoulder to shoulder as she waited on Mortimer Bradley's doorstep. His house, The Outpost, turned out to be a large and ugly orange brick building on the Scorsdale Road, only a few doors from the late Mr Parrish's wax-scented villa. As Ophelia swayed soothingly in the hideously embellished porch, the baby caught sight of a strand of ivy blowing free from its furbelowed moorings and was entranced into silence.

The door opened, with much grinding of security devices, and Mortimer Bradley loomed above them.

He was a large man, around six foot and burly, but the rigid set of his shoulders and his enormous mane of black hair and beard made him appear larger still. Despite the weekend morning he wore a dark three-piece suit with a tangerine shirt and flamboyant cravat.

'Hello?' he said suspiciously, staring at Dodie as though he had never before seen a baby. Adeodata was similarly enthralled, her little mouth open in a pink O as she contemplated the majesty of his facial hair. 'Can I . . . *help* you?'

'Mr Bradley? Er, hello. My name is Ophelia O.' She paused, intending to offer her right hand but realized too late that it was supporting the baby. 'I, um . . . It's about the chess tournament.'

A smile, more horrifying than his previous scowl, passed over Mortimer's face, joining his two sets of side-whiskers with a crescent of scarlet gums and broken teeth. Dodie burst into terrified sobs and buried her head in Ophelia's bosom.

'The Humbert Havelock Memorial. You'd like to enter? How delightful. Do come inside.'

Mortimer's large boots scuffed the orange and black carpet as he shuffled backwards, opening the door with a complex rolling gesture which culminated in his complete disappearance. Ophelia stepped over the collection of iron boot-scrapers, miniature dogs and flat-irons which lined the doormat and stood in the hall, trying to avoid her tousled reflection in the carved oak mirror. Mortimer reappeared from behind the door and shut it with a clang.

'Hhungg!' he whinnied, entirely through his nose, while his mouth gave another grimace. 'After you.'

Ophelia walked through the indicated door of bubbled glass into a nightmare of peach satin. Everything, from the mammalian three-piece suite to the ruffled tissue-box cover, was immaculate, glistening and the colour of a waterproof plaster. Buttoned peach satin cushions lay about in artful disarray while flesh-coloured Austrian blinds transformed the solid windows into cross-sections of human anatomy. The room was saved from complete Ideal Homedom only by the forcible intrusions of the darker side of Mortimer's personality: squat tables of treacle-dark wood, a thick black carpet, imitation Elizabethan beams across the ceiling and corpulent African fertility goddesses, badly painted to masquerade as ebony.

'Take a seat, Ophelia,' invited Mortimer genially as she balanced on the edge of one of the pneumatic armchairs. 'You'll have a drink with me?'

He opened what appeared from the outside to be a Jacobean clothes press to reveal a backlit array of malt whisky bottles. As he surveyed them, evidently bewildered by his choice, the cabinet played the Skye Boat Song and a small plastic kilted figure rotated above the tumblers.

'Er, it's a bit . . . the time . . .' struggled Ophelia, peering through the distressed glass of the grandfather clock to see that it was still only five past eleven.

'Nonsense,' said Mortimer, pouring himself a generous measure of Glenmorangie and closing the door firmly upon the Bonnie Prince. 'Clears the brain, alcohol. Blackburne always said so, though the temperance milksops never forgave him for it.'

'Blackburne?' said Ophelia brightly, reminded of something Giles had said. 'Was he the one they called the Black Death?'

Mortimer snorted and a couple of crystal drops of whisky landed in his beard. 'There you are again, you see. Lily-livered lot, some of these chess players. Blackburne,' Mortimer's own dark eyes seemed to roll in their sockets as he declaimed, 'Blackburne was a Man.'

'I'm sure he was.' The armchair was so large, so well stuffed and so shiny that Ophelia was having difficulty in preventing herself from sliding on to the carpet. The alternative was to sit right back in the chair but she judged that, were she to do so, her knees would barely reach the middle of the seat and her shabbily loafered feet would dangle awkwardly close to Mortimer's knees. In any case, Dodie was evidently finding the rocking motion by which Ophelia balanced herself soporific, and was now snoring, mouth open, against her mother's right breast.

'A Real Man,' repeated Mortimer, striding up and down on his imitation tiger-skin rug. 'Drank like a man, fought like a man, played chess like a man. No wonder the nebbichs couldn't stand him. Take that 'eighty-nine game against Amos Burn. What a queen sacrifice, eh? Of course, Burn didn't have the guts to take it. Mind you, they're just as bad now, if not worse. These quickplay finish rules, for example. The way I see it is, if a man's not got the stamina to spend all night across the chess board, he's no business calling himself a chess player at all. Win on time? Win by outright thievery if you ask me. Of course, old Fred Lamb couldn't see it, thought a quick finish was quite reasonable. Mind you, I could hardly expect anything else. Grade of one-twenty, he's just a social player. What's yours then?'

'No, really, I . . .' began Ophelia, expecting a re-emergence of Bonnie Prince Charlie. She was feeling even more ill-at-ease than before, owing to the fact that her mammary ducts, unable to distinguish between

Dodie's hungry nuzzling and the present accidental proximity of her mouth to Ophelia's nipple, were busily producing their usual vast quantities. This milk, with no baby to slurp it up, had now soaked the two layers of washable breast pad and was oozing clammily through Ophelia's pale blue sweatshirt. She held Adeodata horizontally across her chest, shielding, to some extent, the widening dark circles but was horribly aware that this could only be a temporary palliative.

Mortimer was standing over her now, looking down with a curious detachment. Ophelia had the sensation of being under a long slow grill.

'What's your grade?' he asked again.

'Oh.' A drop of cooling milk meandered around Dodie's cheek to fall upon the padded expanse of the chair's arm. 'I don't think I've got one. I mean, I'm not really a chess player at all.'

Mortimer's great eyebrows drew together in perplexity. He seemed to notice Dodie for the first time and reached out a tentative forefinger to touch the base of her skull.

'Then why the Humbert Havelock? There is a novice section but only in name, really. It's generally quite heavily contested.'

'No, no.' Ophelia's front was now awash with milk, the two formerly discrete circles merging over her stomach in a general swamp. She wished that she had had the courage to do the African-jabbing-herself-in-the-nipples trick earlier. Now it was a choice between her *amour propre* and a wholesale assault upon the immaculacy of the upholstery. Ophelia and Malachi had never bought

new furniture themselves, having begun on the procrea-
tive trail within a few months of their marriage, but
judging from the Saturday afternoon television adver-
tisements, the contents of Mortimer's living-room must
have been worth a few thousand. Now, to make matters
worse, Dodie was stretching and snuffling in her sleep,
urging the tireless milk ducts to yet further efforts. 'No.
Sorry, er . . . Look, you haven't got a towel, have you?'

'A *towel*?' Mortimer bent lower over her. 'Lord, are
you all right? Should I call an ambulance or something?'

'No, quite normal. Just a towel, if it isn't . . .'

Mortimer slid out of the room, his large boots leaving
tracks in the heavy black pile, and returned within
seconds with an armful of fluffy coral cotton.

'Oh, brilliant,' said Ophelia, swathing herself and
Adeodata. She tried to explain, beginning with Dodie's
having once again slept right through the previous night,
but poor Mortimer looked so bewildered that she soon
gave up and returned to the less terrifying subject of the
Humbert Havelock Memorial.

'So you see,' she concluded, 'my daughter would very
much like to play in the tournament. The novice section,
I imagine. Oh, and Alexander Zhukovsky is interested,
too.'

Mortimer, his very red mouth slightly open, goggled
at her. 'Zhukovsky,' he gaped. '*The* Zhukovsky?'

'Well, yes. I don't know that he'll be at his best. I'm
afraid he's just lost his wife, but he's keen to be
involved.'

'Zhukovsky.' Mortimer sat down suddenly in the other
armchair. He looked at a dark-framed picture on the

wall, a sepia daguerrotype of a Victorian gentleman with narrowed eyes and copious side-whiskers. 'Zhukovsky wants to play in our tournament, Humbert. Ten years I've been running this congress and I've never had more than a county vice-captain.' He turned back to Ophelia. 'Are you sure that's what he said? He doesn't think that he's in Hastings or somewhere?'

'No, he certainly knows this is Rambleton. Do you have some entry forms or something?'

'The forms. Oh, absolutely. And I think this calls for something of a celebration.' He reached, wheezing with sudden laughter, towards the Jacobean cabinet, and Dodie stirred to the repeated tinkle of the Skye Boat Song . . .

Chapter Thirteen

Sister Squares

The congregation at the Sunday morning Mass, remembering the bishop's outburst of the previous week, was subdued, almost abashed. Even Father Jim, who normally bounded up the altar steps like a game-show host, now processed sedately behind his chubby altar-girls, and peered continually about the church before giving his opening exhortation. But he need not have worried. The two front pews which had been occupied by the staff of the Alderman Penbury Comprehensive had returned to their usual beeswax emptiness while the only representatives of Saint Wilgefortis' Convent were the ubiquitous Sisters Hedwig, Felicity and Perpetua, looking rather more weather-beaten than they had on the previous Sunday, and the ancient Reverend Mother.

Ophelia, sneaking in through the side door with Pius and Joan, Malachi and the smaller children having pleaded the after-effects of the previous night's whisky and nougat, was just in time to hear Hedwig completing the First Reading.

'*There is going to be a time of great distress, unparalleled since nations first came into existence*,' she declared, her vowels as confidently rounded as ever, but Ophelia thought that there was a catch in the Sister's voice as she continued, '*When that time comes, your own people will be spared, all those whose names are found written in the Book*.' She broke off momentarily, coughed, and gave her trimly habited person a sharp little shake. '*Of those who lie sleeping in the dust of the earth many will awake, some to everlasting life, some to shame and everlasting disgrace*.' Here her bright blue eyes could not help from wandering over the empty front pews and their balancing tears were visible even to Pius and Joan. The children, paying attention for the first time, frowned and exchanged glances of mingled pity and embarrassment. Then something in their expressions sharpened.

'Mum,' whispered Pius, his nostrils twitching like a puzzled rabbit, 'have you got Dodie there?'

'Of course not,' she hissed, then drew in her own breath. There was certainly a distinct odour in the church, quite unlike the usual mixture of incense and lavender polish. Gently wafted by the ceiling convection heaters, the new smell gradually drifted over the congregation who raised their noses to catch the subtler notes and cast accusatory glances at their near neighbours.

'*The learned will shine as brightly as the vault of heaven, and those who have instructed many in virtue, as bright as stars for all eternity*,' Hedwig concluded, and sat down with a grateful nod towards the sanctuary lamp, relinquishing the leading of the Responsorial Psalm to the enthusiastic but sadly tuneless Mrs Stopp.

'*O-oh, Lor-hor-hor-hor-hord, it is you-hoo* . . .' wailed Mrs Stopp, whose idea of ecclesiastical music was to elongate every syllable into six or seven and to string these up a flattened octave and down again thus creating a form of aural torture which she described as 'plainchant'. Vulnerable newcomers would be bullied into weekly rehearsals at *Casa Carminum* which she translated kindly for the non-classicist as 'The Little Hut of Song'. Mr Stopp, a lugubrious, unravelling sort of man, was rarely seen except in the car park, but was spoken of breathlessly by his spouse as her Inspiration, Mentor and Spiritual Svengali. It was rumoured that he had once been a peripatetic euphonium teacher in Huddersfield, which, Ophelia supposed, explained both the breathlessness and his preference for the car park.

The congregation were hoping, on this occasion, that Mrs Stopp's harmonies might be cut short by the thickening atmosphere into which her deep breaths were taken. Unfortunately, her customary catarrh had been exacerbated by a heavy cold and she alone was unaware of the growing stench.

'My so-ho-ho-ho-ho-ho-ho-ho-houl i-is gla-ha-ha-ha-ha-ha-ha-ha-had!' she yodelled, so that the high clerestory windows rattled and a small child begged to be taken home. Only Ophelia was grateful, realizing that Mrs Stopp's extended melodies at least gave Hedwig time to pull herself together for the Second Reading. This was taken from Hebrews, a nice bracing sort of letter, as Mother Thérèse had put it. Somewhat comforted by the '*eternal perfection of all whom he is sanctifying*', she concluded with a brave, '*This is the word of the Lord*,' to which Pius and Joan almost shouted their response, '*Thanks be to God.*'

Father Jim, sensing, though he could not have articulated, the undercurrents in the morning's congregation, hastily adapted his planned homily. This address, based on the text 'In those days, after the time of distress, the sun will be darkened, the moon will lose its brightness, the stars will come falling from heaven and the powers in the heavens will be shaken', had been written as a short discussion of the vagaries of the weather, enlivened by a couple of anecdotes from Father Jim's large family across the Irish Sea. Now, however, something, if not of iron, then at least distantly metallic, entered the priest's soul, and his extempore sermon, though it still included the funny thing that happened to his Auntie Norah when she went into Killarney without an umbrella, made definite, if confused, allusion to the apocalyptic overtones of the Gospel. He was dimly aware of the smell, but only as something comforting from his boyhood, mixed up with buttercups and the taste of his mother's soda-bread.

'And so we pray,' he concluded, 'that the Son of Man may indeed send his angels to gather up his good sheep, such as our own dear Sisters, and that at his left hand he will be placing . . .' Here he broke off, uncomfortably aware that he was close to calling the chairman of the diocesan finance committee a goat, and stumbled into the Creed.

He was, in fact, confused and shaken by the bishop's

decision. Although brought up to revere the person and opinions of all and every Catholic bishop, inheritors of the apostles' vocation, his conscience spoke strongly against the sisters' loss of their home. Had he been an English Dominican, or even a Benedictine, he would have been able to distinguish the ontological essence of the bishop's office from the political mistakes of its exercise, but Irish Catholicism, at least of the type that had moulded Fr Jim, left no room for such subtleties. 'After all,' he had told himself sternly over the morning's porridge, 'the dear children of Alderman Penbury must be in great need of a Gender Thingummy to go to all this trouble, and I can surely plod along without Sister Hedwig for a year or two.'

But as soon as he passed through the cold corridor which connected the presbytery to the church, and saw the Parish Sister adjusting his bookmarkers and checking the Communion wine, he knew that he could not manage without her. And when Teresa, his housekeeper, appeared, tousled and harassed, in the vestry, to ask whether he might, just this once (again) go to the convent for his Sunday lunch, because his namesake, four-month-old James, was making that awful sort of snuffling noise again, Sister Hedwig had bustled up out of nowhere, tidied Teresa's trailing fastenings, soothed Jimmy into an unconstricted slumber and promised treacle tart for Father Jim's pudding.

'Poor girl,' she said to Teresa's retreating apron-strings, though the housekeeper was barely seven years younger. 'She's convinced that something's going to happen to that baby, isn't she?'

'Aye well, she thinks . . .' Father Jim was not at his best discussing feminine psychology.

'. . . That she's due some sort of punishment for her fling with the plumber. Now, there's no need to blush, Father. I've only taken a vow of chastity, not of ignorance. I only wish we could get completely away from this idea of a cosmic Jehovah dispensing thunderbolts and vengeance. The Old Testament has a lot to answer for, you know. If it were up to me I should replace it all with Celtic mythology. Except Isaiah and the *Song of Songs*, of course.'

'Oh, Heddy,' said Father Jim weakly. 'How terribly I shall miss you.'

That was the end of Sister Hedwig's long week of self-control. Few people ever dared to call her Heddy, and most who tried it received a dusty answer, but when it was used by her favourites, her usual briskness was instantly dispelled. She muttered something soothing and fled to straighten the hymn-books, but after Mass, Ophelia came across her behind the old Missals, unaccustomed tears streaming down her apple cheeks. The strange smell seemed still to hang about her, but in a much subdued form so that it might almost have been mistaken for the odour of sanctity.

'Something,' said Ophelia to her grim reflection in the second-best chalice, 'has got to be done.'

After Mass she took the two elder children into Mr Snodsworth's office to search for the *Podd* file. Pius was concerned at the technical illegality of this, especially on a Sunday, but the promise of chocolate fudge cake for lunch soon quieted his conscience. The Market Square was deserted, for Rambleton had long lost the habit of churchgoing, while not yet replacing it with the delights of Sunday trading.

'What is it we're looking for, again?' asked Joan after half an hour.

'Anything to do with someone called Podd, or a piece of land called Trotter's Bottom.'

Pius and Joan considered themselves too old to giggle at this.

'Trotter's Bottom?' said Pius suspiciously. 'Dad was asking about that the other day. You're not in trouble again, are you, Mum?'

'I'm never "in trouble",' said Ophelia in her affronted Mary Poppins voice. 'I merely have a proactive legal technique.'

At the end of two hours, by which time the chocolate fudge cake was not so much a bribe as an urgent necessity, they declared themselves defeated.

'There's some good stuff here, though,' said Pius. 'I didn't know your Mr Snodsworth specialized in wars.'

'He doesn't notably specialize in anything. Particularly at the moment. Why?'

'I found this. *The Complete Cannon Law*.'

Joan looked scornful. 'That's "canon" with one "n". It doesn't mean guns, you know.'

'What does it mean then?'

'Don't know, really. There's one in *The Box of Delights*. At least, a pretend one. I think it's a sort of vicar. Isn't that right, Mummy?'

'Hmm. What? Oh, yes, I think so. I'll take this book

home with me, actually. You never know when sort of vicars might come in handy.'

Ophelia was experiencing that familiar tingle that came with the beginning of an idea. Not an idea that would help in any way with *Podd*, but an idea, nonetheless, that cheered up the chilly office.

'Come on then, kids. Chocolate fudge cake and Yorkshire pudding.'

On the way out they found the Market Square to be not quite so deserted as before. Sergeant Booking had pencilled himself in for some lucrative overtime, sitting in his patrol car listening to the omnibus edition of *The Archers*. Upon seeing them he wound his window down.

'Funny time to be working,' he commented.

'Yes, it is, isn't it?'

'It's different for police officers. We have to be constantly vigilant, on the look out for anything that might constitute a crime. What's that book you're carrying?'

Ophelia handed it to him.

'You do know the penalties for unauthorized possession of weapons?' Sergeant Booking was obviously afflicted by the same confusion as Pius. 'I don't want no damn firearms on my turf.'

Ophelia, since he could not think of anything to charge her with immediately, took the book back and wandered away, reflecting that it was a shame old *Police Academy* films were repeated quite so often on television.

She spent the afternoon lying on the sofa with the book propped on a cushion beside her and Dodie, occasionally suckling but generally just asleep, across her chest. They were disturbed only once, by Hygenus' habitually aggrieved tone through the flimsy wall of the boys' bedroom.

'We got a letter back, Innie. I 'spect it's for both of us, it says to Hygenus Innocent Esk. Don't know who Esk is, do you?'

'Eggs?'

'No, Innie. You don't write letters to eggs. Not even Easter ones. Then it says: "Your offer has been assepted by the Board." '

'Bawdy!'

'Yes, but what board, Innie? Breadboard, cheeseboard, chessboard, skateboard? Doesn't make any sense. And they haven't even sent us a magazine at all. S'pose they want us to send them the money first. Not really fair, is it?'

Innocent, who had been somewhat out of his depth in the conversation up to that point, recognized a familiar phrase.

'Nock fair!' he joined in happily. 'It nock fair!'

Next morning, to Ophelia's frustration, was entirely taken up with the most pedestrian of litigious matters, an apparently endless stream of clients who during the weekend, inebriated, rushed or simply unlucky, had tripped over the inadequately aligned paving slabs of Rambleton, incurring personal injuries which, though invisible, were, reputedly, 'flippin' agony'. She managed to dissuade most of these from taking their clothes off there and then, instead completing legal aid forms on their behalf so that Horatio could have the pleasure of examining them. They grumbled, having imagined that falling over on municipal property constituted an immediate win on the great lottery known as the British legal system, but were eventually, with the aid of Polly's rather sharp elbows, despatched down the steps. By the afternoon the full force of their outrage had diminished, and Ophelia was able to escape. She packed Dodie into the sling, wrapped the voluminous overcoat around her and set off for Saint Wilgefortis' Convent. Entering through the kitchen door, as usual, she found no Sister Eulalia at her station by the sink, nor were there any sisters engaged in their customary bookmark-weaving in the workroom. Only the soothing sounds of stertorous breathing from the direction of the old refectory gave any indication of life in the building. The breathing, that was, and that same lavatorial smell, particularly strong in the kitchen, which she recognized from the church. Perhaps all Rambleton's drains, untouched since their civic creation in the early nineteenth century, were finally imploding.

The refectory, huge, white and very cold, was rarely used by the sisters these days. It had been built when the community numbered well over a hundred and sat in ordered ranks under the gimlet eye of the matriarchal abbess. Now, especially after the democratizing influence of Vatican II, the few remaining sisters would huddle around the kitchen table for meals, the discomfort of jostling elbows being more than made up for by the warmth for their old bones and camaraderie for their tender hearts. Ophelia had never before seen the refectory, imposing in its swept and polished grandeur, speaking of an older and sterner Catholicism than any she had known. But there was nothing stern about the sight which now met her eyes. Twelve out of the thirteen sisters sat, in two rows of six at the top table, gazing across at one another with various expressions of trepidation, mischief, bewilderment and glee. Between each pair lay a chess board with a grimy set of pieces unusually like those which Ophelia had seen at Rambleton Chess Club. Only the Mother Superior, old Mother Thérèse, had no opponent, but sat at the end of the table, her chin resting on it, watching the movement of twenty-four hands and a hundred and ninety-two pieces with an almost mystical intensity.

'Like the Dance,' she whispered to herself, in her tissue-paper voice. 'The eternal movement from life to death and back again. Here we are, each one a pawn; by grace we might become a Queen.'

'I think you have already, Mother Thérèse,' said Giles, listening from the old Abbess's seat, with *Theoretical Physics – A Revision Guide* propped up on the lectern before him.

'Oh no, my boy. I have a long way to go yet, though little enough on earth. Presumption, Giles, my dear, is as dangerous as despair, even on another's behalf. Or maybe not so bad, for our Father must forgive His children's ebullience. Don't you agree, Ophelia?'

'If His children are anything like mine, then He has a lot of ebullience to forgive,' smiled Ophelia, wondering, though she ought to have been used to it by now, at the old lady's perspicacity, even when apparently deep in meditation. 'But what's going on here? Has the whole of

Rambleton developed chess mania?'

'Not quite,' said Giles, 'although Mr Bradley seems pretty near it. I gather that you've persuaded Zhukovsky to play?'

'He didn't need much persuasion. Have they been in touch, then?'

'Oh yes. Thick as thieves, those two. Mr Bradley's so chuffed that he's decided to come back to Rambleton Chess Club. The committee had an emergency meeting last night about it. I'm secretary, you see.'

'Oh right. But why . . .?'

'The sisters? Well that was sort of my contribution. The Humbert Havelock's always been held at my school, you see.'

'The Alderman Penbury Comprehensive?'

'That's the one. But this year the teachers have voted against allowing it.'

'Why? Has there been damage caused in the past or something?'

'Oh no, nothing like that. It's even a non-smoking congress so they haven't got that to worry about. Not that they would anyway, the staff room's like a chimney. No, some of the teachers reckon that chess is intellectually elitist. Oh, and it's sexist as well, because not many girls enter. They're not sure which is worse, the girls' not doing very well in the main sections or there being a special ladies' prize. I suppose it might be better if it was called the Women's Award.'

'Hmm. "Award" might be a bit patriarchal. Don't many women play, then? I know there weren't any at Rambleton Chess Club, but I thought it might just be the

Ratchet-Crampers that put them off.'

'No, I'm afraid not. There are a few, of course, and some at the very top. But on the whole – hang on a minute. Sisters Mary-Joseph and Albertine seem to have got themselves into a stalemate.'

'Young Giles has told you our news, then?' crinkled Mother Thérèse as he bounded down from the dais.

'No – no, I don't really think he has.'

'This chess tournament, the, what did he call it? Humbert Havelock Congress. It's going to be held here.'

'What, in the convent?'

The Reverend Mother nodded, and into her distant grey eyes came a fleeting spark of malice. 'That'll show those comprehensive heathens, eh? Yes, we'll use the refectory here, and spill into the parlour if necessary. It should be marvellous publicity, or so they tell me.'

The old lady let the other-worldly mist fall back over her features.

'So that's why Giles has got all the nuns learning to play? Are they all going to enter?'

'Not just Giles, my dear,' Mother Thérèse's voice was more fragile than ever as she returned to her contemplation of the moving pieces. 'That kind Russian, Mr Zhukovsky came to help us this morning as well. But I'm afraid that he didn't stay very long. He went to the kitchen for a glass of water and came out looking dreadful.'

'What, is he ill?'

'Not ill, I would have said, so much as in shock. But what could have upset him in the kitchen? And Sister Eulalia's not well, either. She's gone up to the Infirmary for the first time ever. Over fifty years she's been here and never so much as complained of a sore throat. I don't understand it, I'm afraid.'

Ophelia, who suddenly thought that she might understand it, changed the subject quickly.

'You're not going to play yourself, then?'

'I may do, my dear. My brother taught me the moves many many years ago. But the tournament's what, in a week's time?'

'Something like that, I think.'

'Exactly. The chances of my living until then are so mercifully slight.'

Ophelia remembered with a shock that the Reverend Mother was over a hundred. But that made it more imperative that Ophelia find her answers quickly. The enigma of Zuke and Eulalia, fascinating though it was, would have to wait for a little while.

'I am sorry to bother you, Mother Thérèse . . .'

The old lady smiled with an unexpected radiance. 'Nothing "bothers" me any more, child. Everything is part of the design. What is it that you want to know?'

'The convent. Is it the only house of the Order?'

'Institute, my dear. The Institute of Saint Wilgefortis. We're not a full-blown Order, you know. Oh yes, there's only ever been this House. The Institute was founded in France in seventeen-forty-eight by Louise Thierry. Then, in eighteen-hundred-and-one, when the political climate for religious houses was better in England than France, we were invited here by Anne Trellist, a Rambleton gentlewoman. She was an ancestor of our own dear Beatrice, you know.'

'Beatrice?'

'Lady Tartleton.'

'Oh, of course.' Ophelia had been invited to call Lady Tartleton by her Christian name, but had never dared to do so, nor even to think of the familiar martinet without her title. 'And, um, you wouldn't call yourselves a contemplative order, I mean institute, would you?'

The Reverend Mother smiled again. 'I don't know that we really call ourselves anything any more. When we were teaching, of course, we were what they classify as an "active" house, but now, apart from dear young Sister Hedwig's parish work, we're all too decrepit to do much else but contemplate. Is that all, dear? I'm feeling a little tired, I'm afraid.'

'Oh, I didn't mean . . . Please, just one more thing. You haven't any idea how much this house is worth, I suppose?'

Mother Thérèse laughed, like the whistling of the wind in faraway beech trees. 'Half of the moon and a pocketful of stars. Or maybe less than this.' She took a pawn from the nearest board and weighed it in her furrowed palm. 'You must excuse me now. I have some matters to deal with before I go.'

Chapter Fourteen

Pawnstorming

The second enamelled pig was found after school on Monday. The children were in the larger pigsty with Claire, rehearsing their Saint Wilgefortis performance when Urban, tiring of his part, which was to say, 'Where's my mummy? I'm frightened of ghosts!', turned instead to investigating the earthy gaps between the crumbling bricks. He had just found a conveniently pointed twig with which to root, when Pius' commanding voice came from the other end of the sty.

'Urban! It's your turn now. You've got to say, "Where's my . . ." '

'Know. Don't want to.'

'But it's your part. We all have to say our parts, otherwise it won't work. If you don't say "Where's my mummy? I'm frightened of ghosts!" then the bishop mightn't know that Claire *is* a ghost. He might think she's just some sort of wandering loony.'

Claire, retrieving half of her beard from a nearby

trough, thought that this was exactly what the bishop would think, in any case, and that he wouldn't be far wrong. She was missing a double lecture on Headlining Techniques to stay in Rambleton for this farce, which she'd only agreed to because Giles had asked her, and now he was off coaching the nuns in the English Opening, which sounded faintly improper.

'Don't want to,' repeated Urban, who had found something interestingly rubbery protruding from the sandy ground.

'But why not?'

''Cos it's babyish.'

'Well you *are* babyish, Urbs,' commented Hygenus before either of his elder siblings could sit on him.

'Don't be silly,' cried Joan desperately. 'Of course he's not babyish. He's just more *sensitive* than the rest of you. We don't all want to be great clods like you, only interested in food and rugby.'

'Dad's only interested in food and rugby. D'ye call him a clod, then?'

'I might,' said Joan darkly. 'But you will say it, won't you, Urban?'

'No.' The rubbery thing proved incomprehensible for further along there was a metallic corner to be excavated.

Pius, less optimistic than Joan, was already trying to coach Innocent as understudy in the part.

'Say "Where's my mummy", Innie.'

'No.' Innocent drew himself up to his full two foot four, thrust his thumbs in the pockets of his dungarees and grinned wickedly. There was nothing he liked better than a battle of wills.

'Why not?' Pius began to feel that there was a certain inevitability about these fraternal encounters.

'Dowant Mummy.'

'Well pretend.'

But for Innocent, who was, as a matter of routine, Fireman Sam, an uncaged tiger, the beggar outside the bus station and the entire cast of Tots TV before breakfast, this concept was unattainable.

'Want Daddy,' he said, with the air of one who waves a tempting morsel in the vicinity of a hungry dog's nose. Pius leapt for the bait.

'Say "Where's Daddy" then.'

Hygenus, Innocent's main ally in these skirmishes, delivered the final blow.

'But he knows where Daddy is. He's in the kitchen, eating up our breakfast Weetabixes.'

The impasse was broken by Urban's emergence from the hole he had dug, bearing a small rust-flecked object in his grubby palm.

'Look what I've found. It's a sort of badge.'

The others gathered around, relieved at any diversion from Pius' unremitting leadership. Claire, temporarily divested of the sheet, but with long moustaches hanging down one side of her face, joined them.

'It's got a pig on,' explained Urban, rubbing the pin on his jumper to better display its glories. 'Same as Mrs Pockebonce's. I'm going to wear it.'

'You can't,' said Hygenus.

'Can. You can't stop me. I found it, not you. Didn't I, Claire?'

Claire, who, as an only child herself, found these

exchanges rather awkward, made a non-committal sound. She was beginning to wonder whether she would manage to see Giles at all before she caught her train back to Manchester.

Hygenus gave a long-suffering sigh. 'I didn't mean that you're not *allowed* to wear it, if you really *want* to. I just wouldn't have thought, achully wouldn't have thought in a zillion years, that anyone, any boy I mean, 'specially any boy in our family, even you, would ever achully *want* to wear it.'

'Why not?' asked Urban, looking down at the badge with rather less confidence. 'I like pigs.'

'Oh, Urbs, you are stupid. Of course you like pigs, everyone with any sense likes pigs. But look what colour it is.'

Urban looked, and his heart fell. It was true. However burly and masculine the pig, however gleaming the emerging brass of its background, however sharp the pin, for emergency use in battle, one thing was uncompromisingly clear. The pig was pink, a bright, bold, unambiguous pink.

'But of course it's pink!' expostulated Claire. Pushed far enough, she rather enjoyed the children's arguments, viewing them with the detached interest of the journalist and even deigning to become involved, especially when Urban, as often, was the underdog. 'All pigs are pink. Well, most of them, anyway. It doesn't matter whether they're male or female. It's just a piggy colour, like you being, er, sort of mud coloured.'

The boys were just beginning to be persuaded, looking at one another with guarded expressions, none wanting to be the first to relent, when Claire spoiled it all.

'Anyway,' she said blithely, 'I think he looks really sweet.'

Ophelia, meanwhile, was finding her loyalties torn. As soon as she had finished her conversation with Mother Thérèse, she made her way up the narrow staircase to the Infirmary. Eulalia was lying in bed, the crisp sheet pulled up to her chin and an expression of miserable resignation on her broad face. As soon as she glanced in, Ophelia knew that her sudden intuition had been right.

'Dilys?' she said softly.

The sister's grey eyes snapped open and seemed to flicker with fear. 'You know, as well?'

'I saw Hilda when, after . . .'

'When she was dead. After she'd been murdered.'

'Yes, I suppose so.'

'I'd never seen her in all that time. Never saw any of them, nor heard. I sent Father a card for my Solemn Clothing but he didn't reply. I didn't know that Hilda had married, that she was in Russia. Anything at all. So I suppose it's daft to mind now, isn't it?'

It was more words than Ophelia had ever heard from Sister Eulalia, through all the fragrant teatimes of the past year.

'I . . . don't think so.'

'He wonders if I killed her. For the land, or for revenge. He doesn't want me to know, hardly knows himself, but that's what he wonders.' The grey eyes looked bleakly at Ophelia. 'Are you wondering that, too?'

Ophelia clutched the baby more closely to her as she considered the question. Of course, she had been looking for Hilda's sister who would, inevitably, be a prime suspect, particularly since the attack on Mr Snodsworth. And there was something, not quite sinister, but chilling about Sister Eulalia, as she lay here, stiff with misery, the unaccustomed words hanging in the cold antiseptic air.

'I've done very wrong,' came a whisper, so bleak that it seemed to have come from the iron bedstead itself.

'Of course you wouldn't want the land,' said Ophelia at last, fastening on the simpler motive. 'Did you even know that you and Hilda owned it?'

'Yes.' She spoke slowly, more unwilling than before. 'That is, I knew that there was some land, somewhere. I don't think we ever saw it. To be honest, that birthday was overshadowed by what happened afterwards. It was only a few weeks later that Father found out that I'd been receiving Instruction from the parish priest. He was furious. He threw me out of the house and so I went to stay with the sisters. Then later, after I'd been received into the Church, I joined them. I left everything behind, except the plane. I sneaked back at night, with a couple of other postulants, to fetch that.'

With the last two sentences Eulalia's voice had regained some of its usual Yorkshire warmth. Ophelia remembered the aeroplane, that had rusted for so long in the side chapel before being called into service that summer as an emergency windmill.

'That was the only thing I regretted,' she said, dreamily now, 'especially with it being wartime. I could have been a fighter pilot, but I don't expect they really took women.'

'No, I don't imagine that they did. But the land?'

'Oh yes, the land. Trotter's Bottom, was it called? Well, after my Solemn Profession, I made a will leaving everything I had to the convent. And, of course, I gave them the little bit of money I'd saved. But at the time, with all the excitement . . .'

It was impossible, now, to imagine Sister Eulalia becoming really excited about anything.

'I forgot about the land. A few months later I came across the papers but I didn't want any more squabbles between Father and the Institute – he'd already sent them some pretty threatening letters, so I just stuffed them away somewhere and tried to forget about the whole thing.'

'Can you remember where you put them?'

'Mr Zhukovsky asked me that, and, yes, I'm pretty sure that I put them under the big drawer in the kitchen table. You see, the drawer has a space to fit into, and there was room to slip the papers underneath, where they can't be seen. But we checked this morning, and they weren't there.'

Ophelia had the idea that she had heard something else about that kitchen drawer lately, but could not remember what it was. Nothing of importance, probably. It did not seem, in any case, as though she were likely to find out much more from Eulalia that afternoon. Obviously, her movements would have to be checked, for both the time of Hilda's poisoning and that of the attack on Mr Snodsworth, but that could be

227

done later, and more tactfully. Sister Eulalia was such a landmark in her kitchen that the other sisters would have been bound to notice if she had been missing. It would also be worth while checking with Letitia Lamb as to whether Eulalia had been seen in the public library at all. Ophelia could not imagine the gentle Eulalia to be a killer, and yet there had been a shudder of guilt as she spoke that was not entirely explained by the shock of her sister's death.

On her way back from the convent, Ophelia called in to the Grand Hotel to find Zuke in a similar state of collapse.

'They were so much the same,' he kept repeating, from the disintegrating horsehair armchair in which he was propped. 'It was like seeing my poor Hilda brought to life once more.'

But he had obviously discovered no more from his interview with Eulalia than Ophelia had herself. Reluctantly, therefore, she left him to his tea and vodka, promising to call again in the morning. As she closed his door and began to walk down the corridor, the manager, Jason Spikewort, shimmered from the shadows.

'Poor *dear* man,' he said in a hushed voice. 'He came back here in such a state this morning. I've just been popping in from time to time all day. Tea and sympathy, you know, all I can offer. On the house, of course. We can't have him worrying about the hotel bill, after everything else he's been through. You know, I think seeing poor Hilda's sister has brought it *all* back, worse than at the beginning. Like seeing a ghost, you know. Positively Shakespearean.'

'Absolutely,' agreed Ophelia. 'Look, I have to go now, but . . .'

'Oh, I'll be keeping a close eye on him, don't you bother about that. I'm generally about, you know, checking up on my guests, especially the elderly ones. I think of them more as aunties and uncles, really, than as clients.'

The reference to uncles reminded Ophelia of where she had heard his name before.

'I'm very grateful to you, and I'm sure Mr Zhukovsky is as well. By the way, were you related to James Spikewort, that used to own our house? Moorwind Farm, you know.'

Jason smiled sadly. 'I do know, I'm afraid, only too well. I was brought up there. Yes, James was my father, but *not* a very sympathetic one. Rather a rough sort of fellow, though I'm told that he meant well. I like to think that I've rather grown away from his influence.'

'Oh, I'm sure that you have. Now thank you again. I really must dash.'

She went home, feeling much comforted and cheered by the thought of the letter which she had to write that evening. It took several more hours with Mr Snodsworth's book, and some experimenting with the fonts on Malachi's computer to find the most impressive, but eventually it was printed.

'But is it Italy?' the children, from their bedrooms, could hear her mutter. 'If it's Italy then that's the EU, and only a first-class stamp. Well, I'll bung two on, just to be sure.'

Urban, who had never heard his mother use the word

'bung', lay awake long into the night wondering what could be going on. He was not fond of mystery, and Moorwind Farm was considerably more mysterious at the moment than he liked. He thought about the books he was learning to read at school, where parents and brothers did nothing more unusual than visit the zoo, and wished he could jump into their pages, just for a few days, for a bit of a rest.

Chapter Fifteen

The Bryan Counter-Gambit

Neither Ophelia nor Joan batted an eyelid as they passed through the Ratchet-Crampers' Gents on their way to the chess club on the next Wednesday evening. Some of the Ratchet-Crampers muttered dialect oaths under their breath and one even turned around in mid-flow to expostulate, but to no effect. Joan, who had been practising her openings against the chess program on her father's one functional computer, was anxious to confront a live opponent, and preferably one who would not, at the vital twenty-seventh move, have his cable ignominiously pulled out by Innocent. Ophelia, meanwhile, had since the weekend found herself, upon entering any building, sniffing about her like a trained beagle. This was not, she soon discovered, the most salubrious way to traverse the urinals, and she entered the hallowed precincts of the chess club coughing painfully. She had established, however, that whatever municipal affliction was permeating Rambleton, it had not reached the Ratchet-Crampers, whose methane was entirely of their own creation.

'Sshhh,' hissed Major Lamb from the far end of the room, without turning around to see who it was. 'An inevitable draw, I think?' he continued to his opponent.

'I think not,' said Simon lightly, removing the Major's queen from the board.

'Hurumph.'

Mortimer Bradley, meanwhile, was greeting them genially.

'Mrs O., what a pleasure. I'm so pleased you decided to come along.' No one would guess from his magnanimous demeanour, thought Ophelia, that he himself had been absent from the club for the past six years. 'But you haven't got your, er . . .'

He gestured in the vicinity of her left breast, as though expecting a dangling appendage to materialize.

'Baby,' supplied Ophelia. 'No, my husband's looking after her.' Sort of, she added to herself, remembering the two gallon bucket of butterscotch Instant Whip into which Malachi and the boys had been taking it in turns to dip the delighted Dodie as they left. 'This is Joan, my elder daughter. She's getting quite keen on chess, aren't you?'

Joan shot her mother a sharp I-can-speak-for-myself look before ruining the principle by nodding dumbly at the overpowering Mortimer.

'Marvellous, *marvellous*. So I hear you'll be entering the Humbert Havelock? And you, Mrs O.? Can I persuade you to take a board?'

'Oh no, I couldn't,' began Ophelia but Joan interrupted her.

'Please, Mummy.'

Ophelia, startled, realized that it had been several years since Joan had used that tone of voice. The idea of competitive chess was gruesome, involving, she was sure, ritual humiliation of an intensity unknown outside the more barbaric rites of cannibals or American college students, but if it was so important to Joan . . . And she would at least be able to keep a close eye upon any potential suspects among the entrants.

'All right then. In the novice section, mind.'

'Splendid!' roared Mortimer, and Major Lamb, who was now, in addition to the queen, three pawns and a bishop down, turned around again.

'Will you please,' he began, paused for a moment upon seeing Ophelia and then, his eyes bulging apoplectically, stared at the badge on the lapel of Joan's gabardine coat.

'You as well!' he gasped, in the tones of a dying Caesar. 'Children?' He goggled ineffectually, then seemed to notice Mortimer for the first time. 'Aha,' he said in a lower voice. 'Now I understand. It's all been a blind, hasn't it, all this talk of reconciliation. You've still not forgotten the quickplay finish rules. Well, let me tell you, Mortimer Bradley. *Neither have I.*'

Despite this dramatic commencement of the evening, Ophelia noticed that Joan was looking particularly cheerful in the car on their way home. This tournament must mean a lot to the little girl, she thought, and resolved to tie Innocent up well away from the power cable during Joan's next practice sessions. But it was only partly the prospect of being a Novice in the Humbert Havelock

Memorial that was causing Joan's suppressed explosions of glee. As Mortimer Bradley had painstakingly filled in their entry forms, in wet black italics, she had looked over his shoulder at the pile of completed forms on the table. The top one, an application for the Major section, had been completed by a Cuthbert John MacBride of Scorsdale, whose occupation (an inquisitive innovation of Mortimer's this, for no other chess congress requested the information) was given, in self-effacing pencil as 'R. C. bishop'. Joan was jubilant. The children had been avoiding the question of where and when the haunting of the bishop was to take place, the younger ones relying on Pius' unflagging, if not unerring, leadership and Claire secretly hoping that the whole idea would fizzle out for lack of opportunity. What Pius thought, no one knew, but Joan was confident that her solution would be seized upon with enthusiasm, though almost certainly without acknowledgement.

'Everything all right, love?' asked Ophelia, as a particularly mirthful snort came through the darkness from the passenger seat.

'Perfect,' said Joan ingenuously. 'You know, Mummy, I'm really looking forward to the chess congress.'

With Adeodata quietly snuffling in the cardboard box which Ophelia had purloined from Freezaland as a makeshift crib, one of Polly's cups of enthusiastic coffee (three teaspoons of Nescafé, double cream borrowed from her mother's fridge, and a crumbled Flake on the top) and a nice juicy divorce petition, Ophelia was having a good morning. It was true that the fan heater under the desk produced a stream of tepid air so narrow that the slightest movement of her stockinged feet propelled them into the polar atmosphere of the rest of the office, that her monthly pay cheque had been returned by the bank, eclipsed with red ink, and that Polly had typed up an entire affidavit yesterday without noticing that her fingers were on the wrong keys, so that 'The petitioner alleges' came out as 'Yjr \\\[ryoyopmrt s;;rhrd' and they had to send a cryptoanalyst along with the private detective to serve it on the wayward respondent. Nonetheless, as days at Snodsworth Parrish Ranger went, it was going reasonably smoothly, and might, within six hours or so, have gone entirely, when there was a self-important rattling at the front door and Major Lamb marched in.

He observed no formalities, but strode, his fondly nurtured limp forgotten, straight into Ophelia's room.

'Apology!' he barked.

'I'm very sorry,' gasped Ophelia.

'No, no. *I'm* apologizing.'

'Are you?' His demeanour, brusque and red-faced as ever, scarcely suggested contrition.

'Of course I am. Last night. Of course, I quite see that it wasn't the little girl's fault. That blasted Bradley gave her the thing to wear, I suppose?'

'The badge, do you mean?' Ophelia had scarcely noticed it until the Major's outburst. Joan had, she thought, shown it to her before they left, but she had been busy removing a chocolate chip from the baby's nostril and not in the mood for art-and-craft appreciation. There had been something familiar about it, she had vaguely registered, but it was only on the drive home that she remembered seeing its twin, rather less rusty and battered, on the yellow tweed frontage of Edgar Pottle-bonce. 'No, I'm sure it wasn't anything to do with Mr Bradley. I think the child found it somewhere. You know what they're like.'

'Hmmm,' growled the Major in the tones of a convinced conspiracy theorist. 'There'll be more behind it than that. "Found it somewhere." You don't expect a man who's been through the Bedulan Campaign to believe that sort of weak story, do you? Now then,' he interjected quickly, as Ophelia's expression became dangerously set, 'I'm not saying that you had anything personally to do with it, nor the kiddies. But a man in my position . . .'

'Would it be a good idea if you were to tell me about it?' asked Ophelia philosophically, pushing aside the petition, in which she had just reached an interesting allegation about a window-cleaner's bucket, with lingering regret. 'What is it that so upsets you about these badges anyway?'

Major Lamb had obviously been longing to be asked. He pushed back his chair with a prolonged screech, and began.

'I wasn't always a military man, Mrs O. As a lad, you might almost say . . .'

But he got no further. The high-pitched squeak of his chair had enraged the dozing Adeodata, who had just been getting comfortable against the *Beauties of Brid-lington* tea-towel which Polly had found in the codicils deed-box. Her voice (Dodie's, not Polly's) was currently in the transition stage between the naked cry of the new-born and the more verbal and varied demands of the older baby. Consequently, no one ever knew quite what sound she was going to make next, and often the resulting grunts and shrieks were as great a surprise to Adeodata herself as to her auditors. This was one such occasion, and the sound produced was, to Ophelia's utter humiliation, an unmistakable squeal.

'What?!' roared the Major, and Dodie, perhaps realizing that she had committed something of a *faux pas*, tried a different register. This time it was a grunt.

'You!' cried Major Lamb, pointing at Ophelia with the righteous fury of a wronged deity. 'You!' Realizing that he could not simply stand there saying 'You!' until lunchtime, he tried again. 'Pretending not to know, putting on all your innocent looks, asking me for the story, and all the time you've got a . . . a *piglet* under the desk.' His voice trailed off at the end of the sentence and he seemed almost lost for invective. 'I shall go to the library,' he concluded with dignity, 'and find Letitia. A wife is what a man needs at a time like this.'

And with a reproachful final look at Ophelia, who, if a wife, was certainly not a virtuous one, he left the room, remembering to limp, albeit with the wrong leg.

Much confusion, both that morning and subsequently, might have been avoided if the Major had concentrated less upon perfecting his limp and more upon where he was going. As it was, he met the full force of the Law.

'Hello, hello,' said Sergeant Booking in time-honoured fashion, though not, perhaps, with the bonhomie that tradition required. 'If you could *just* watch where you're going there.'

His tone was subdued, utilizing sarcasm rather than all-out brutality, for he could not, off-hand, be absolutely positive that Major Lamb was not a magistrate.

'All very well to say watch where you're going,' blustered the Major. 'All very well for someone who isn't being plagued by blasted piglets everywhere they go.'

'Piglets, sir? Did I hear you say *piglets*?'

'Yes, blast you. There's no need to keep going on about it. A man does have feelings, even if he has fought alongside Montgomery and shared his hip-flask with General Eisenhower.'

'Quite so, sir, quite so. But you see this, er, *gentleman* has just reported the theft of several piglets. Something of a coincidence, I'm sure you'll agree.'

From behind the lamp-post where he had been skulking appeared a familiar stooped figure in a dirty overcoat, a battered cigarette protruding from amidst his grey stubble.

'Mornin', Major,' said Albert Skate. ''Ow's business?'

'Can't complain,' said the Major, although in fact he could, and did, albeit not to his social inferiors. The novelty of a ten-pin bowling alley having slid from the fickle consciousness of Rambleton, it had now returned to its more traditional pastimes of soap operas and mild domestic violence. 'But I didn't know you kept pigs, Skate?'

'It's my new hoccupation, in't it? Chief Pigman to her ladysworth. I allus knew as she had a soft spot fer me.

'Oping fer a bit of the other behind the sty, I reckon, except that she ain't got no sties, just a couple of bairns' paddlin'-pools. Daft, I call it, and Sir Edgar, he says the same.'

'He's not Sir Edgar yet.' It rankled with Major Lamb that Lady Tartleton, who had for so long confided in him, should have turned instead to Pottlebonce who was, when all was said and done, nothing but a clod-hopping farmer. It did not help that it was probably his own fault, for making that scene at Tartleton Court. All the same, when it came to pigs . . . 'How many have been stolen, then?'

'Aahhh.' Albert aided his cogitations by languidly scratching his crotch. ''Ard to say, reely, pigs being such slippery buggers, 'specially when they're all over muddy water. I reckon there's bin eight or ten gone. Seems like they take a couple at a time, like. At night, it must be.'

Sergeant Booking, who had been nodding judiciously, now turned again to Major Lamb, his pencil ready licked for rapid note-taking.

'And you say Mrs O. is keeping pigs in her room?'

'I didn't say that, exactly. Not pigs plural. I couldn't smell anything, for one thing. It might be, it might possibly be that I've been mistaken altogether. That is, there might be one pig. A very small one.'

'I understand your chivalrous instincts, sir,' said Sergeant Booking, in the same tone of condescending disgust he might have used if the Major had confessed to a spot of bestiality before breakfast. 'But this is an extremely serious matter. I think it might be best if I had a word with the . . . the accused myself.' He looked towards Ophelia's window, a look of delicious anticipation, and he licked his pencil once again.

'Afternoon off?' asked Gordon, coming into the kitchen to fetch his post-lunch, pre-teatime snack from the fridge, and finding the kitchen table occupied by Giles and a lot of closely-written paper.

'Not exactly. The school boiler's on the blink, so I thought it might be warmer here than in the library.' Giles' wistful tone suggested that he wasn't convinced, in this case, of the scientific validity of his theory. He looked longingly towards the wall where, pre-explosion, the Aga had purred. The new cooker, however gleaming and space-age the halogen hobs (and they hadn't stayed gleaming for long, with Tansy's level of housekeeping), didn't do much in the general way of warmth.

'Right.' Gordon hovered in front of the open fridge door, trying to choose between blueberry cheesecake and a Wensleydale sandwich. 'Er, right. You, um, do a lot of work, don't you?'

''Bout average, I s'pose. "A" levels aren't that easy, you know. Not unless you're a genius.'

'Hmmm,' agreed Gordon, taking this as a compliment. 'But I mean, you do a lot of extra physics, don't you?'

'Well, the bloke we had last year wasn't much good, so Mr Stephens, he's new, said he'd give us some extra lessons to catch up. It's been really useful; I think I'm getting the hang of it all now.'

'Great, great. I mean . . . excellent. What about experiments?'

There was something in Gordon's agitation to suggest

that it was not merely the choice of a sweet or savoury snack that exercised him.

'What about them?'

'Are you redoing them from last year? Or doing any extra ones? I'm very concerned, you see, that you should be getting sufficient time in the lab. It's the one thing, really, not all this swotting, that makes the real scientist.'

'It's great that you're so concerned, Dad. You didn't seem to take much notice before.'

'Oh, never mind all that. I mean, of course I've always been concerned. But what I really want to know is, have you got a key to the lab so you can do extra work? I mean, I was just wondering, idly, for your own good, you know . . .'

Confused, Gordon snatched a salami and a chunk of ungrated Parmesan and fled upstairs.

'What was all that about?' asked Claire, coming into the kitchen with a pile of last year's washing. Philip had asked her to help out at the *Courier* for a few days, his other reporter having gone down with 'flu, and she was taking the opportunity to help Tansy with her backlog of housework. 'Why's he after a key to your school lab?'

'I don't know that he was exactly *after* a key. He was just interested . . .'

'Oh come on, Giles. When's your dad ever been interested in anyone except himself and his precious work? What's he up to in that shed? Have you looked in recently?'

'No, of course I haven't. It's private, isn't it?'

'Is it?'

Giles grinned. 'Actually it's locked. I tried yesterday.

241

There were some awfully funny noises coming out of it. Squeaking and grunting. And no, it wasn't him and Mum up to some practical biology.'

Claire laughed, but she was worried. The lead story for that week's *Courier*, the story that was taking up all her investigative energies, was the mysterious theft of piglets from Yardley Farm. The police, she knew, were taking it terribly seriously, and if it turned out that Gordon was taking them for scientific experiments . . . She shuddered, having encountered the wrath of animal rights protesters one day in London, when she had recklessly worn one of her grandmother's rabbit skin coats on the freezing Underground. He would be safer being arrested, she thought, than falling into their hands, though of course Giles and Tansy would be targets, too, and Rambleton police cells were scarcely large enough to take them all into protective custody. As she sorted wool from cotton, she resolved to keep a closer eye upon Gordon's enigmatic activities.

Chapter Sixteen

A View of the Board

'Wet Nose Solutions, may I help you?'

'Hiya. Er . . . d'ye sell Megadrives?'

'Megadrives? Oh, those sonic thingies. Yes, yes, I'm game for anything. How much do you want for it?'

'Wor? Oh, nah, nah. I wanna *buy* one, see?'

'You want to buy something . . .' Malachi tasted the unfamiliar words. 'You want to buy something. Marvellous. Hang on, I'll just go and see if there's one in stock.'

He vaulted over the mountain of Labrador in the doorway and crashed into the boys' room. Innocent was sitting on one of the bottom bunks, dismantling a mobile phone.

'Teddyphone broke!' he explained cheerfully. 'Innie mend it.'

'Oh good. Look, Inn, have your brothers got a Megadrive, d'ye know?'

'Megging-eyes?'

'No, it's . . . Oh, it doesn't matter.' Malachi plunged

into the nearest cardboard box and started throwing toys out at random.

'Mess,' commented Innocent dispassionately, and turned his attention to Ophelia's clock radio.

Malachi piled a few items on to the useful shelf which he discovered unaccountably attached to his chest and jogged back to the phone.

'No Megadrives, I'm afraid, but I could do you two jigsaws and a battery-powered Hulk Hogan. Say three quid?'

'No, ta.'

'Tell you what then. I'll throw in a headless Sindy and half a box of Misfits. Can't say fairer than that, can I?'

But the potential purchaser had gone, and a squawking from under the pile of toys revealed the useful shelf to be Adeodata's head. Ophelia had strapped her sling across Malachi's broad stomach first thing in the morning, telling him that he would hardly notice she was there.

'But, Oaf,' he had objected, 'you remember what it was like last time. She hates me. Why can't you go on taking her into work with you?'

'Don't be silly, of course she doesn't hate you. No child has ever hated you. They recognize a kindred spirit. That and the inexhaustible supply of chocolate buttons in your back pockets.'

'Oh. I didn't know you knew . . .'

'You might have noticed that I do the laundry around here. Even the most incurious washerwoman's suspicions are aroused by a delicate film of milk chocolate over her best pink knickers.'

'Lovely ones they are too,' murmured Malachi,

running his free hand, the one that wasn't being chewed by Dodie, over Ophelia's tweed-covered bottom. 'Got them on today, have you?'

'Certainly not, and stop trying to change the subject. Dodie's matured a lot over the past weeks.'

'Sounds like port and Stilton.'

'And I think she's ready for the added, er, stimulation of the home environment. Anyway, when it comes to being accused of keeping pigs under my desk . . .'

'Booking wasn't convinced?'

'You're dead right he wasn't. And I didn't dare show him that it was Dodie. He'd only insist that the office be registered under the Children Act for the purposes of crèche provision.'

'Silly old sod,' said Malachi with feeling. Things had been going rather well lately, with just Innie around, although it wasn't as though Wet Nose Solutions was exactly thriving. He'd sold a screen cleaning cloth a couple of months ago, but, because of forgetting about VAT, he'd ended up three quid down on the transaction. He supposed, in view of the fact that it was Ophelia who kept them, however inadequately, fed, clothed and roofed, he had better show a bit more enthusiasm for the house-husband bit.

'All right then, I'll look after her. But I'm warning you, she'll just scream all day again.'

It was then that Ophelia, fastening the sling straps rather excessively tight after his substantial breakfast, had said her little piece about his not noticing Dodie was there. Well, she had been right about that anyway. It was nearly two o'clock, and the baby had been asleep, or in silent contemplation of his Fair Isle chest, since half-past eight. Struggling with Ophelia's Girl Guide sheepshank, he went through to the kitchen. He did not look behind him, his mind on puréed semolina, and so did not see Innocent, quietly climbing into the big leather chair to take his father's place.

Polly wasn't sure whether, apart from school, which didn't really count, she had ever been in a library before. Ophelia had asked her to go and insinuate herself with Letitia Lamb, in the hope of discovering who had mutilated the *Courier*, and she had readily agreed, grateful both for the relative warmth and for the opportunity to take an active part in the investigation. Now, however, she wondered what to do. Should she inspect the Romance shelves, as she saw several plump ladies doing, searching for the one tale of hospital passion they had not yet read? Or perhaps she should pretend to read the notices that advertised blood donor sessions and training for disobedient dogs? She hovered by the desk and Letitia, who had been straightening a row of picture books into a precision of which her husband would be proud, clicked on Cuban heels over to her.

'Yes?' she said, quite kindly. 'You'd like to join the library, I suppose?'

'Oh yes please!' said Polly with rather unnecessary enthusiasm.

But Letitia had been waiting, through half a century of librarianship, for just such a display of fervour.

'A . . . a *voracious* reader are you, dear?'

'I think I'd like to be.' Polly was not sure what 'voracious' meant, having always thought that it had something to do with mice, but was anxious to agree.

'Wonderful. Now, if I could just take your name and address?'

Polly sighed with relief. She had just remembered that she had once been in the library before, with Ophelia, when they had been working on Mr Snodsworth's *Geranium* case. On that occasion, she seemed to recall, Mrs Lamb had practically expelled them both. Luckily, she did not seem to remember. Polly gave her name and address, at which Letitia smiled pityingly over her half-moon spectacles.

'From the council estate? Oh, I do so admire you.' The spectacles clouded over as Letitia remembered the excitement of reading *Room at the Top* for the first time, and her fantasies of finding a clever young working-class lad to encourage, though perhaps not quite in all the ways that novels like that tended to suggest. A working-class girl would, of course, be much more suitable, especially now that she was far beyond all that sort of business. 'And now you feel the need to immerse yourself in some really *great* literature?'

'Mmm,' said Polly, rather desperately. 'Er . . . what would you recommend?'

'Aahhh,' sighed Letitia, flinging her arm out in an expansive gesture, as though to suggest that the full riches of the English canon were spread out on the shelves around them. In fact, once you discounted the Mills & Boon and the Ministry of Agriculture manuals, there was little left but the poems of Longfellow and a bit of dog-eared Dickens. 'Have you tried Virginia?'

'Not yet. My auntie went to Disney World last year but Mum wants to stick to Ibiza. Says you get enough of America off the telly.'

'No dear, not the state. I meant Virginia *Woolf*. *To the Lighthouse* and *The Waves*.'

'I don't really like the sea-side, I'm afraid. I like newspapers better. You know, old ones, from the war and that. Do you have many people looking for that kind of thing?'

'Oh yes,' said Letitia with a vaguely disappointed air. 'There's a lot of interest in local history, especially among the older generation. But for a young girl like you . . .'

'I suppose you're too young to remember the war yourself then?'

'Me?' Letitia pinkened and mellowed again under this blatant flattery. 'Bless you, dear, I'm quite old enough for that. I was at school, mind you, and we didn't get much in the way of bombs around here, but I remember the little ones being evacuated and all of us helping with the harvest.'

'Was that when you met Major Lamb?'

'Oh, our families were friends from way back. But he was courting another girl, older than me, at the beginning of the war. I only got a look in much later, after she had gone halfway round the world, to Russia.'

'Russia!'

'Yes, she married a Russian soldier, I believe. Poor Frederick was quite cut up about it. That and losing the pig.'

'Oh, did he have a pig?'

'He did, yes. A charming little thing, from what he tells me, though I don't imagine it can have been little for very long. I gather that he and Hilda, that was the girl's name, had plans to marry and run their own pig farm, after he had left university. Quite what use a Cambridge degree would have been in pig-farming I don't know, but his family insisted that he go up. I don't think they knew about Hilda; I gather that she wasn't exactly from his background. Anyway, he had this pet piglet, a sort of first instalment, I suppose, and he took it with him in nineteen-thirty-eight when he went up to Cambridge. Well, dear, you know what undergraduates are like – or perhaps you don't – take it from me, anyway, it was bound to happen.'

'What was?' Polly longed for her shorthand notebook. Surely there could not have been two Hildas from Rambleton who had married Russian soldiers? Never mind the boring question of who had mutilated the newspaper – this was real evidence. Just wait until she told Ophelia that the Major had been the corpse's boy-friend. There must be a motive in that, somewhere. 'What was bound to happen?'

'Why, the kidnapping. A group of Frederick's friends took the pig and hid it away somewhere. Just as a joke, you know. They had special badges made, nice enamel pins, quite expensive I suppose, and they wore them on their jackets whenever poor Fred was around. Such a tease, as Miss Mitford would say. Anyway, I'm sure they meant to tell Frederick where the pig was, but the war came so suddenly and they all dispersed and lost touch.

To tell the truth, I imagine most of them were killed. Fighter pilots, you know. And then, to make matters worse, he wrote to Hilda and she never replied. He may seem like a crusty old military gent to you young people, but, believe me, he has a romantic heart. It took him many years to get over that blow, a "double whammy" I believe they call it these days, or is that a hamburger? Anyway, he can't look a pig in the eye without sniffing a bit, even now.'

'And Hilda's dead and so we'll never know,' said Polly dreamily.

'Dead? I suppose she might well be. A lower standard of living in Eastern Europe, I understand, though they do say that the diet's very healthy. All that beetroot.'

'But she died here in Rambleton!'

'What?!'

'Oh.' Too late, Polly realized that Letitia had probably not even heard of the body at the Grand Hotel, the existence of which had been efficiently hushed by Jason Spikewort, and that, if she had, it had not yet been named. She supposed that she had better make a clean breast of it. 'A lady died last week at the Grand Hotel. Hilda Zhukovsky. She used to be Hilda Podd.'

'And this was Frederick's . . .?'

'Sounds like it, yes. Ophelia, I mean Parrish's—'

'I thought I'd seen you somewhere before.'

'We're acting for Mr Zhukovsky. That's why Ophelia was looking for that article on Trotter's Bottom. It was owned by Hilda and her sister, you see. Her sister's a nun, by the way. She's been here all along. Do you know anything about it?'

'Just slow down a moment, would you?' Letitia was caressing her temples, like a nineteenth-century lady with an attack of the vapours. 'Do I know that Mrs Zhukovsky was in Rambleton and that she has now died? No. Do I know anything about Trotter's, er, rear end? No. Do I know Mrs Zhukovsky's sister? Not that I am aware of. Do I consider it grossly impertinent of you to come here under false pretences and interrogate me about my private life? Certainly.'

But Polly had already fled.

Innocent swung himself around in his father's chair, faster and faster, until the seat balanced precariously on top of the swivel mechanism. ''Paceship,' he reminded himself. This was more fun than the stapler, which had made a cowardly attack on his thumb and more exciting than the hole punch, which, once Daddy's only tie had been perforated, was really rather dull. The telephone rang, but Innocent knew what to do.

''Ello?'

'Mr Innocent?'

'Yes!'

'Mr Innocent, this is Bernard at Mottleberry Holdings plc. May I say, first of all, how delighted we are that you've taken on *Zugzwang!*'

''Ello.'

(*sotto voce*) 'You were right, he is a foreigner. Lithuanian, possibly. The thing is, Mr Innocent, we've had an approach from the owners of *Practical Gerbils*, wanting to know whether we're interested in purchasing the title. They envisage a merger to appeal to the rodent-keeping chess market. Apparently it's a rapidly growing sector with particular strength in the lower B and C(I) social groupings. Our own analysts forecast particularly vigorous activity in and around the East Midlands area.'

Innocent, who was experiencing particularly vigorous activity in and around the bladder area, was getting bored with the conversation.

'Bye-bye.'

Bernard was impressed. 'I like a man who makes up his mind quickly. Buy, then, you think? At the best price we can get, obviously.'

'Bye-bye,' repeated Mr Innocent, and fell off the swivel chair.

'But I didn't really suspect Letitia!' protested Ophelia, who was celebrating her babyless state by sitting with her feet on the desk and a bottle of gin beside them. She had no intention of drinking the gin; not before lunchtime at least, but it was a symbol of liberation.

'No one is above suspicion,' said Polly sententiously. 'You've got to admit, she's got a motive now.'

'Only if she thought the Major was likely to run off with poor old Hilda. And she was hardly a *femme fatale*. Letitia must be nearly ten years younger and a good deal better preserved.'

'But it doesn't always work like that, does it? I mean, Hilda was his first love.'

'After the pig, yes. Of course, you could argue that he had a motive, too.'

'Who, the pig? Wouldn't it be dead by now?'

'Major Lamb, you idiot. If he's really been brooding

for all these years . . . I wonder whether Sister Eulalia knew anything about the relationship? I'll have to go back and—'

A thump and then a splintering sound came from the front door.

'Freeze!' called the hectoring voice of Sergeant Booking. 'No one move. I've got you covered.'

He scuttled into the room like an overheated crab, followed by his apologetic constable. Both carried the type of cardboard tubes that are used for delivering posters. Ophelia looked quizzically at them.

'We're not allowed guns,' explained the constable. 'Sergeant Booking asked the Chief Constable, but he called him a blithering—'

'Pigeon! Pigeon, we do not discuss operational strategy with suspects. Now, no more procrastination. Where is he?'

'Where is who? Look, why don't you put those things down? Surely the modern Nineties police don't need these confrontational tactics?'

Booking looked a little disorientated, but held on to his cardboard tube even tighter. 'Where is he? Gareth Macmillan Grobbett? Come on, quick, quick, quick.'

'Gareth Macmillan Grobbett? You've just made that up. I've never even heard of anyone called Grobbett.'

'Yes you have,' said Polly in an unusually subdued voice. 'It's my Gary.'

'You mean you're seriously thinking of calling yourself Mrs Grobbett?'

'Only if he asks me.'

'Oh,' said Ophelia. Polly's Gary had been in the

background for so long, occasionally glimpsed lurking at the bottom of the steps waiting for Polly to finish work, or swathed in blood-stained white behind the counter of Mr Whitworth's butcher's shop, that she had almost forgotten that he had an independent identity at all, never mind a surname. 'Why Macmillan?'

'Oh, his mum hoped he'd grow up to have a moustache. She thinks they're dead distinguished. Gary did try once, but it turned out a bit fluffy and one side grew faster than the other.'

'Ladies!' Armed resistance Sergeant Booking imagined that he could cope with, similarly deliberate obstruction, but feminine discussion of facial hair was too much for him. 'Is he here, or he is not?'

'Of course he isn't. We're running a solicitors' office here, not a refuge for escaped butchers. At least, we *were* running a solicitors' office until someone smashed the front door in. I hope your Chief Constable appreciates getting the bill for that. It's a couple of centuries old, you know. Practically listed.'

Sergeant Booking blanched, while Constable Pigeon tried not to snigger. 'I did suggest that we knocked first, sir.' Booking silenced him with a basilisk stare.

'What do you want my Gary for, anyway?' asked Polly, wishing that she had worn her six-inch heels so that she could have drawn herself up to a more impressive nearly five feet.

'My auntie Clarrie's friend . . .' The Sergeant recollected himself quickly. 'Certain *sources* have indicated to me that Grobbett . . .'

'*Mr* Grobbett, please,' said Ophelia.

'That Mr Grobbett, in the course of his mobile butcher's rounds – I trust, incidentally, that he has obtained statutory certification for the business – that Mr Grobbett has indicated a certain frustration at not being able to obtain sufficient pork for his customers' requirements.'

'Oh aye,' said Polly, following this with difficulty. 'He said to me as he always runs out of bacon by the time he gets to Shedd.' Shedd was a small hamlet some few miles outside Rambleton. 'But what's it . . .? Eh? Eh?' The blood of generations of Yorkshirewomen in defence of their menfolk bubbled in Polly's veins. Ophelia could suddenly imagine her in forty years' time, stout and red-faced, impregnable in her pinny and slippers. 'Are you calling my Gary the piglet thief?'

Sergeant Booking suddenly seemed less sure that he was, while Constable Pigeon feigned intense interest in *Paterson's Licensing Law*.

'That's ridiculous, anyway,' said Ophelia, authoritative from Lady Tartleton's lectures. 'Those pigs are only weanies – weaners, I mean. You couldn't get bacon from them, not for ages yet.'

'He might be fattening them up somewhere.' But the policeman's voice had lost its conviction. 'You tell him, he hasn't heard the end of this.' He turned on his rather meagre size eight heel and tried to make a dignified exit.

'What about that front door, then?' Polly called after him.

'Oh. Oh. Well I'm sure the Chief Constable won't want to be bothered about it. You'd better not risk a prosecution for wasting police time, not in your situation. I'll, er, send Pigeon here round with a piece of hardboard and get a proper job done on it tomorrow.'

'Very well,' said Ophelia coolly.

'And by the way,' added the Sergeant, thinking thereby to have the last word, 'I trust that I *won't* see you at Mrs Zhukovsky's post-mortem tonight. Strictly *in camera*. Members of the public absolutely not admitted.'

Ophelia opened her eyes very wide. 'Oh goodness, no, I wouldn't want to get into trouble with the Home Office. And actually,' she wondered whether it was too late to appeal to Sergeant Booking's masculine instincts of protectiveness. Well, it was always worth a try. 'Actually I'm most awfully squeamish about that sort of thing. I'd be terrified to even think I was within half a mile of where a thing like that was going on.'

Polly was goggling at her in astonishment. Ophelia tried not to catch her eye.

'And I was going to work late tonight, until eight o'clock or so. I'm not in any, any *danger* of seeing anything, am I?'

Sergeant Booking was relieved, but not really surprised, that the rather fearsome Mrs O. had proved, at heart, to be just another delicate little popsie.

'Oh, don't worry about that, dear,' he oozed, giving her a little pat on the bottom. Ophelia vowed that he would pay for that one day. 'We're not due to start until nine and it'll be at Mr Marrow's funeral parlour, which isn't on your way home, is it?'

'Not usually, no,' said Ophelia, and hazarded a quick wink in Polly's direction.

Chapter Seventeen

A Poisoned Pawn?

Ophelia was so horrified to find Zuke waiting in Mr Marrow's ante-room, that she forgot to use her practised Oliver voice.

'You shouldn't be here! Really, it's . . .'

'Ophelia?' He looked momentarily perplexed at her costume and then remembered that she was, after all, an Englishwoman, and free to dress in whatever eccentric manner she pleased, especially after dark. 'Ophelia, I was a soldier. I have seen worse sights than the interior of my poor Hilda. And, in any case, I must know what really happened.'

'Quite right,' said Horatio, who came through the door bundled to the neck in Barbour and Burberry, looking as though he were off for a day's grouse-shooting. 'You know, I can't apologize enough for cocking the whole thing up in the first place. Trouble is, a chap never thinks of foul play. Not in a sleepy little place like Rambleton. Oh, hello, Ophelia. Didn't recognize you in that get-up.

Very fetching, I must say, but I wonder, have you got a problem . . .?'

He gestured vaguely in the direction of Ophelia's upper lip, upon which was Sellotaped the bluish-grey tail of an indeterminate soft toy. As moustaches went, it was marginally more successful than Gary's, but hardly flattering.

'I think it's only temporary,' she assured him. 'And I'm not Ophelia, not for this evening. I'm Oliver, okay?'

'Absolutely, yes,' said Horatio with enthusiasm. He had read about this sort of thing but had never imagined that he knew a real live transvestite. Zuke just nodded, feeling somewhat out of his depth.

The remainder of the party consisted of Mr Marrow, fussily straightening curtains and trying to help the others off with their coats, which they resisted, Sergeant Booking, severe and magisterial, Mr Snodsworth, who still said nothing but 'client confidentiality' and a suspicious looking pathologist. Horatio recognized the pathologist as the man over whom he had spilt a goblet of brandy at the last BMA social function, and retreated hastily, with Ophelia, to the shadows.

The procedure was not as gory as Ophelia had feared, most of the time being taken up with removing and replacing plastic cartons from little polythene bags. Sergeant Booking, unusually, said nothing, but stood upright beside Hilda's feet, a distant expression on his face, evidently thinking about Lady Tartleton's missing piglets. Mr Snodsworth's pebble eyes blinked intelligently, and he nodded to Ophelia a few times, but no new words came. So it was only Mr Marrow, fidgeting with combined anticipation and shame, who questioned the pathologist.

'What do you think? Was I right? Do you think she was poisoned?'

'It appears likely,' said the man, in the tone of one who makes an unprecedented concession, 'but I prefer not to commit myself at this stage. A full report of my findings will be sent in the next twenty-four hours to the appropriate bodies, i.e. the police, the Home Office and the deceased's solicitors. That is yourself, I believe, Mr Snodsworth?'

'Client confidentiality,' said the old man seriously.

'Quite so. But the report should be addressed to you?'

Ophelia stepped forward, hoping that her moustache was straight.

'*For the attention of Oliver*, er, *Smith*,' she said, in what started as a magnificent bass but somewhere around the middle became unsustainable and turned into an alto. 'I'm Mr Snodsworth's assistant solicitor.'

Sergeant Booking looked curiously at her but without any real suspicion. Ophelia O. was now safely bundled away in his pigeonholed mind along with his wife, female colleagues and all other irrational and emotional women. He did not expect to hear any more from her about this ridiculous business, not now it had turned messy, with real blood on the table. Not that he had stopped suspecting her of being the Mrs Big behind the pig-rustling outfit. Animals, in his experience, brought out the worst in that sort of woman, as his own wife had proved when she had come home with that disastrous rabbit. He shivered at the memory.

'I shall also,' continued the pathologist, with a glare in Horatio's direction that made it quite evident that he had not forgotten the brandy, 'be considering whether to submit the file to the General Medical Council. The negligent completion of a death certificate is, in my opinion, a particularly serious offence, even when committed by a mere G.P.'

Horatio made some vaguely conciliatory noises but, for a change, was lost for actual words. He cheered up a few minutes later when the pathologist declared the proceedings to be at an end and snapped off, followed by Sergeant Booking. Mr Marrow invited Mr Snodsworth through into his private quarters for a glass of port, at which the old man smiled beatifically, opened his mouth to say 'Cli' and then thought better of it.

'Have you got your car, O— Oliver?' asked Horatio.

'No, Mal needed it to take the boys to Beavers.'

'To what?'

'It's a sort of mini-Cubs, I think. I'm sure they'll hate it, except perhaps Urban, but they wanted to try out being normal for a change. I thought I'd get a taxi if the last bus has gone.'

'Oh, don't worry about that. I'll give you a lift. We'll take Mr Zhukovsky back to his hotel first.'

Zuke, who was leaning against a wall, looking rather pale, smiled weakly, but by the time that they reached the Grand, a mere three hundred yards away, his complexion was positively green. It had turned out to be hard work to wedge him in the back of Horatio's Morgan and even harder work to extricate him again. With all the confusion, Ophelia almost forgot to remove her moustache, and had to run back hastily and stow it away in the glove compartment. Eventually, however, he was helped upstairs and Horatio telephoned room service for three medicinal whiskies.

Jason, when he brought them up, was horrified.

'My *dear* Mr Zhukovsky! Why, you look worse than ever! Mrs O., whatever has he been up to?'

Ophelia explained, to the accompaniment of Jason's genteel shudders.

'But how ghastly! A post-mortem? Whatever could be the point? I saw the poor lady with my own eyes, you know, and it was nothing but a heart attack. Terrible for the bereaved, of course, but at least it's a nice quick way to go. Not like these dreadful *lingering* things.'

'The problem is, Mr Spikewort . . .'

'Oh Jason, Jason. We can't be formal, not at a time like this.'

'The problem is, Jason, that it doesn't seem to have been a heart attack at all. We're afraid that she may have been poisoned.'

'Poisoned? In my hotel? Oh, surely that's impossible. We cater for the most exclusive sector of the tourism market. And the food – well, I can't deny that the breakfasts aren't quite up to the wine bar standard yet, but there's certainly no question of actual *infection*. Dear me, it all makes me feel quite faint. Perhaps . . .?' He looked longingly towards the whisky.

'Oh, take mine,' said Ophelia. 'I shouldn't really be drinking at all.'

Jason did so, draining the glass with astonishing speed. 'I don't usually, you know. But this, this has been a bit of a shock for me. Though of course nothing to what Mr Zhukovsky has been going through. I wonder if he'd like . . .'

But Zuke, worn out by the rigours of the day, had fallen asleep in the armchair.

'Ought we to get him into bed?' asked Ophelia.

Horatio looked horrified.

'Oh, don't worry,' said Jason. 'I'll tuck him up for the night.'

'Awfully good of you,' said Horatio. 'By the way, Spikewort, Spikewort . . . aren't you some relation of that chap who died falling off Ophelia's tractor?'

A light breeze of annoyance passed over Jason's pleasant features. 'My father. And he didn't die falling off the tractor or trying to move the tractor or any other variants of the myth. He died in Scorsdale General Hospital of cirrhosis of the liver. Now if you don't mind . . .'

'Oh, of course, of course.'

'Seemed a bit touchy about his old dad, didn't you think?' said Horatio when they were back in the Morgan, speeding out on the road towards Yardley Farm.

'Oh, I think it's just that he's trying to avoid mentioning his origins. Upwardly-mobile, you know.'

'Instead of downwardly, like us. What does your mother really think of Moorwind Farm, Ophelia?'

'About the same as yours thinks of you being a G.P. in a scruffy little town like Rambleton, instead of taking up residence in Harley Street.'

'True. Last time I went back she was telling people the

surgery was "just outside Harrogate". Anyway, if that pathologist gets his way then I won't be practising anywhere.'

'I shouldn't worry,' said Ophelia, with the deceptively casual air of one who still opened every communication from the Law Society with trepidation. 'Why are we going this way? It's at least five miles further.'

'Oh, it's a lovely evening for a drive. You family types don't know how lonely it can get, sitting night after night in front of the same video, with only a microwave curry to keep you warm.'

'Perhaps you ought to get married.'

'I would, Ophelia, if I could find someone like you. Trouble was, when I was a medical student and actually knew some girls, I was too busy drinking and playing rugby. Now I've matured—'

'You're still too busy drinking and playing rugby.'

'Come on, Ophelia, that's hardly fair. I play golf as well, now. I say, what's that?'

They were now passing Yardley Farm and could see that, by the side of the house, two enormous floodlights, like those used at football matches, had been erected. Beneath them the two paddling pools glinted as their occupants enjoyed a nocturnal wallow. At the edges of the pools, where the light was lost in shadow, crouched a few dark figures.

'Looks like fun,' said Horatio, parking the Morgan at random. He clambered out and began to spring towards the lights.

'Freeze!' called an imperious voice and Horatio recognized the small circle approaching his forehead as the barrel of a shotgun. He obediently froze, as did Ophelia, some ten yards behind him.

Lady Tartleton kept the gun steady as she looked them up and down. 'My lawyer and my doctor,' she said in a contemplative tone. 'Hmm. I suppose you *might* be the thieves. That idiotic policeman certainly seems to suspect you, Ophelia. On the whole, though, I think not.'

'Oh, I quite agree, Beatrice,' said Edgar Pottlebonce, puffing up, rather out of breath, in a green padded waistcoat and wellingtons. 'Not at all the sort of person we'd be looking for.'

'Perhaps we ought to check the car just the same,' suggested Monica, her great voice booming out of the shadows. 'One can never be *quite* sure. And if Dr Hale has been keeping pigs in it, then there ought to be some evidence.'

'Keeping pigs in my Morgan?' said Horatio, aghast. Amidst the anarchy of his daily life, the Morgan alone remained pure, ordered and gleaming. Not even a stray rugby sock, a sweet wrapper or a petrol coupon was allowed to sully its perfectly buffed leather. 'Keeping *pigs* in my Morgan? Why on earth should I want to do that?'

Ophelia, Lady Tartleton, Edgar and Monica all, simultaneously and with much contradiction, told him about the pig-rustling.

'So this is a stake-out? Fantastic. Mind if Ophelia and I join you?'

'The more the merrier,' said Lady Tartleton, who was always more cheerful with a gun in her hand. Ophelia tried to demur, thinking of Dodie, who would be expecting her midnight feed, and Malachi, who, apart from a brief respite when she had gone home for supper, had been in charge all day and was liable to complain about being a latch-key husband. Not that things had looked too bad that evening, apart from toys strewn over every square foot of floor and the swivel chair demolished. But Lady Tartleton was insistent.

'Might come in handy, a lawyer, when we make our citizen's arrest. That is, if I don't just blast the blighter's head straight off. I've already had one chap turned yellow on me – who d'ye think? – the Major of all people. I asked him along to our little ambush, thinkin' it would be just his sort of thing – military, y'know, and he made some excuse about not wantin' to be near pigs. "Are you a man or a mouse?" I asked him and he just muttered somethin' pansyish and stalked off. Got his limp wrong again, too. If I didn't know the chap better I'd suspect he had somethin' to do with it. Ha!'

But Ophelia was not so amused. Major Lamb's behaviour had certainly been aberrant lately, so much so that stealing pigs no longer seemed to be beyond him. And if he was the pig-rustler, then what had set him off? Was it really only the discovery of the badges, or did he have some more sinister reason for demonstrating pig-mania? Pigs, for the Major, might be inextricably linked with Hilda, with the innocence of their youthful love and with the horrors of her death at his own hand. She shuddered, and Horatio, mistaking the shiver for one of cold, offered her one of his four cashmere scarves.

'Thanks,' she whispered, but they did not have long to

wait. Lady Tartleton was still explaining how the pigs were disappearing, two at a time, almost every night, under the inebriated gaze of Albert Skate (who had been summarily dismissed that morning) and Edgar was telling Ophelia, in response to her question, that it had not been he at all, but Lady Tartleton herself who had found the original pig badge. At this Lady Tartleton interrupted herself (never an easy feat) to say that she must have picked it up somewhere when she was out with the dogs, but she had no idea where, and would have left it there if she had known it would cause this much trouble. She evidently had not heard the story of the Major, Hilda and the pig, so Ophelia, who wasn't supposed to know about it either, said no more. Instead she changed the subject to that of the Podds.

'*I* remember,' said Monica, who had been silent for so long that the others had almost forgotten that she was there. 'My father used to have a garage business and when a customer needed a really old spare part, that he couldn't get any more, we all used to go up to Podd's and have a good rummage. He owned the scrap yard, you know, on the Clipkirk Road. It's quite near you, isn't it, Ophelia?'

'I'm afraid so.' In fact the scrap yard, with its perpetual columns of burning tyres, made up the principal facet of Moorwind's view, the rest being mainly occupied by the glue factory.

'Not that we were allowed to talk to Mr Podd himself,' continued Monica, 'even if we'd wanted to, which we didn't. He was a terrifyingly morose individual, enough to put anyone off living in sin.'

'Oh, of course!' boomed Lady Tartleton. 'He wouldn't marry that poor woman he lived with, would he?'

'Was that the twins' mother, then?' Ophelia was too interested to be discreet.

'Hilda and Dilys, yes.' Lady Tartleton had now taken over the tale. 'Wonder what happened to them in the end? Surprised you've even heard of 'em. Nice girls, I remember, if a bit on the podgy side. I suppose they just stayed to look after their father after their mother buggered off.'

'She what?'

'Oh yes, she hopped it pretty quickly as soon as they were old enough to fend for themselves. Well, by all accounts, old William Podd had led her a merry dance over the years, and not even a wedding to show for it. Before the war, that must have been. I was only a child, you know, but one heard the servants gossiping. The story was that she'd found another chap, not much better than Podd, but at least he married her. I don't know who he was. After the war, with that dreadful Labour government, we never had a full staff again, just a little couple "what did", so I lost touch with the lower orders.'

'Do you know anything about Trotter's Bottom?'

'No, I told you, we never mixed with the hoi polloi after 'thirty-nine, so I didn't get the chance for all that Lady Chatterley stuff. Not that we ever had a game-keeper. Father liked to do all his killing personally. Who was this Trotter, anyway?'

Ophelia explained, but the others all declared themselves baffled.

'He was a close man, was Podd,' said Edgar approvingly. 'Owned plenty a-land, all about Rambleton. Reckon it were fer the tax, if he gave it to his bairns.'

'What happened to it when he died? He is dead, I assume?'

'Oh aye, some thirty year back. He had some business partner, I reckon. It maybe went to him. That scrap yard's bin leased to young Mick McIsles fer twenty-five year or more.'

Ophelia knew Mick McIsles by sight, a brown, weather-beaten man of indeterminate age and taciturn manner, who had once, in a fit of gruff generosity, given Hygenus an ancient and rusty set of pram wheels to make into a go-kart. Perhaps she could call in the morning to find out who his landlord was. An enquiry to the Land Registry would be more conventional, but Ophelia was growing impatient.

'This business partner of his . . .?'

'Sshhh!'

Creeping into the fringes of the floodlights, their dim torches suddenly extinguished by the glare, were two bulky figures. They reached the edge of the first paddling pool and bent down, their rather short arms stretching out towards the wallowing pigs. Lady Tartleton raised her shotgun and aimed.

'No, don't—' began Ophelia, and Lady Tartleton turned angrily. At that moment one of the dogs barked and the two pig-rustlers dropped their burdens and fled. Lady Tartleton fired after them.

'I got one!' she cried in jubilation. 'Peppered him in the arm. Come on now, after them. Tally-ho!'

But the dark figures, with a surprisingly efficient jogging shuffle, had already reached the woods which fringed Yardley Farm and not even the dogs, who had become distracted by last month's smoked salmon sandwiches in Horatio's pocket, could hope to find them again.

Chapter Eighteen

Opening Preparation

'I have not the slightest hesitation,' said Sergeant Booking portentously, 'in declaring that the brains behind this operation is . . .'

'Are,' Claire corrected him.

'What?'

'Brains are. Brain is.'

'Brain or brains, what does it matter?' Sergeant Booking, along with most of Rambleton, mistrusted an excess of either. 'The brains behind this operation are those of Ophelia O.'

'But Mrs O. was there when Lady Tartleton saw the thieves.'

'Exactly. And very conveniently, too. She turned up at Yardley Farm, in the middle of the night, with no rational explanation,' (Ophelia, of course, when questioned, could not admit to having been at Hilda's post-mortem) 'and just happened to provide herself with a clever-sounding alibi. But who was it that distracted Lady

Tartleton and allowed the thieves, or perhaps I should say *her accomplices*, to get away scot free? Answer me that one.'

'Lady Tartleton doesn't think they got away scot free. She says that she shot one of them. Do the Rambleton police condone that type of vigilante action, Sergeant Booking?'

'The Rambleton police,' said their representative stiffly, 'are on the side of the law, order and the maintenance of social discipline. Our task would be quite considerably assisted if the media were to adopt a more responsible attitude. I'm sure the *Courier* has no real desire to stir up anarchy and mayhem in our happy little town.' He said this stoutly, trying not to think about the pathologist's report lying on his desk. *Certainly poisoned*, indeed! These people watched too much television. And, even if it was true, where was he to start, looking for a proprietary kitchen scourer so common that even the woman who cleaned the police station used it? He supposed he'd have to call in the C.I.D. at Scorsdale after all, but meanwhile he would single-handedly recover Lady Tartleton's pigs. So much more appropriate to Rambleton, and undoubtedly a better class of victim.

'Of course not,' said Claire, thinking, after a week back in Rambleton, that a little anarchy and mayhem would make a rather pleasant change. 'Er, these accomplices? Would you hazard a guess at their identities?'

'Certainly. They are:' he made a gesture as though reading from a notebook. 'Number One: Malachi O., a noted troublemaker, unemployed, Irish (which almost certainly means terrorist links) whom I caught, recently, climbing out of a town centre window with no trousers on. Number Two: Pauline, *alias* Polly Dragoman, Mrs O.'s secretary and close confidante. Number Three: Gareth Grobbett, Pauline Dragoman's boyfriend, self-employed butcher heard recently complaining about the scarcity of pork. And all four have form.'

'Really?'

'Oh yes. Mr and Mrs O. – driving with excess alcohol. On the same occasion, mind, and causing a mutual collision. One could practically call it conspiracy.'

'Sounds dreadful.'

'So it was. I know the officer who arrested them, their next-door neighbour, actually. It seems that they thought moving their cars around on their own drive was an activity exempt from the ministrations of the Law. But as the Inspector said, what about his clematis? Eighteen month ban, they both got. Pity it's run out now.'

'And the other two?'

'Oh yes. Miss Dragoman was cautioned for cycling on the pavement. Eleven she'd have been then, quite old enough to know better. And Grobbett's been convicted for criminal damage to a municipal litter bin. Lit a firework in it, by all accounts. A dangerous crew, Miss Lamb, a dangerous crew. We're counting on your efforts to get them under lock and key as soon as possible.'

Claire nodded dumbly, wondering whether there could be anything in it. She was growing rather fond of the O. family, now that she was used to their ebullience, and could not imagine any of them involved in a major porcine heist. On the other hand, Ophelia had never provided an explanation for that old matter of the mortgage bandits and Claire was almost sure that she had seen her, the other evening outside the Grand Hotel, desperately tugging a luxuriant moustache from her upper lip. Claire hadn't liked to look too closely, but that kind of thing was scarcely *normal*.

On the other hand, Gordon's credentials as the pig-rustler were growing daily. Claire had offered to take over the Glade-Rivers' laundry entirely, much to Tansy's relief, and had used the excuse to carry bundles of soggy clothing through the yard, past Gordon's shed, to the rotary drier by the back gate. The washing, of course, hung in the drizzle with hardly even a breeze, never grew any drier, but none of the family noticed that, and it gave Claire an excellent opportunity to audit the peculiar sounds from the shed. And they were remarkably peculiar sounds: squeaks, grunts and the scurrying of very small feet. The grunts and the louder squeaks, she would have said, were definitely piggish in origin, but even the smallest piglets would surely scamper with a heavier tread than this, and Lady Tartleton's weaners, by all accounts, would by now be growing quite hefty. The smell, too, as she discovered when she placed her nose to the edge of the door, although rancid and foul, had something too acrid, insufficiently earthy, to be derived from a pig. Unfortunately, she had little time now to find out, for she was due back in Manchester on Monday morning, and an inordinate amount of the weekend was likely to be taken up in the Saint Wilgefortis charade. She sighed, and went to see a woman about a prize-winning Yorkshire terrier.

★ ★ ★

This, thought Mortimer Bradley, standing in the middle of the refectory and surveying the bustle around him, was his favourite part of the whole weekend. It was Friday evening, half an hour before the first round was due to begin, and the room was filling up nicely. Already there was a hint of the comfortable stuffiness which, by Sunday evening, would become a thick fug of sweat, weak coffee and cheese and onion sandwiches with the faint whiff of forbidden tobacco. Now, however, the heat and fetor were only hinted at by the haste with which his assistants set up the last few boards, enjoying their own manufactured panic, the weary energy of the bookstall proprietor and the first few chess players, relieved at finding the unfamiliar venue, who threw their drenched anoraks over the backs of chairs while they greeted old rivals and ostentatiously practised sophisticated lines which they had no intention of playing in the actual tournament.

Major Lamb strutted past, his scarlet face manifestly averted. During their brief reconciliation, Mortimer had invited the Major to act as controller for the Novice and Minor sections and, despite the resumption of hostilities, Major Lamb was determined to hang on to his authority. Mortimer hoped that it would be all right. The intricacies of the Swiss pairing system could be tricky, especially during the final rounds. The problem, for example, of whether a player on two and a half points should be challenged by an opponent on three points, or rewarded with one on only two, was always a difficult one, and liable to lead to bitter exchanges, especially if one of the players was forced to be Black twice or three times in a row. These dilemmas, feared Mortimer, would not be amenable to resolution by military discipline. Never mind, he told himself, no use in anticipating trouble. He wished he knew, though, what he was supposed to have done to old Fred this time. They had agreed to differ on the adjournment rules, though it broke Mortimer's heart even to think of these dreadful quickplay finishes, but all this pig business was quite incomprehensible. Too much bully-beef, thought Mortimer, whose brief period of National Service had given him no great affection for the Army, and who was serious about his food.

Anyway, the draw was up for the first round, and there was unlikely to be anything badly wrong with that. Around the room, Sellotaped to the ancient oak panelling, were small sheets of paper with lists of names and board numbers. The lists for the top two sections, in Mortimer's large italics, were visible from several yards away, but the Novice and Minor lists, inscribed by the Major in a style intended to save valuable paper and prevent enemy interception, required close inspection and a degree of lateral thinking which was, thankfully, quite common among chess players.

Mortimer was making a final check of the arbiter's table, ensuring that sufficient ball-point pens were available, when the door into the refectory opened with a bang. He frowned, hoping that not too great a proportion of the Novice section would have taken a detour *via* the Ram's Leg. But the procession which now entered, although chattering excitedly, was not drunk on wine. At its head strutted Zuke, his worries temporarily forgotten, a proud beam spreading across his round face. He stopped in front of Mortimer and gave a brief bow.

'Mr Bradley? I am Alexander Zhukovsky, grand-master. You have perhaps heard of me?'

'Oh certainly, certainly, Mr Zhukovsky. And I understand that you will do us the honour of playing this weekend. Board One in the Open section.'

Zhukovsky nodded. 'Excellent, excellent. And these ladies?'

Mortimer looked, aghast, at the neat line of sisters behind Zhukovsky. A few reddened beneath their short grey veils and one gave a smothered giggle.

'What? They all want to play?'

'Precisely. They have been specially coached for the occasion. Haven't you, ladies?' One or two of the sisters smiled beatifically and then wondered whether they were being immodest.

'But there's, what, twelve or thirteen of them?'

'Fourteen,' said Zuke proudly. 'Even the Reverend Mother is to do us the honour of taking part.'

'Or, er, excellent.' Mortimer dared not offend the first grandmaster he had ever netted, and it was, of course, quite usual to have one or two late entries, though they did spoil the wall charts rather, but fourteen all at once! It was almost enough for a section in itself. That gave him an idea.

'A wonderful suggestion, Mr Zhukovsky. But I'm sure the nuns wouldn't want to play in any of the main sections of the tournament. They'd have to, you know, play against *men*. Perhaps if we were to set up some more tables over here at the edge of the hall . . .?'

'Certainly not,' said Mother Thérèse with the quiet authority that had terrified postulants for the past sixty years. 'We are doing this to draw attention to the plight of our Institute. We can't do that by hiding ourselves away in a corner and not competing against anyone else. Why, we could do that in our own recreation room.'

Mortimer couldn't see why that was such a bad idea.

'We need *victories*, Mr Bradley. Solid victories that will put the public on our side. I understand that the Press will be attending this event?'

'Sort of,' muttered Mortimer, the abundance of whose beard was not affording him his usual authority. The *Rambleton Courier*, as usual, had promised to send someone, and he had heard that the old *Weekend Chess Player*, what was it called now, *Zwichenzug*? were covering the tournament, but neither was exactly a mass-market publication.

'I defy anyone to counter my Scandinavian Defence,' said Mother Thérèse, with a ferocity that Mortimer had not imagined a nun to possess.

'Very well. The Novice section, then?'

'I'm afraid not. "Novice" has rather a particular meaning for us religious, you know. For us, as professed Sisters, to enter a Novice section would be tantamount to unmaking our solemn vows. I'm sure that you understand.'

Mortimer had never been less sure of anything in his life.

'I think I shall try the Major,' continued Mother Thérèse in the tone of a discerning customer at the cheese counter, 'but I believe that most of the others prefer to remain strictly Minor. Like the Friars, you know.'

If Mortimer did not, then this was certainly not the time to admit it.

'I'll, er, go and fill in some more pairing cards,' he mumbled, and shuffled away, glad that he had had the foresight to pack a bottle of whisky in with the spare pieces.

Though neither Mortimer nor Mother Thérèse knew it, one of the representatives of the Press, of whom so much was expected, was already in the room, clinging to a chair against the wall and wishing that he wasn't. It was all Arabella's idea as usual, that he should play in the tournament himself as a way of approaching Zhukovsky.

'It's really time you overcame this phobia,' she had said, the stridency of her voice diminished not in the slightest by the minuscule nature of the negligee she had been wearing at the time. 'The days of fashionable neuroticism are over, Markie. It's all tough love now. Anyway, I can't be here to hold your hand for ever. Or any other bits of you, come to that.' She had disappeared under the bedclothes at that point and somehow the thread of conversation had been lost but it was still true that only one thing frightened Marcus more than the idea of actually playing competitive chess, and that was defying Arabella. He had even phoned Head Office to confess and ask what to do, but when he had asked for *Zugzwang!* the switchboard girl had claimed not to know what he was talking about.

'D'ye mean *Chess'n'Cheese*?' she said eventually.

'It's merged with some gerbil magazine, see. Who shall I say is calling?'

This had been too much for Marcus, who had replaced the receiver and headed for the library. The lady there had proved much more helpful, nodding at him through her half-moon spectacles as though there was nothing strange about his request. He was still holding the book now, gripping its sweaty cover as though it were a talisman. He looked down at the title, *Enjoy Hamsters*, and gave a hollow laugh. Sometimes he wondered whether he would ever enjoy anything again.

'Can you see us, Mummy?' piped a voice from the back of the throng which pressed against the Novice pairing list.

'Grumpphh,' replied Ophelia, fighting her way to the front and taking a mouthful of her neighbour's donkey jacket. 'Oh, here we are. What's this one. *Calipher Q.* I think that must be me. Board twenty-three, Black. And *Toon C.* must be you, I think. Board five, and you're White.'

'Who'm I playing?' asked Joan, entering the details in her brand new scorebook, but her mother had been trampled underfoot by a pair of rampaging twelve-year-olds and was in no condition to reply.

'Ladies and gentlemen!' thundered the voice of the Tournament Director. The surreptitious whisky had done its work and Mortimer had regained his confidence. 'If you would just take your seats now. The Humbert Havelock Memorial Congress is about to begin!'

Chapter Nineteen

Bishop's Ending

If any of the chess players arriving at the convent in the driving rain, parking on the soaked gravel and flinging themselves into the sanctuary of the warm, dry hall, had, from some masochistic impulse, paused on the drive and peered into the dark shadows of the Alderman Penbury Comprehensive School next door, they might have seen a small dancing point of light in the distance, where the last of the school buildings met the tussocky games field. But none did, for they were sensible men (and a very few women), prepared to make reasonable sacrifices for their sport but with no unhealthy desire for pneumonia or the nasty shivery sensation of sitting for four hours with a damp collar.

So (for the caretaker, suspecting, after forty years of janitorial experience, that despite the chess congress's change of venue this year, he would end up having to sort something out, extra chairs or a faulty sandwich toaster, had gone to stay with his sister for the weekend), there was no one to witness the bulky figure, muttering beneath his breath, who struggled with his torch, a piece of wire, and the lock of No. 2 Physics Lab.

'Twist it up, hold it tight, one, two three and jerk the bugger!' recited Gordon Glade-Rivers, suiting his actions to the words, but once again the piece of wire stood impassively in his fingers and the lock remained unbroached.

A fruity cough came from behind him.

'I told yer that you'd not manage it by yerself. Here, let's 'ave a go.'

The speaker, a wiry middle-aged man engulfed in a large and smelly overcoat, elbowed Gordon aside and gave the wire a confident flick. The lock made a quick cracking noise. The man opened the door and gestured, with an ironic bow, for Gordon to enter.

'Thank you. Er, thank you, Mr Skate.'

The man wagged a yellow-stained finger at him. 'Albert, Albert. We bin colleagues too long now t'bother with that Mister lark. Any road, burgling were me dad's trade, like. I could've done that lock when I were in nappies. When I,' he repeated emphatically, 'were in soddin' nappies.'

'And it was very kind of you, Albert. Now . . .'

'*Now*,' echoed Albert, perversely taking up the cue, 'now you'll not see a decent job like that fer love n'money. Take our Darren. Criminal damage, ABH, carryin' a 'fensive weapon. In't no skill in them lot, is there? 'Spec' you find the same with your lad, do yer?'

'Not at all,' Gordon had been about to reply loyally, but then he remembered Giles' unhelpfulness on the matter of the keys. 'Well actually . . .'

'Fought so. Bloody ungratification. Blame 'is mother, I do. Give 'im fancy ideas. D'je know, age of eight, what that kid says 'e wants to be when 'e grows up?'

'Er, fireman, train driver, policeman?'

Albert spat on the path and the little heap of phlegmy bubbles glinted under the light of Gordon's torch.

'Nah, wan't that bad. No, 'e wants to be a con-man, dun't e? Effing con-man! You in't got the brains, I telled im, and I were right, weren't I?'

'I couldn't say,' equivocated Gordon, remembering that the only time he had met Darren Skate, an anaemic nineteen-year-old, the boy had been vomiting into Tansy's bicycle basket. 'Now, I'm very grateful . . .' The chink of coins could have been heard, if the caretaker had been there to hear anything, followed by Albert's grunt of contempt and the apologetic rustle of paper. Albert stuffed the notes into his pocket and scurried off into the darkness.

Meanwhile, inside the convent, the first round of the chess tournament was well into the opening moves. Ophelia sat at the end of the room, under a portrait of the Founder, Louise Thierry. She had taken a beginners' chess book out of the library that lunchtime, basking, like Marcus before her, under the approving half-moon spectacles of Letitia Lamb, and had spent the afternoon memorizing its first chapter, concealed inside the *Law Society's Gazette*. She could scarcely get used to the peace in her office this week, and often found herself gently stroking the now empty cardboard box with a stockinged foot, or whispering maternal endearments to the fan heater. But, although the long slumber of Dodie's first day back with her father had not been repeated, according to Malachi she was apparently contented, thriving, as had her elder brothers and sister, under his erratic care. Ophelia wondered how much earlier she could have left the baby, or, were it not for Major Lamb's outburst, how much longer she would have kept her in the outgrown cardboard crib. She was certainly glad that she had not had to bring Dodie that morning, when she had called in at the scrap yard on her way into work. The noise of drills and heavy-duty saws, the particles of rust filling the air and the smell of leaking engine oil had been almost enough to make Ophelia herself cry, never mind the baby. And it had been a wasted journey for all that, for Mike McIsles had been away 'pickin' up a write-off', and all his assistant could say about the rent was that it was generally collected by some posh bloke with a name like Thistle.

A suppressed cough from her opponent brought her back to the game, and she realized that she had forgotten to press her clock after her last move. Even so, she had only used two minutes of her allotted two hours, while he, a serious elderly man, had already taken half an hour, although they were only on the seventh move. Perhaps he was musing about his week, too, though from his creased forehead and silently moving lips she thought not. He kept darting quick glances at her king, which worried her slightly, although she could not see how he could checkmate her in the next two moves, which was as far as she could calculate. It was not that she expected to win, or even draw, but to be the first to be beaten might be humiliating, and prove a distraction for Joan, who was playing at the other end of the Novices' section, close to where it bordered upon the Minors. She looked down the tables towards her daughter, and was struck suddenly by the hundreds of pieces, and thousands of squares, no board showing the same position, each pawn poised or active, the servant of its master's skill, hazard or inattention. For a moment she saw what Mother Thérèse had meant by 'the Dance', felt herself caught up by the magic of the ancient game, dizzied by the forces of will, desire and intellect which were concentrated in the tiny figures.

Her opponent reached out his hand, and, with a smile, took her queen from the board.

At that point Ophelia decided to use the remainder of her time, of which there was still an inordinate amount, in making a general survey of the tournament, and to give up trying to devise a strategy at all. As she looked up from the board, the first pair of eyes to meet her own were those of Sergeant Booking, who was standing guard on the doorway, accompanied by the sweating Pigeon. The constable had been warned by his brother-in-law, who used to play in his bachelor days, that chess congresses were always freezing cold, and so he had put on two vests and a woolly waistcoat under his navy serge. He was not to know, of course, that the sisters, solicitous for their guests' welfare, had installed extra heating especially for the weekend. Pigeon was feeling anxious, as well as uncomfortable, for he had heard strange noises coming from the school next door, noises which, even after his mere three years on the beat, he recognized instantly as being those of a break-in. But Sergeant Booking refused even to let him go and check.

'Our business here,' he had hissed, 'is with that O. woman. What's she up to, anyway? She doesn't look like a chess player to me.'

'Perhaps she just wants to start,' suggested Pigeon, but he knew that it would be of no use. Booking was of a monomaniac nature and all the force of his old obsession with his wife's infidelity had been entirely transferred to his new preoccupation. And, after all, it was not entirely a change for the worse. Hot and itchy as he was, this was better than walking up and down the road outside the Bookings' bungalow, watching for roving Inspectors, or even, as the Sergeant's suspicions had reached their summit, an elderly Superintendent with distinguished greying temples.

Ophelia nodded to Sergeant Booking and looked around to see how the sisters were getting on in the Minor section. They seemed to be managing better than she had feared, due rather, she suspected, to the paralyzing effect of their habits upon the young men they played, than to any innate chess-playing ability. Some of the older competitors had sisters who had been educated at the convent, and all had heard apocryphal tales of their supernatural powers of detection and punishment. Only Giles, playing steadily under Claire's devoted gaze, was at ease. Sister Hedwig seemed particularly keen, bouncing up and down on her chair as she cogitated and making her moves with little noises of excitement which flustered her opponent so thoroughly that he had already thrown away a knight and two pawns. Sister Eulalia, as might be expected, was less enthusiastic, although she had recovered from the shocked state in which Ophelia had seen her in the Infirmary. She obviously found it hard to concentrate on the game, however, and made constant trips through the small side door which led to the kitchen. In these expeditions she was frequently joined by Felicity and Perpetua, one of whom, Ophelia noticed, had her arm in a sling. Surely they had no need to check up on the refreshments, she thought, for Jason Spikewort, anxious to assist with anything that might, even tangentially, be of comfort to Zuke, had offered to prepare and serve these himself. Probably the sisters were merely taking the long way around to the lavatories.

Mother Thérèse, in the Major section, was already creating something of a sensation, with players leaving their own games to come and watch her. From where she was sitting, Ophelia could see the old lady's grey-veiled head bent low over the board and her papery thin hand reaching confidently for the pieces and the clock. Next to her sat Arabella, who was playing against the bishop. The combination of Arabella's cleavage and the proximity of the Reverend Mother, about whom he still felt guilty, had evidently been too much for him, and he was standing forlornly on the other side, munching one of Jason's corned beef sandwiches. Finally, Ophelia looked towards the Open section, the smallest group, but arguably the most diverse. Zuke was the only entrant whom she recognized, playing against a nervous young man who still clutched, under his left arm, a library copy of

Enjoy Hamsters. The only thing the others had in common was that they were all male. One, a dusty little bearded man who looked as though he were kept in a sunless attic, and only brought out for chess tournaments, kept a lit pipe in one pocket and a newspaper in the other. Periodically he would wander to the doorway, where smoking was permitted, and refresh himself with either or both of these diversions. Ophelia watched him in fearful fascination, waiting for the moment at which he would replace one or other item in the wrong pocket, and set himself on fire. His opponent, by contrast, was a huge blond Scandinavian. He and his equally blonde girlfriend, who sat nearby reading a magazine, seemed, in their glowing perfection, not so much of a different nationality from the grubby English, but of a different quiddity, as though a contingent of Norse gods had descended on this all too mortal gathering.

The evening wore on and the games became more intense, as the early finishers, finding no bar at the convent, adjourned to the Ram's Leg. Jason was obviously busy in the kitchen, for Ophelia could hear, in the quietness, the sounds of cupboards and drawers being opened and closed as he searched, for the cheese-grater, perhaps, or some extra teaspoons. She smiled apologetically at her opponent, who had evidently expected her to resign some two hours ago. She could not explain to him that this seat, on the raised section at the end of the refectory, was such an excellent and inconspicuous vantage-point that she was reluctant to relinquish it. She looked at her watch. Five to ten. She had asked Malachi to collect her at ten, if she had not telephoned him first.

In any case, there was no evidence of murderous intent on the part of any of the chess players, not even that of the inscrutable Scandinavians, who could, presumably, strike the whole company with a thunderbolt if they so desired. Carefully, as Joan had showed her, she laid her king upon his side, stopped the clock and held out her hand to her opponent.

He never had the chance to take it. Suddenly, through the cerebral hush of the hall, came a blood-curdling shriek, like that of a small animal caught in a trap. It came from the direction of the school laboratories, through the doorway patrolled by Sergeant Booking and the now wilting Pigeon. The chess players froze, hands in mid-air, offers of draws hanging unanswered, but none left his seat.

From the depths of the convent, on the other side of the kitchen, came answering squeals and the clatter of small cloven feet on the flagged stone floor. A squawk of a slightly lower timbre, which Ophelia recognized as Jason's, heralded a stream of thundering weaners from the kitchen door, followed by Innocent, his face lit up with delight, crying 'Piggie! Piggie!' After him came Malachi, clutching Dodie to his woolly chest and finally, elbowing each other to reach the pigs, Pius, Hygenus and Urban.

The piglets fled out of the main door, past the two guarding policemen. Constable Pigeon made a gallant attempt to catch one, but it slid through his large hands and escaped with its fellows.

'Don't waste your time with that, man!' snapped Sergeant Booking.

'But I thought we were looking for the pigs, sir?'

'We're looking,' corrected his superior, 'for the pig-*nappers*. And now we've got them.' He grasped Malachi's sleeve just as he, too, was about to trot out of the door. 'Mr O., I am arresting you on suspicion of theft. You are not obliged to say anything, but if you mention anything, I mean if you do not mention something . . .'

As Sergeant Booking struggled with the newly worded caution, Ophelia, abandoning the attempt to shake hands with her apparently catatonic opponent, thundered down the hall.

'You ridiculous little man!' she shouted. 'Why on earth should Mal want to steal Lady Tartleton's pigs? He's obviously just trying to catch them.'

'I was *trying*,' said Malachi mournfully, 'to catch Innocent. I don't care about the bloomin' pigs, but Innie wanted a wee, and goodness knows where he's going to do it now.'

'Quite right,' said Sister Hedwig. 'This is blatant police harassment. I shall complain to the Chief Constable.'

'You can't,' said Sergeant Booking as Innocent trotted back into the hall, rather wet, especially around his trousers. 'He's gone to the Seychelles for a fortnight. But I've got his deputy with me. I asked him along especially, in case of encountering this type of Bolshevism. Mr Snodsworth?'

The old man uncurled himself from the chair in which he had been sitting, almost invisible in the shadows. 'Client . . .' he began.

'Mr Snodsworth,' began Malachi, in whom Ophelia had, in what had, up to that point, been wifely wisdom, not confided her alternative identity as Oliver. 'You know me, don't you? I'm married to your assistant solicitor, Ophelia. Look, here she is. You do realize, don't you, that there must have been a mistake?'

Mr Snodsworth looked slowly from Malachi to Ophelia and back again. He opened his mouth, placed his tongue against its roof in preparation for the sound 'Cl' and then, with a little click, recovered his full powers of speech.

'Oh no,' he said, with dreadful distinctness. 'I don't employ any lady solicitors. That's a man, you know, dressed up as my daily woman. I can't think what the world is coming to, allowing people like that out in public.'

'Oh *no*,' groaned Joan, her irritation at having the tournament interrupted now superseded by the prospect of having to bring up four brothers and a sister alone, with both parents serving long terms of penal servitude. The same idea occurred to Pius, with the sole difference that he imagined himself doing the upbringing.

'Quick!' he said. 'Let's do the haunting now!'

'But where's the bishop?' In mufti, with neither mitre, dog collar nor crozier, he could be any one of thirty or forty mild and middle-aged men. Helpfully, he stood up.

'If I can be of any assistance—'

'Right. And what about Claire?'

'There she is,' said Urban. 'I think she's trying to hide.'

'Come on then, Claire. We won't bother about the

beard. Let's just get started. It might distract them a bit.'

If Claire had previously had any mild misgivings about her role as Saint Wilgefortis, they were overcome now by the definite and unequivocal knowledge that there was nothing in the world that she wished to do less than stand up in front of a room full of chess players, on a floor now smeared with evidence of the pigs' traversal, and pretend to be a medieval princess with a facial hair problem. Unfortunately, she was unable to think of an alternative.

'I am the lovely Wilgefortis,' she recited, as if in a trance, as she wove her way through the chairs and tables towards the front of the hall, 'otherwise known as Uncumber, daughter of the King of Portugal. I have vowed never to marry, but to devote my life to the service of God.'

'I am the King of Sis-silly,' roared Hygenus. 'No one knows what my name is, but it might have been Bert. I want to marry her. (Not in real life, of course,' he hastened to assure his audience, '''cos she's got a boyfriend and I don't like girls anyway.) Can I marry her, King of Portugal?'

'Yes, my dear Bert,' said Pius seriously. 'You are worthy of my lovely daughter, and in any case it'll be useful having another king in the family. We can borrow each other's crowns if ours are being mended. How about Saturday?'

'No!' shrieked Claire with a hysteria that was not entirely manufactured. 'I've told you that I'm not going to get married!'

'You'll do as your parents tell you,' snapped Pius in a tone that Ophelia recognized, unpleasantly, as her own after a long day. 'Come along, young lady.'

'Oh God, please help me! What shall I do? Oh, gosh, what's this growing on my face?' Claire rummaged in her handbag and improvised with a tissue. 'Look, Father, I've grown a beard. Does King Bert still want to marry me?'

'No, I bloomin' well don't,' said King Bert stoutly. 'You look horrible. What shall we do with her, King – what's your name, Pi?'

'I haven't got one,' hissed Pius. 'I'm just the King of Portugal.'

'What shall we do with her, just-the-King-of-Portygall?'

'I think we'll have to kill her.'

'Then I'll be a saint,' said Claire calmly, feeling that Wilgefortis' crucifixion was possibly preferable to this public humiliation.

'I want my mummy!' wailed Urban, remembering half of his one line, and meaning it.

Ophelia stepped forward to pick him up as Pius and Hygenus began to manhandle Claire towards the arbiter's table.

'Get off me now,' she said, pushing them away. 'We've finished it. I'm not really going to die, you know.'

It was only a gentle push, but Pius' foot slid on a slimy patch of pig dung and he was forced to perform an uncharacteristically athletic somersault in order to regain his footing. A piece of paper fell out of his pocket and fluttered down beside Urban. Ophelia picked them both up at once.

'But this is Trotter's Bottom!' she cried, and, indeed, it was an exact copy of the map which Zuke had given her, though with the corner containing the name and pig motif torn off.

'Don't be silly,' said Pius. 'You're assessed with that place. And it's not a treasure map either, like Hygenus thought. We worked it out in the end. It's just a map of Moorwind Farm before the bungalow was built. Look, you can see all the barns and the pigsties and the biggest of the trees. We found another piece of paper with it but that's really boring. *Deed of Gift*, it's called, all about someone called Mr Podd. Look, I've got that as well.'

He delved into his pocket and brought out, together with half a Snickers bar and some football cards, a rubbed and dog-eared legal document. But by then, the collective attention had switched to a board halfway down the Minor section, where Sister Eulalia had fainted into her few remaining pawns. With a little chirrup of freedom, the last piglet ran out from under her habit.

Chapter Twenty

Recording Moves

'Look, sir!' cried Constable Pigeon, as the piglet nipped between the Sergeant's legs and out into the cold night. 'It must have been the nuns all along.'

'That's right,' said a piercing voice behind him. Sisters Perpetua and Felicity stood in the kitchen doorway, rueful expressions on their walnut faces. 'We'll come with our hands up. Well, three out of four hands, anyway. Lady Tartleton shot Felicity's other one.'

'But . . . but . . .' Sergeant Booking was reluctant to relinquish his arrest of Malachi. 'What on earth did you want with a load of pigs? You're trying to shield some-one, aren't you?'

'We were called,' said Sister Felicity simply, and then, catching a stern look from Mother Thérèse, 'At least, we thought we were called. Just after we'd had to give up the hedgehog sanctuary, Mrs Pottlebonce came round with that badge on her coat. Then we were walking one afternoon near Yardley Farm and we saw them all, so miserable and cold in those awful great paddling pools. We just thought it was our duty to rescue them. We've looked after them terribly well, in the little outhouse and fed them with the kitchen scraps. Eulalia helped us, you know. She said she'd got pigs in the blood.'

At the sound of her name, Sister Eulalia raised her head from the board. 'Do they know, now?' she asked in a tremulous voice.

'Yes, dear, they know all about it. And Father Jim will hear our confessions. I'm sure he won't be too harsh on us, even if we do get sent to prison.'

'Is that what you were feeling guilty about?' burst in Ophelia. 'Just looking after the stolen pigs?'

'Yes of course.' Sister Eulalia's face had resumed its old tranquillity. 'What else could there be?'

'Er, nothing. Nothing at all.' Ophelia's mind, honed by the chess game, was thinking fast. If Moorwind Farm was actually Trotter's Bottom, then it had not belonged to Jas. Spikewort at all, regardless of all the rumours about the tractor's part in his death. But she was sure, when they had bought the property, that the vendors had been the executors of his estate. Suddenly she realized who it was that was so desperate to suppress that Deed of Gift, desperate enough to murder the sister who remembered it and came home to claim her rights, desperate enough to steal the file that referred to it, to attack the only solicitor to have read the file and to search for the deed itself—

'Quickly!' she shouted. 'Never mind the pigs. Just get him!'

She dashed into the kitchen, followed by the thundering Constable Pigeon. They were just in time. Jason had taken the opportunity afforded by the weaners' escape to make one final and chaotic search of the kitchen, pulling out drawers, ripping open boxes and rifling through the bins of flour and rice. Thus engaged, he had not at first heard the conversation about the map, and did not realize that the deed had already been found. Only with Ophelia's final cry was he certain that the game was up. Unfortunately for him, the old sink was high and needed a chair to reach it, while the window above was stiff with the cold and its haphazard layers of paint. He had just managed to open it and raise one foot to the frame when Constable Pigeon grasped him firmly around the waist and set him back down on the floor, with no more difficulty than if he had been a tiny child. He stood beneath the policeman's great paw, floury and dishevelled, and scowled across the pine table, that had kept his secret for so long.

Ophelia ran back through to find Sergeant Booking, but he, along with the sisters and the rest of the O. family, had finally followed the weaners outside.

'Don't you worry,' said Constable Pigeon, producing a pair of handcuffs from beneath the woolly waistcoat. 'He won't be going far. You go and find out what's happening with them pigs. Funny, I'd always thought of this as a peaceful sort of place.'

Outside it was still raining heavily and the light in the No. 2 Physics Lab beckoned across the gleaming asphalt. Inside, it was a different matter. Halfway down one of the long benches stood Gordon in his third best corduroys, staring in horror at the squelching mass of pig that besieged him. In front of him stood a piece of electronic apparatus from which, at thirty second intervals, a faint and caressing moaning sound was emitted. At each of those moans the weaners went wild, raising themselves up on their hind legs in yearning towards the machine and rubbing themselves affectionately against Gordon's Hush Puppies.

'Do you have an explanation for this, sir?' asked Sergeant Booking. He spoke with a quiet confidence, sure that this time his arrest could not be thwarted. It was disappointing that the man was not an O., even rather shocking that he should have a double-barrelled name, for Sergeant Booking held old-fashioned ideas of social hierarchy, but an arrest, after all, was an arrest, and a mere Glade-Rivers was nothing in comparison to a real Lady vindicated.

'Do you mean an electro-physical explanation,' asked Gordon, 'or a biological one?'

'An explanation,' blustered Sergeant Booking, going rather red in the face, 'as to why you have enticed twenty valuable stolen animals into this laboratory like a modern day, a modern day—'

'Pied Piper,' supplied Pius helpfully.

'That's exactly it,' said Gordon. 'Clever lad. This is my prototype Hamelinoscope. I came across the story in one of my wife's poetry books and it occurred to me that, in these days of animal liberation, a humane method of removing pests might make my name – I mean might be of great value to society. I've been experimenting for some time in my shed – my personal laboratory – but I haven't managed to get the frequency quite right yet. The idea is, you see, that the electronic emissions mimic the call of the mother rat to her offspring. Unfortunately all the baby rats I tested it on took no notice, just finished polishing off my Bath Olivers. Very expensive, too, those Bath Olivers. I get them sent up from Fortnum's especially.'

'Very nice too, I'm sure,' said Sergeant Booking with some asperity, for his own supper had been sacrificed to the importance of his mission. 'But it doesn't explain . . .'

'Oh, it does, officer, if you'd take the time to listen. You wouldn't, if you don't mind my saying so, be a very sympathetic television interviewer. Create the space for your guest to create his own story. That's the idea. After all, you're not trying to become a celebrity yourself, are you? Now then, what do you know about the behaviour of sound waves within a graduated environment? Not much, I'll bet. Well, basically, my idea was that if the Hamelinoscope could be utilized in an enlarged internal space, preferably with audio monitoring equipment available, then the experiment might achieve a satisfactory outcome.'

'You thought the rats would come if you made the noise in here?' confirmed Sergeant Booking, busy with his notebook.

Gordon sniffed. 'Put very crudely, yes. Sadly, I had omitted to calculate the effect of the laboratory benches, which served to diminish as well as to amplify the sound. Evidently the Glade-Rivers Hamelinoscope has proved effective, although upon a different species than was its original intention. I imagine, however, that there may be a significant market for the product within the agricultural sector.'

'You're not in league with these nuns, then?'

'With *nuns*? Certainly not. Outmoded personification of a pre-scientific superstition. Why, I imagine that they scarcely know the value of a truly empirical observation, never mind how to lay out a decent press release.'

'Quite so, sir, quite so.' Sergeant Booking ripped four or five pages from his notebook with sudden ferocity. 'Well, it doesn't look as though I can charge you with more than breaking and entering, and that's really a matter for the school to decide. Just keep these pigs safely in here, will you, and I'll get Lady Tartleton to send someone down for them. Bloody hell, what a Friday! My famous pig-rustlers just a bunch of dotty old nuns – can't see the CPS bothering with that one, and their accomplice turns out to be the original mad professor. I could have been in the pub by now. They do a good steak-and-kidney pie on a Friday night. A policeman's lot, eh?'

'We've got a murderer for you in the kitchen, if you like,' offered Ophelia.

As they walked back through the refectory it was as though nothing untoward had happened. Other than the three sisters, Ophelia and Joan, all of the chess players were continuing their games with no more signs of agitation than if the central heating had temporarily become a little noisier. Even Zuke seemed not to have noticed that anything had happened, for he was pursuing his game against Marcus with relish, their heads close together over the few remaining pieces on the board, the same expression of sharp animation on the old and the younger face.

There were now four people in the kitchen: Jason and Constable Pigeon, handcuffed together in mock intimacy, Sister Eulalia, phlegmatically tidying away the spilled foodstuffs, and the tall, saturnine figure of Nick Bottomley.

'He had the right to call his solicitor,' said Pigeon miserably. Nick gave a languid smile.

'I'm pleased to see that you train your junior officers to comply fully with the provisions of PACE,' he drawled. 'And, talking of provisions, I think one of those statutory refreshment breaks is probably called for. I had to leave a rather good dinner to come here, you know. Oh, the trials of being a duty solicitor! Of course you wouldn't know, would you, Ophelia? Parrish's hasn't woken up to the scheme yet, has it?'

'We prefer to leave criminal work,' replied Ophelia, 'to those with a natural inclination for it.'

'I think that refreshment break would be a good idea,' put in Sergeant Booking, cheering up a little. 'One must, as Mr Bottomley says, be very careful to meet with all the legal niceties. Wouldn't do, eh, for your client to get off on the grounds of having had his statutory Rich Tea biscuit denied. You do have some Rich Tea, Sister, er . . .'

Sister Eulalia, without speaking, brought a large tin from the pantry. It proved to contain a sumptuous fruit cake, at which even Jason's sullen expression brightened somewhat.

'So,' said Nick Bottomley, a few minutes later, his

mouth still half full, 'my client is now ready to make a statement.'

'No hurry,' said Sergeant Booking, spraying little pieces of glacé cherry across the table. He had a small tape recorder in his pocket for just these eventualities, but imagined that his own gravitas might be diminished if, when the tape was replayed by the Crown Prosecution Service, or even in court, the sounds of munching were too evident. 'Tell him to have another piece of cake and think it over. He wouldn't want to say anything that he might regret later.'

'No,' said Jason, speaking for the first time. 'No, let's get it over with. There's no point in wasting any more time. You all know that I did it and however much fruit cake you stuff yourselves with, you're not going to forget it. I'll tell you what happened, and then go off to my cosy little cell. It can't be much worse than the Grand Hotel was, before I took it over.

'My father, as I suppose you all know, was Jas. Spikewort. He was William Podd's partner in the scrap yard business. Partner, that was, in so far as the work and the responsibility was concerned. Podd owned all the land and took the lion's share of the profits. My father was pretty feckless anyway, and spent everything he was given, on drink, mainly, and a bit of gambling. Anyway, he didn't complain, because Podd was a good twenty years older than him and it was a sort of understood thing that he would leave Dad the business and all the land in his will. He wasn't married, after all, not legally, and the woman he'd been living with left him so he didn't owe her anything. As for the girls, he couldn't see what a woman would want with a scrap yard and he supposed they'd find husbands to look after them.

'Towards the end of his life, though, when he got ill and spent all his time in hospital, he started brooding over things and got some peculiar ideas. Not quite peculiar enough to be insane, unfortunately, but certainly not characteristic of the stingy old Podd. He got to thinking that he'd not been fair on that woman of his, Peggy, I think she was called, nor to his daughters. It was too late by then to do anything for the girls, as Hilda was off in Russia, which, in those Cold War days, this was the early sixties, mind, was like being dead, only more so, and Dilys was locked up in the convent . . .' He looked up suddenly at Sister Eulalia as though recognizing her for the first time '. . . which wasn't any better. But he decided that Peggy ought to get everything, wherever she was, and to make a will saying so. Now, he'd found out how to draw up a will properly, so he got one of the nurses and Dad, when he called in, to witness it. The nurse, as you'd expect, was pretty busy, and probably didn't really realize that she was signing a will at all, never mind what its provisions were. Dad read it, of course, and felt a bit fed up that he wasn't going to get the scrap yard after all, but he figured that Peggy would need someone to run it for her, so he'd not be destitute. So, it would have all ended there, if it hadn't been that Dad had just started courting. A bit late in the day, he was over forty, but he'd never exactly been the romantic kind. Well, his girlfriend, my mother, was cut from a different cloth. Jas. Spikewort was good enough looking, but hardly smart or sophisticated, but she'd thought that, with the scrap yard doing well and old Podd on his last legs, there'd be a decent enough future in that direction. And I'm afraid that the post of foreman of Peggy's yard wasn't quite what she'd got in mind.

'So, when Old William finally kicked the bucket, and Dad, being his only visitor, was asked to sort out his things, Mum made sure that she was there too. She found the will and saw – Mum was sharp about that sort of thing – that it was all quite legal and binding, so she got rid of it pronto, but not before she'd taught herself to copy the old man's signature. Luckily the nurse had left the hospital, so Mum copied her signature, too, and forged one for the old man who'd been in the bed next to William's and had conveniently popped off the week before. Then she just wrote out a new will, making Dad the sole beneficiary and executor. The will was proved without any difficulty, after all, it was what everybody had expected, and they married and built Moorwind Farm for themselves. Mum thought they'd gone too far up in the world by then for Dad to be working in the scrap yard, so they let it to Mike McIsles and started a little smallholding at Moorwind, or Trotter's Bottom, as it used to be called. Mum thought that the old name was a bit common and, anyway, she didn't like pigs. Hilda had looked after one up there during the early years of the war, for a boyfriend, Dad had said, but the boyfriend never wrote, or, more likely, Podd destroyed the letters, so that in the end she gave up, let her father have the pig for bacon and went off with the Women's Royal Ambulance Corps.

'Well, everything would have been fine if Mum hadn't

been so greedy. The will old Podd had made at the hospital, you see, had referred only to the scrapyard and one or two other pieces of land, but Mum couldn't see why he'd left Trotter's Bottom out of it, so she stuck it in as well. She never knew, you see, and dozy old Dad never remembered, that William had given it to the girls.

'Mum never knew her mistake. She died eight years ago and I took over the deeds. Snodsworth & Ranger had handed them all over to us when the forged will was proved and Mum had kept them under her bed. Well, there was a copy of the Deed of Gift in there, that no one had noticed, and a note – what do you call it?'

'A memorandum of sale,' said Ophelia, whose conveyancing law was better than Nick's.

'That's right, on the last conveyance, so I had to destroy them both and, when Dad died and I wanted to sell Moorwind Farm, I had to swear a statutory declaration that the conveyance had been lost. I didn't mention the Deed of Gift at all.'

'Oh, I remember that now,' said Ophelia. 'It all sounded genuine enough, I must say.'

'It was meant to. I suppose you'll want to know now why I didn't just confess what they'd done and give up the land. After all, it was before I was born that the fraud was carried out. I wouldn't even have known if Mum hadn't told me about it, just before she died. Well, the truth was that I couldn't afford to. Mum's ideas, you see, had got grander and grander as time went on. She encouraged me to be extravagant, and, well, I'm afraid I inherited some of Dad's vices as well. The drink I can generally keep under control, but I'd already run up a string of gambling debts. I know they're not legally enforceable, but I wouldn't last long in the hotel trade with a reputation as a welsher. Anyway, I didn't think it was doing anyone much harm. Peggy, wherever she was, and she'd probably been dead for years, never knew what Podd had intended, and his daughters, as I'd said, were as good as dead. Towards the end of her life Mum had convinced herself, and me too, that William had meant to leave everything to Dad after all, and that the will had just been a temporary aberration, a piece of mischief to amuse him in those final weeks. Probably he had meant to revoke it at the last minute, but left it too long. So, I'd practically forgotten that it wasn't all above board, when the letter came from Hilda reserving the room. Silly cow, instead of just a normal business letter, she rabbited on for pages, all about how she'd been Hilda Podd and was coming home to reclaim Trotter's Bottom and wasn't it a good thing that she'd kept the map after all these years, though she thought that her sister had the actual deed. The only thing she didn't say was what name her sister had taken when she'd taken the veil – perhaps she didn't know – so I wasted a bit of time searching the obvious places in the convent. I managed to get to the library, too, and got rid of that newspaper cutting, though I was so flustered, cutting it out with my nail-scissors while that battle-axe of a librarian watched me over her specs, that I didn't realize until I got back that I'd missed off the headline. I didn't dare go again, though, and attract even more attention.

'Then all I could do was wait for Hilda. Poisoning her was pretty easy, especially with that cat's paw of a doctor, and I thought I was safe once he'd signed that certificate. Her husband knew about Trotter's Bottom, of course, but not where it was. I remember Dad telling me that the name wasn't really used, even in Podd's day, and I never heard anyone call it anything but Moorwind Farm, so I wasn't too worried. Before Podd built the scrap business, it was all part of the same piece of land, so it wasn't mentioned in any legal documents apart from that Deed of Gift. I tried to pinch the map, of course, but I assume he must have given it to you,' here he looked again at Ophelia, 'pretty early on.' She nodded.

'Well, after that there wasn't much point in polishing old Zuke off, even if he had gone blabbing his paranoid suspicions all over the shop. I knew you wouldn't take any notice of him, anyway, Booking.'

Sergeant Booking took a deep breath, but, in consideration of the tape recorder, dared do nothing but sniff.

'I was slow, too, in realizing where Hilda had gone that night. I thought she'd probably been to see her sister, which was safe enough. In any case, not knowing which one her sister was, I could hardly get rid of the whole convent, even given the run of the kitchen like tonight. I'm not really cut out to be a serial killer, you know.' He smiled, a little of the old camp manner returning. '*Much* too fastidious. It was lucky that I'd thought of bugging Mr Zhukovsky's phone. It was very kind of you, Mrs O., to telephone and give me the chance to do something about old Snodsworth before you did. Mind you, I'm glad I didn't actually kill him. At the time I wasn't sure.

In any case he was sufficiently knocked out not to be a threat any more and I was able to grab the file with all the correspondence. It even had another copy Deed of Gift that someone had forgotten to send to the Yorkshire Deeds Registry. But I still didn't have the original document, which *had* to be in the convent somewhere. Offering to do the refreshments tonight was the best way I could think of to get in again. I thought that, if anyone caught me wandering about, they'd just think I was a lost chess player in search of the Gents. It was only when I got here and Sister Eulalia came to show me how to use the tea urn that I saw her up close and knew that she was Dilys. Then I guessed that the deed was somewhere in the kitchen. And I'd have found it, too, and none of you been any the wiser, if it hadn't been for those blasted children.'

He stopped, as the doorway was darkened. It was the blasted children.

'Lady Tartleton's taken the pigs back,' announced Pius, 'and she doesn't want the sisters to be arrested.'

'She's taken Professor Glade-Rivers with her too,' added Joan. 'They're going to work together on a – a commercial application for the Hamelinoscope.' She finished in a rush.

Hygenus noticed the handcuffs.

'Ooh, is that a burglar?'

'Murderer, actually,' said Constable Pigeon cheerfully. Urban began to cry.

'Is that so?' said Zuke, coming in arm-in-arm with Marcus. 'I wondered whether it might be Mr Spikewort, but it seemed, how do you say it? – discourteous to suggest such a thing, after so many cups of tea on the roof.'

'On the house,' Jason corrected him, 'though it's kind of you to mention it. I suppose I should apologize for poisoning your wife. She seemed a very nice lady, the little I saw of her.'

'She was,' said Zuke sadly. 'She was indeed.' He turned to Marcus. 'At least now you have a good story for your *Zugzwang!* There cannot be many chess tournaments at which murderers are unmasked.'

'I don't even know whether it is my *Zugzwang!* any more. It's been taken over, apparently, and merged with a gerbil magazine. Never mind. After that game, I think I'll take up competitive chess again. I'd forgotten how much I enjoyed it.'

'It was an excellent game,' said Zuke judiciously, 'and the draw was a very fair result. I'm sure the new owners of your magazine will be delighted to keep you as their editor.'

'Yes,' said Hygenus thoughtfully. He grasped Innocent's sticky palm. 'Yes, I should 'magine they will.'

Epilogue

The Immortal Game

'May perpetual light shine on her for ever, for You are rich in mercy,' concluded Fr Jim, and the bishop joined him to give the final blessing. No one wanted to be the first to leave the graveside, but the cold wind blew along the backs of their legs and turned their valedictory prayers to thoughts of the funeral tea.

Sister Hedwig caught up with Ophelia on the church path.

'I'm glad Father Jim gave the sermon, aren't you? He might not be the Church's greatest theologian, but he always manages to say what's really important.'

'Well, it would have been a bit embarrassing for the bishop, considering how she died. Giles was watching the game, you know, and he said it was a marvellous checkmate. Even Zuke was impressed. It's a shame she didn't take up chess earlier.'

'Oh, I don't know. I can't see Mother Thérèse regretting anything. I'm sure she's celebrating her victory now.

We're wondering what to do with her prize money. Perpetua and Felicity want to buy a chess set for the recreation room, but it hardly seems worth it, just for a few months.'

'I suppose you could take it to Scorsdale with you.'

'Mmm. It wouldn't be the same, though.'

'Look, Sister Hedwig, I do wish you'd reconsider taking Moorwind Farm. After all, you are its legal owners, or, at least, Sister Eulalia is.'

'Nonsense. We've been through all that. It's your family home, you paid for it and you've brought life to it. It's not as though it would make any difference anyway. The bishop's determined to close down the Institute.'

The two women walked down the path in silence until Lady Tartleton joined them.

'Heard about my pig man, then?' she boomed.

'Albert Skate? No. I thought you'd sacked him.'

'Wish I hadn't. He's worth a damn sight more than I am, now. He called around to tell me, full of dribbling glee, said he wanted me to be the first to hear. You remember that Peggy, old Podd's common-law wife, was supposed to have married again after she left him?'

'Oh yes?'

'Well, they've traced her. Turns out she married old Josiah Skate, and Albert's her son and heir. He inherits the scrap yard. Bloody gold mine, that place.'

'Oh, so he's a man of property?'

'He is, for the moment, but he says he's going to sell it to Mike McIsles. Mike's wanted the freehold for years, you know. Albert wants to buy this magazine, the one that your little boys got involved with. Fancies himself as an "inter-lectual". Bosh, I call it, but I suppose it gets you out of a sticky wicket.'

'Oh, it wasn't really a problem. Minors can't be bound by contracts, you know, especially ones they never meant to enter into in the first place. Poor Hygenus, he only wanted to buy me a single copy so I'd be able to find out a bit of chess background.'

'Well, you've had enough by now, I expect.'

'Maybe. Joan's so keen, after winning that Novice section, that I think we'll have a fair amount of chess still around the place. With any luck the next tournament won't be quite so eventful.'

They had reached the gate, where a postman was standing a respectful guard.

'Mrs O.? Your babysitter said I'd find you here. I've got a special delivery letter, and she didn't like to sign for it.'

'That doesn't sound like Claire.'

'Well, it is a rather grand one.' He handed her a heavy cream envelope with a foreign postmark, embossed with a familiar coat of arms. Sister Hedwig gasped.

'You certainly believe in going to the top, don't you?'

'It's the only way to get anything done.' Ophelia opened the letter hastily, tearing through the solemn crest. *'Thank you for your kind letter, considered matter with the Vatican's canon lawyers, quite agree with your interpretation, only your humble servant entitled to close down a religious institute, no intention of doing so* – Yes! Sister Hedwig, you're safe!'

'I don't understand,' said Lady Tartleton crossly. 'Who is this letter from, anyway?'

But Ophelia was still reading. '*I wonder whether the convent, while still retaining its primary contemplative purpose, might also be of some more tangible benefit to the school children. A small farm, perhaps, run on organic and humane principles, would surely be of more use than a Gender Redefining Centre?*'

'But who *is* it?'

Ophelia handed her the letter, folded at the signature: John-Paul II. For once, Lady Tartleton was lost for words. Sister Hedwig was silent as well, the old smile creeping back across her apple cheeks. Ophelia, watching them, felt a sudden brush on her forehead and looked up in surprise. Then she too smiled.

In the darkening sky the first flakes of snow had begun to fall, like the papery touch of the Reverend Mother's fingers.